OCT , 2002

Bohannon's Women

Bohannon's Women

Mystery stories
by
Joseph Hansen

Five Star • Waterville, Maine

Five Star First Edition Mystery Series.

Published in 2002 in conjunction with Tekno-Books and Ed Gorman.

Set in 11 pt. Plantin by Elena Picard.

Printed in the United States on permanent paper.

Library of Congress Cataloging-in-Publication Data

Hansen, Joseph, 1923–
    Bohannon's women : mystery stories /
by Joseph Hansen.
       p. cm.—(Five Star first edition mystery series)
    Contents: Storm damage—Widower's walk—
Confessional—Survival—Home is the place—
Widdershins.
    ISBN 0-7862-4177-2 (hc : alk. paper)
    1. Detective and mystery stories, American.   I. Title.
II. Series.
PS3558.A513 B65 2002
  813'.54—dc21   2002025196

Table of Contents

Storm Damage

The storm kept waking me. The wind blew hard. It drove the rain hard. Thunder cracked and rumbled. Lightning flared. We're not close neighbors with anybody, but looking out from my darkened room, I could see a couple of lighted windows through the trees. People were too nervous to sleep. Then a tree fell somewhere and the power went off.

Arlene yelled to me, "Don't panic, Jason." As if I was five years old. Hell, I'm fourteen. She'd been in the front room. I heard her blunder along the hall to the kitchen, and in a minute she was at the door of my room with a kerosene lamp in her hand. We kept three of them. Always filled. Power outages happened a lot in Settlers Cove. She hadn't changed for bed. She wore corduroy jeans, scuffed suede boots, a big old bulky sweater, and a watch cap. The lamplight showed tears on her face, and I scrambled out of bed.

"What's wrong?"

"Sam's still not home."

I looked at my watch. "It's only a little after midnight. He's drinking someplace—Schoonover's."

She shook her head, bit her lip. "I've been on the phone. He's not at Schoonover's—he's not anywhere."

"What about Cap's Pier?" Cap Willard takes people out on boats to fish, and rents them gear, and sells them bait, and all that. My father, Garland Moore, used to be a pilot for

7

Cap. They were friends, they still are. But Garland lives in San Francisco, now. Alone. He and Arlene got divorced. Sam Dexter is my stepfather. He came to know Cap through my real dad. "Did you try Cap's?"

"Often. But I only get the answering machine." She headed back toward the kitchen. "Cap is probably out with the Coast Guard, trying to help them find his boat."

I shivered. The night was cold, and I got my bathrobe. Gusts of wind kept slamming against the house, shaking it. The rain hit the windows like gravel. The trees creaked. I went down the dark hall to the soft light in the kitchen.

I said, "You don't know for sure Sam took a boat out. There were storm warnings all day. I heard them on Miss Touhy's radio in the gym." I went to see what Arlene was doing at the stove. She'd poured two mugs full of milk into a pan and was heating the milk carefully, stirring it to keep it from boiling. I said, "Sam must have heard them too."

She sketched me a smile. "I hope so."

I took down the orange-colored Ghirardelli's box from a shelf and spooned double helpings of powdered chocolate into two mugs. I was going to enjoy this. It was a long time since Arlene and I had been alone at night in stormy weather sitting here drinking cocoa together by lamplight.

I was sorry she was worried about Sam, but I couldn't see why, really—the way he treated her. If you want the truth, I hoped she was right, and he had gone out fishing today, like he planned, that the storm had caught him, a big wave had swamped the boat, and he'd drowned. You weren't supposed to feel that way about anybody—I knew that. But I couldn't help it. Sam Dexter was a son-of-a-bitch.

Arlene poured the hot milk into the mugs while I stirred it into the cocoa powder. She set the pan in the sink, where it sizzled. When the brown powder dissolved in the milk, I brought the mugs to the table and set one down for her and one for me. She was in her chair, but now she got up.

"Where you going?"

"I'd better try Cap Willard again." The phone is on a little chest in the hall. There were soft beeps as she punched the lighted buttons. After a minute, she told the answering machine her name. "It's after midnight. I'm worried about Sam, Cap. Call me as soon as you can."

He called. But not till we'd drunk the cocoa and washed the pan and the mugs, and I'd gone back to bed and fallen asleep in spite of the racket the storm was making outside. There's a clock by my bed with big red LED numbers but of course that wasn't working, and there was no way to read my watch, so when the phone woke me I didn't know how late it was. I heard Arlene run to snatch up the receiver. I scrambled out of bed, opened my door, stood watching her. Her face lit up.

"Oh, thank God," she said. "Thank God."

And half an hour later, good old Sam was home. The boat he'd taken out with two drunk friends had lost its rudder, and wallowed for hours in high seas, but the Coast Guard had located it before it sank. Just before. It was the *Argo*. Named that because my name is Jason, and Cap Willard took delivery on it the day I was born. Jason was an ancient Greek who went to sea in a ship called *Argo* to find the Golden Fleece. Cap told Garland the boat was mine as soon as I grew up. And now Sam Dexter had sunk her. Arlene was crying with relief, getting the wet clothes off him, toweling his hair, wrapping him in a blanket, giving him coffee. I was crying too. Luckily, neither of them asked me why.

Carlotta Wright is my grandmother. She drives a Bronco and lives up in Sills Canyon. Apples—she grows apples. You say the word grandmother to people and they get the idea of somebody creaky and frail and bent over, but that's not Carlotta. She's sturdy and rosy and there's not a gray hair on her head. What I'd liked her best for when I was little was her apple pies, but what I liked her best for now was that she hated Sam Dexter as much as I did. Once, at the jail, after he'd beaten Arlene up, Carlotta told him if it ever happened again, she'd kill him. And she meant it. She went and bought a revolver. I know. She showed it to me the next time I was at her house.

Anyway, around seven, the morning after the storm, Arlene and I were eating breakfast in the kitchen, being very quiet about it, because Sam was still asleep, when Carlotta slammed the door of the Bronco out back of the house and came charging in with mud on her boots.

"Well, he nearly got his comeuppance this time, didn't he?" She unwrapped a red wool muffler from around her throat and let the long ends hang down. "Drunken fool."

"Hush, mother. You'll waken him. He's exhausted."

"Hah." Carlotta marched to the stove and poured herself a mug of coffee, brought it to the table, pushed my school-books aside to make room for it, and plunked herself down. "I'm not sorry for him. It's the Coast Guard boys I'm sorry for. In a storm, I always keep the short wave on. I heard the whole stupid affair. Sam Dexter endangered the lives of half a dozen brave officers and men with his craziness."

"He's alive, mother," Arlene said. "That's what they're out there for. To save lives. I'm sure they didn't mind."

"Didn't mind?" Carlotta snorted. "In weather like that?"

Arlene said to me, "Jason, what's the matter? You've hardly touched your food. It's a cold day. You can't go to school on an empty stomach."

"Not hungry," I mumbled.

"Sam's all right." She stroked my hair. "Everything came

out all right. There's nothing more to worry about."

I wasn't worried. I hadn't been worried. But of course I couldn't say that to Arlene. I'd tried telling her what I thought of Sam before. She never let me finish. She said he'd been good to us and I had no right to hate him so. That was her answer every time. I'd given up. But I had to tell somebody. I really felt very bad. I turned to Carlotta.

"It was the *Argo* he sank," I said. "It was my boat."

The sky was blue with only long, drawn-out trails of cloud all morning. But by noon the temperature had dropped again and the sky had darkened. Westward, far out over the Pacific, thunder muttered. From where I sat on a bench under a big old eucalyptus tree, not eating my lunch, not even opening the bag to learn what was in it—you can't see the ocean. Buildings are in the way. But I knew from times past that there'd be lightning flickering under the black low-hanging clouds out there. Sometimes these storms never make it ashore. I tested the wind with my finger. This one would.

Sean Touhy sat down beside me. In jogging pants, a duffel coat, and a green knitted ski cap. Her cheeks and the end of her nose were rosy from the cold. She's the gym teacher. And the art teacher and the drama teacher. She thinks I'm good at all of these things and pays me more attention than she should. The kids are always sniping at me about it. "Not shooting baskets today?" She touched the lunch bag. "Not eating, either. Sick?"

"I'm all right," I said.

Jeff Van Slyke in Nikes that looked like dirty bandages, dribbled the ball across the tarmac that was patchy with damp in places and strewn with twigs and pods and leaves blown from the trees. "Your old man, the drunk nearly bought it last night," he said. "It was on the news this morning."

"He's all right," I said, "but he's not my old man. He's only my stepfather."

"Yeah, yeah," Jeff said, and dribbled the ball away, and tried a hook shot, and missed.

"What happened?" Sean Touhy said.

I told her. "I wish he'd drowned."

She spoke my name sadly and patted my shoulder. She didn't do more than that, for fear of over-stepping the guidelines—what's okay for a teacher to do and what's meddling. She'd meddled once, and almost lost her job.

Sam had come home on a rampage and started a terrible fight with Arlene. I'd been showing her some drawings I'd made at school to illustrate a book about gray whales our class was writing. I yelled at him to quit hitting Arlene. So he went for me. I scrambled out of there. He chased me but he was drunk and fell down. I got my bike to find a phone and call the Sheriff, but the front tire was flat. So I hid up in the trees. When the house got quiet again, and I tiptoed back inside, the drawings were all torn up and kicked around on the floor.

When Miss Touhy asked me for them next day, I should have made up some story, but instead I told her the truth. And she went to our house, where Sam has his office, and read him the riot act. She got real emotional about how brainy and talented I am, and how if he kept abusing me, she'd put a stop to it—and like that. Well, in the days before he boozed his good name away, he used to be a member of the school board—and he went to the Principal, and tried to get Miss Touhy fired. And since at that time he was thought to be a reformed character, it almost worked. So I guess you can't blame her for being cautious about discussing Sam Dexter with me.

"You don't need to say it." I looked into her eyes, pink-rimmed and teary from the cold. "I know how you feel."

She gave a short laugh and stood up. "Poor old Jason." She wiped her nose with a crumpled Kleenex. "I sincerely hope you don't."

In American History class, Sandra the Rabbit brought me a note from the office. Even when she doesn't have messages to deliver, she jogs. Everyplace, not just at school, but all over town. That's where she got the nickname. She's seriously overweight, and her plan is to jog the fat off, but jogging only makes her hungry, and eating just puts the fat back on.

Anyway, after she handed me the note, panting, and jogged out of the room, everybody was quiet, watching me, including Croaker Cogan, the teacher, so I opened the note and read it. It said my mother had been unexpectedly called out of town, and I was not to go home after school: I was to go stay with my grandmother, till she got back. I frowned at the note. Who would call Arlene out of town? She grew up around here. She didn't know anyone anyplace else—not that I ever heard of. What did "out of town" mean, anyway? Where to? Garland lives in San Francisco. Was he sick or hurt or something? Even if he was, would he send for Arlene?

In his croaky voice, Mr. Cogan said, "I take it Jason's note doesn't mark a new epoch in American history, so perhaps we can go on, now, with Lewis and Clark."

Cogan was right—it didn't mark a new epoch in American history but it marked a new epoch in mine. At the end of last period, I went to the office to check up on the message. But Sticks Everly, the tall thin woman in charge said the note was exactly what my mother had said. Sticks was rattling a computer keyboard, while charts came up on the screen, then craning forward to peer at these through horn-rim glasses.

"Was she all right?" I asked.

"She didn't say she was ill," Sticks said.

"How about upset?" I said. "Did she sound upset?"

"She seemed to be calling from a pay phone," Sticks said. "On the highway. I heard trucks roaring past."

I felt cold in the pit of my stomach.

"Isn't it likely something about your stepfather?" She threw me a glance that said I wasn't using my brain. "After all, he had a terrible experience last night." With a ballpoint pen, Sticks made a note on a paper chart on the desk, then turned to the computer again. "She did seem worried about one thing. She stressed it several times."

"What was it?" I asked.

"That you were not to go home," Sticks said. "That you were to go straight to your grandmother's."

"Thank you," I said, and left the office.

Outdoors, the sky was smudgy with low clouds, and the wind smelled strongly of the ocean. I pulled the hood up on my parka and headed for the bike rack, thinking it was probably something about my stepfather, all right, but not the way Sticks meant. Maybe after I left for school, and Carlotta went home, Arlene took after Sam about my boat. She goes into this mother-bear-protecting-her-cub act sometimes. Mainly Sam isn't jealous of me, he just ignores me. But when she brings me up to him, he can get vicious. I unlocked the bike from the rack, dropped the lock into my pocket, hunched my book bag on my back, and rode off. For home. She was probably afraid if I went there, Sam would hurt me. But if I was going to stay at Carlotta's, I had to take clothes.

Riding along, my ears beginning to ache from the cold even with the hood up, I puzzled as I often did what it was about Arlene and alcoholics. See, Garland drank too. Did he ever. Only Garland never got mean like Sam. He was a sweet drunk. People liked him. They just got tired of his not showing up for work, until the only person who would hire him was Cap Willard. And the little Cap could pay him, he drank away. He just couldn't remember there were bills to pay. But he loved Arlene, and Arlene loved him and put up with him for a long time. So did I. He wasn't around much, but when he was, he gave me smiles and hugs and even sometimes took me with him up the canyons hunting, or out fishing on the *Argo*.

Garland never meant anybody any harm. But he did harm. And when he stole and blew away the money Arlene had earned waitressing—she would waitress when there wasn't any food left in the house and they'd turned off the electricity and telephone, and the taxes had to be paid or we'd be homeless—she said he'd have to quit drinking or she'd kick him out. It's her house, a gift from Carlotta

And so Garland joined Alcoholics Anonymous, and never took another drink. And changed. Some people think it's funny, but it isn't, not to me. He was a different man. A distant man. The laughter went. He was still gentle and sweet natured, but he stopped joking, he never took his hunting and fishing stuff out of the closet again. He wore business suits. And not just the suits. He was all business. And the laugh people get is that once he stopped drinking, Arlene stopped loving him. And they got divorced.

He had a sales agency here for a while, and chalked up such a record the company gave him the San Francisco office to manage. Meantime, he'd introduced Arlene to Sam Dexter, the man who had been a special help to him in kicking the bottle, the guy you call up in the middle of the night when you think you're going to die without a drink.

At that time, Sam had a good job with a big salary and, like I said, he was on the school board and stuff like that. Even so,

I thought he was a nerd. And I don't know anything about love, but on TV I've seen people marry people on the rebound after they're divorced and lonely, and that's what Arlene did with Sam. I think. Anyway, they got married.

And then, a year later, the company where Sam was such a big shot went belly up, and everyplace he applied to for work said he was overqualified, and he started drinking again. Secretly at first. But after a while not bothering to keep it secret. And daring Arlene to say anything about it. He was mean, the way he talked to her. But that was as far as it went for a while. He took spot jobs keeping the books for small businesses, starting with Cap Willard's, and began to earn a living again. I figured he'd stop drinking then, but he didn't. He wasn't the head honcho anymore, issuing orders to a department full of peons—and that rankled him. And soon it wasn't just words he hit Arlene with. But you already know that.

Like I said, our place is back in the pines, and pretty isolated. Our road doesn't get a lot of traffic, so I was pedaling the last stretch right out in the middle of the road when a car came fast around the bend, a silver Mercedes. I swerved one way, and it swerved the other way with squealing tires, and we missed each other. But I wobbled and the bike fell over and spilled me. Not because I was scared. I was shocked. The driver of the car was Garland. My father. He hadn't come to Settlers Cove in a couple of years. What was he doing here? I must have been wrong. I was a little dizzy, getting back on my bike, and I remembered I hadn't eaten all day. I was always privately wishing Garland would come back. He never would.

When I pedaled up the driveway the first drops of rain began to fall. Sam's Thunderbird was in the garage, but not Mom's ten-year-old Wagoneer that used to be Carlotta's.

Mom was gone, all right. But called out of town? No, that was a lie, and it worried me. Had Sam hurt her so badly she'd run away to save her life?

Except for the whisper of the rain in the trees, everything was deadly quiet. I prayed Sam was drunk and passed out. I sure as hell didn't want to wake him, and I was very quiet using my key, and hardly breathed while I passed through the silent rooms. I stuffed a canvas airline bag with T-shirts and briefs and socks, clean jeans, a couple of favorite shirts. I zipped the bag shut. On the desk was the wooden case I keep my pencils and brushes and paints in. And I'd need my sketching pad. And books to read. And music to listen to— my Walkman and a bag of tapes.

Hell, it wasn't going to work. I couldn't take all this junk on my bike. It would be heavy, and it's a long ride to Carlotta's, most of it uphill. I tiptoed into the hall to phone her. Maybe she'd come pick me up. But the phone rang and rang and she didn't answer. And then, just holding it to my ear, listening to it ring, I turned, and this way I could see the door to Sam's office. It was half-open. Beyond it, the computer monitor glowed blue.

And I saw a pair of legs stretched out on the floor. My heart gave a thump. I put the receiver back, crossed the living room, and stopped. Printouts and other business papers strewed the floor. Sam hadn't passed out drunk. Blood had soaked the papers under his head. He lay in front of the desk, his face turned away from me. And the back of his head was a bloody mess. He was dead, had to be. My stomach heaved. I ran to the bathroom, hugged the toilet, and breathed slowly in and out until the sick feeling left.

Then, avoiding even looking toward the den, I went back to the phone. Emergency numbers are on a printed label glued to the instrument, and I started to punch out the one for the Sheriff's station in Madrone, and then I stopped and put the receiver down.

What if, this morning, Arlene had fought back? What if she was the one who'd killed Sam? That would be a real reason to run away, wouldn't it? And her strict orders for me not to come home were because she knew Sam was lying here dead, and she didn't want me to be the one to discover the body. That added up, didn't it? I pushed the idea away.

But one just as bad took its place: what if it really was Garland I'd seen in that speeding car just now? Garland knew how things were going here because I'd telephoned him in a panic at least twice lately and begged him to come save us. He'd always tell me to keep calm and he'd come later, soon as he could clear the time. So maybe today he saw on the TV news about Sam sinking my boat and that brought him. What if he chewed Sam out, and Sam went for him, and Garland killed him? Garland is a lot bigger than Sam.

I took my hand off the phone. I couldn't call the Sheriff on my own mother and father. What should I do? Carlotta wasn't home. Who could I ask for advice? I picked up the receiver and punched out the number of the school. Miss Touhy usually stays late, taking the teams through practice. Not today. She had a cold, and she'd left early.

I yanked a blanket off my bed and, trying not to look at him, went into the den and covered Sam up. It was wrong to leave him lying there. But there was something very important I had to find out. I got my money out of the coffee can in my closet, picked up the airline bag, and left the house, wondering if I'd ever go back.

If it had been raining hard, I guess I wouldn't have made it, but the rain was scattered and fitful, so I arrived at Cap's Pier only half drowned. The *Emily*, old, broad-beamed, rocked and pitched beside the pier. Gulls perched on her, looking miserable. The pier shook from the storm tide swirling around its stakes. I felt an ache in my chest, looking at the empty place where the *Argo* used to moor. Tears came to my eyes, and I was boiling mad at Sam all over again. But he was dead, now, wasn't he, beyond my reach. If he'd ever cared how I felt, he didn't care any more.

A big old wreck of a man, Cap sat at the cluttered desk in his shacky office that was hung with all kinds of ship's tackle, lines, and pulleys. Fishing rods stood in racks. Rolled sails were stacked against the wall. Shelves sagged with engine parts, radio parts, and galley supplies. The air smelled of bait. Cap was shuffling bank statements. I cleared my throat, and he looked up with his faded blue eyes.

"Come in," he said, "I've been expecting you."

"You shouldn't have let him take the *Argo*," I said.

"I wasn't here. Place was locked up. Didn't learn he took the *Argo* until he'd been out for hours. Not the stupidest thing I ever knew a man to do, but close. Close."

I was relieved. I wanted to go on liking Cap. I went and sat by the desk. "You didn't let him, then."

He shook his head in its greasy old captain's cap. "Somebody came into Schoonover's and said did I know one of my boats was missing. First I heard. Four in the afternoon. Dark, windy, rainy. Surf way up. You know how it was."

"You would have stopped him," I said.

"I'm sorry it had to be the *Argo*," he said.

"I guess you couldn't help it," I said. And then I asked the question I'd come all this way for. "Was Garland here today?"

"Garland?" There were no lights on in the place. I couldn't make out his expression in the gloom. But he sounded surprised.

"I thought I saw him," I said, "on my way home from school. Driving a car. Not far from our house. I thought maybe he'd come looking and found—nobody home. Was he here today? He wouldn't come all the way from San Francisco without stopping to see you. You were his best friend."

Cap had listened to me closely. When I quit talking, he waited a few seconds before he drew a breath and slowly nodded. "Yup," he said, "he was here."

"Great." I jumped up. "Where's he staying?"

Cap waved a horny, thick-fingered hand. "Jason. He ain't. He was just driving through. Business trip. He sat and had a cup of coffee with me, looking at his watch every two minutes. Wanted to see you, but he had to be in Frisco by six." Cap chuckled wryly and shook his head. "Hard to believe. A man of responsibilities."

I made a face. "He didn't used to know the meaning of the word."

"Too bad you missed him. Been good for you to meet up with your dad right now," Cap said. "Considering how you just lost the *Argo* and the way you lost her and how it was that son-of-a-bitch Sam who lost her for you. I knew you'd be feeling bad."

He almost made me cry. I hung my head. He said, "I'd like to say, don't worry, we'll see you get another boat. But I'm not going to lie to you, Jason. The insurance ran out. Business is bad, not earning enough to pay the bills. I've about used up my savings. There's not going to be any new boat."

"It's okay," I said, but I felt hollow. All my life I'd dreamed of someday piloting the *Argo* around the world. Little kid stuff, right, not realistic. Anyway, now that I knew for sure Garland had been to the house today, I had grimmer worries. Should I tell Cap the whole story, and ask him what to do? I couldn't. Sitting there in the darkening room, he looked pathetic—old and defeated. I'd only lost a dream. The *Argo* had been his livelihood, half, anyway. He might not be able to keep going at all, now. I couldn't load him with my troubles. He had too many of his own.

I was winded and my legs ached by the time I'd ridden up Sills canyon to Carlotta's. I was also wet, because the rain had come on in earnest. It was almost dark. Her garage door was down. I heaved it up. The Bronco stood there shadowy, ticking while it lost heat. I could feel the heat. She hadn't been home long, had she? I leaned my bike against the wall, shut the garage door, unstrapped the airline bag from behind the seat of the bike, and went into the kitchen. The house was cold. Brown sacks of groceries sat on the table.

"Hello?" I called. "It's me—Jason."

I heard the toilet flush, and a minute later Carlotta appeared. She said, "Where did you come from? Look at you. You're soaked to the skin. Don't tell me you rode your bicycle all the way up here? Oh, Jason."

"Sam is dead," I said. "And Arlene's gone."

"What?" The rosiness left her face. Staring at me, she groped out for a chair and sat own. "What did you say?"

"She phoned the school and left word for me not to go home, to come and stay here until she came back."

"Back?" She couldn't seem to take it in. "From where?"

"She didn't say. But I went home. I mean, I had to, didn't I? To get clothes. And Sam is lying dead on the floor in the den, Grandma. There's blood. His head is bashed in, blown away, I don't know."

"Oh, my God," she said. "Oh, my God."

"I didn't know what to do," I said. "I tried to phone you, but you weren't here."

"Go put on dry clothes." She stood up, the chair legs stut-

21

tering away behind her. "I'll phone the Sheriff."

"Don't," I yelped. "He'll think Arlene did it."

She had the kitchen phone down from the wall. But she turned back and stared at me.

"Because she ran away," I said. "That's, like, an admission of guilt. That's the way the police mind works."

Her laugh didn't have humor in it. "Honestly, Jason—life is not a television show." She punched the number. Waiting for someone to answer, she said to me, "When did Arlene phone this message to the school?"

"American History," I said. "One o'clock."

"And you got home at what time?"

"Three fifteen, three twenty."

"She may not even know Sam's dead," Carlotta said. That made me feel even worse about Garland than I had before. Now Carlotta said into the phone, "Yes, this is Carlotta Wright. Sills Canyon. Mmm, the apple ranch. My young grandson has just arrived here with the news that his stepfather is lying unconscious from a severe head injury at home in Settlers Cove. Excuse me?" . . . "Jason Moore." Pause. "Sam Dexter. No—stepfather." . . . "Thirty-four eighty-seven Old Bridge Road. No, I'm afraid there's no one home. Do you want me to—?" A final pause. "Yes, of course. Yes, we'll be here if we're needed." And she hung the receiver back on its wall bracket. Not on the first try. She missed on the first try. She looked at me.

"They'll be taking paramedics," she said. "It's the paramedics you should have phoned for."

"His skull was smashed," I said, "he couldn't be alive."

"You should have checked." She began taking cans and boxes and plastic bags out of the sacks, and stowing them in refrigerator, freezer, cupboards. Her hands were shaking, and she was putting things in the wrong places.

"You might have saved his life."

"I didn't want to save his life," I said, and sneezed.

"If you don't get out of those wet clothes," she said, "you'll lose your own. Oh, rats." She started off.

"Don't go," I said. "Where are you going?"

She stopped and looked at me with her head tilted. "Only to the car. I left the little bag from the drugstore. My medication." She half smiled, half frowned. "Jason—I'll only be a minute."

"No," I said. "Let me go." I'd begun to be afraid. I didn't know what of, but I was shaking inside. It was childish, but I was scared if she went out that door she wouldn't come back. I'd be all alone. First no Garland, now no Arlene, not even any Sam. I had to hang onto Carlotta. "You stay here," I said, and darted out the door before she could stop me.

Carlotta doesn't lock doors. She's lived on the Central Coast too long. In small towns, and out in the boonies like this. There never used to be any crime here, and she can't get it through her head that somebody might walk in and steal from her or hurt her. Arlene and Garland used to try to tell her to lock up. So did Sam. She said she didn't want to live in that kind of world, anyway.

So the Bronco wasn't locked. I pulled open the passenger side door and looked for a bag from the drugstore in Madrone. It would be white. They always were. It wasn't on the seat. She often set small stuff on the dashboard, but it wasn't there. Maybe it fell off. The Bronco's ceiling light had winked on when I opened the car, but it was feeble, and the garage was dark. I groped around for the drugstore sack on the carpet, gritty the way the floors get in vehicles used for farm work. Back under the seat? Ah, there it was.

I reached for it, and my fingers brushed something else, something hard and cold. Metal. I drew the thing out. Heavy.

A revolver. It gave off a sharp smell. I couldn't tell if it was the gun Carlotta showed me that time after Sam beat Arlene up so badly. But I guessed the smell meant it had been fired, didn't it? I felt sick again.

"Jason?" The door from the kitchen opened, and light fell into the garage, and Carlotta's shadow. I pushed the gun out of sight quickly. "Are you all right?"

"It was on the floor." I got out, slammed the door, and jiggled the little white sack at her. "It took me a while to find it."

"Thank you." She took the sack from me, set it on a counter, picked up my airline bag, grabbed my arm and propelled me across the kitchen and down the hall. "Now you take a hot shower, young man, and get into dry clothes. Then we'll have supper."

"What about Arlene?" I sneezed again, and wiped my nose on my cold wet sleeve. "Where did she go? Where is she?"

"She'll telephone." Carlotta pushed the carry-on bag into my hands. "She'll want to know you got here safely." Carlotta ran down the zipper of my parka, turned me around, and yanked the parka off me. "I'll ask her where she is."

"But what if she doesn't call?" I said. "What if she's too scared of the police? They might tap this phone."

"Jason," Carlotta said sharply, "please stop. She probably doesn't even know Sam's been hurt. I'm sure there's a perfectly simple, harmless explanation for this—trip she's taken." She clucked. "Scared of the police, indeed." She reached for me. "Now, you get out of those wet clothes, or I'll get you out of them myself. You want me to bathe you? I did that, when you were little, many a time. I can still manage, if you can't do it yourself."

I backed off. "I'll do it, I'll do it."

"I should hope so," she said, and closed the door on me.

* * * * *

The storm was going strong when the man in the black slicker and sou'wester arrived. It must have been around seven. Carlotta and I had just finished off half an apple pie for dessert when the doorbell rang. My heart jumped again. I dropped my fork. Carlotta looked at me. Gravely. Pale-faced. She didn't get to her feet. I think she wanted to, but fear kept her from moving. I got up. My legs felt watery, but I made them work. My napkin was still tucked in at my collar. As I passed Carlotta, without a word she just mechanically reached out and pulled it off me.

I switched on the porch light and opened the front door, and rain and cold blew in. The man in black flashed a badge, said he was Lieutenant Gerard, and could he come in, please.

"It's about your father," he said.

"Come in," I said, and he did, and I shut the door, and told him, "but he's not my father."

He busied himself getting out of the wet rain gear and draping it on a brass hanger by the door. He took off the sou'-wester. He was getting bald. His uniform was tan and neatly pressed, but the cuffs of the trousers were wet. "Is your mother here?"

"No, I'm his grandmother—Carlotta Wright." She came forward. "How is Sam?"

Gerard looked doubtfully at me. Was I too young to hear this—that was what he was wondering?

"He's dead, isn't he?" I said.

Gerard looked over my head at Carlotta. "He'd been dead for hours before you called us."

"What did I tell you?" I said to Carlotta.

She told the lieutenant, "Sit down, please. You look cold. Let me get you some coffee."

"Thank you." He sat down and looked at me. "When did

25

you find him?" I told him. He asked, "You didn't see anyone else in or near the house when you got there?"

I swallowed hard and lied. "No, Sir."

"Why didn't you phone us when you found the body?"

"I—I thought an adult should do it." To my own ears, it sounded flimsy. "I was scared, mixed up. It's the first time I ever—saw a—dead person."

"Why didn't you call your grandmother? She's an adult. She could have called us."

"I tried. She wasn't home. So I rode up here. On my bike. She called you then. Well, it's a long way."

He eyed me interestedly, as if he was hearing something he'd never heard before. New facts. "It takes two and a half hours to get here on a bike from Settlers Cove?"

"It was raining," I said weakly.

"You must have left the house later than you thought. Maybe you waited around, hoping your mother would come home."

"Yes, right." I nodded hard. "That's what I did."

"You're sure? You didn't go anywhere else before you came here? Looking for some adult friend?"

He was scary. How did he know that? He couldn't. He was bluffing. I shook my head. "I—I tried to phone my gym teacher at school. Miss Touhy. But she'd gone home."

He said, "Where is your mother, Jason?"

Before I could answer, Carlotta came in with mugs of coffee on a black tin Mexican tray painted with gaudy flowers. She set this on the coffee table in front of the couch where Gerard was sitting. He gave Carlotta a quick smile, picked up his coffee mug, and looked straight at me. Or through me. His eyes were steely. "Jason?"

"I—don't know. I'm worried about her."

Carlotta sat down, looking rosy again, and acting as com-

26

fortable as if she served coffee in her front room every week to sheriffs investigating murders in her family. But she didn't stay nonchalant long. Gerard said:

"I'm worried about her too. There was a fight in that office. The blood there isn't only your father's—"

"He's not my father," I said hotly. "He's my stepfather."

"There's someone else's blood, as well. Two broken teeth. Handfuls of hair. They could be your mother's. We know Sam Dexter was a wife beater. We think he beat your mother again, today." He glanced at Carlotta, then back at me. "If either of you knows where she is, please say so."

"I simply don't know." Carlotta looked crumpled and ready to cry. She shook her head helplessly. "Why didn't she come here? I wasn't home, but the doors are never locked. You've checked the hospitals, of course? And the halfway house for battered women in Morro Bay?"

Gerard nodded. "All those places." He drank some of his coffee, reached to his breast pocket, paused. "May I smoke?" Carlotta waved a hand to say she didn't care, and he lit a cigarette. Then he said, "We used her phone book to check with her friends. No one's seen her. We're looking for her car. A 1982 brown Wagoneer, is that right?" He recited the license number.

"You think she killed him," Carlotta blurted.

"She couldn't," I said. "Not my Mom. She can't kill anything, not even a bug. Anyway, she's not strong. And she's not brave. She's scared of him. She never fights back. He can do anything, and she just—" I shut up.

"Sometimes," Gerard said quietly, "meek people get fed up with being knocked around. And you don't have to be very strong to pull the trigger of a gun."

Before I could stop myself, I looked at Carlotta. She was sitting there stiffly, white-faced, just staring at him.

27

I said, "It looked to me like somebody'd bashed his skull in."

"That was the exit wound," Gerard said. "They can look that way. He was shot in the throat. At close range. It appears the murderer was someone Dexter knew and trusted. The bullet went upward and out the back of his skull."

"No," Carlotta said, "it couldn't have been Arlene. Not my little girl."

"There was no gun in the house?" Gerard said.

"We're not that sort of people," Carlotta said.

Gerard looked at me again, eyebrows raised.

"My real father kept a Winchester," I said, "for hunting, and he left it behind, but Mom sold it after the divorce. We were short of money."

"Mr. Dexter was shot with a handgun, a .357 magnum. We found the bullet. But not the gun." Gerard gulped the last of his coffee, put out his cigarette, stood up. "Thank you. For the coffee and for your help." He crossed to take his slicker down from the hook and shrug into it. The stiff rubber rattled and rustled. "If you think of anyplace Mrs. Dexter might have gone, please call me." He put on the sou'wester and pulled open the door. The storm was still out there and it made a gusty try to come inside. Gerard closed the door against it, and said to us, "I'm sorry, but we'll need a positive identification by a family member. It's the law. Mrs. Wright?"

"You mean going to the morgue," Carlotta said faintly, "and looking at the body?"

"I'll do it," I said. "Just to be sure he's dead."

Gerard gave me a startled look. But all he said was, "I'll send a car to pick you up tomorrow morning." Then he went back out into the storm.

My plan was to stay awake. I kept my clothes on under the

28

covers. I tried reading one of the old children's books of mine Carlotta keeps in the room where I always sleep when I stay there, but my eyes kept falling shut. I was dog-tired from all the bike riding I'd done. And in a way, that saved me. Leg cramps woke me. Bad ones. I wanted to yell. But I mustn't wake Carlotta.

I sat up in the bed wincing, whimpering, and kneaded my calves, the way Garland used to do for me. And finally the pain eased a little. I switched off the reading light, got out of bed, hobbled to my door, softly cracked it open, and listened. Except for the patter of rain on the roof, the house was quiet. I put on my parka and, cautious, in my stocking feet, I passed Carlotta's door. Beyond it, I could hear her snoring. That was good.

I crossed the kitchen, went down into the garage, eased open the door of the Bronco, and got the revolver from under the seat. I didn't close the door tightly. It would make noise. In the kitchen, by the very small light on the stove, I found a plastic bag and wrapped the gun in it. Then I peeled off my socks and rolled up the cuffs of my jeans.

The rain was cold on my face, the planks of the rear deck cold under my feet. I didn't like going on, but I had to, didn't I? I went into the apple orchard where the trees were bare of leaves. I made myself stumble on over the lumpy ground, mud oozing between my toes, until when I looked back, I couldn't make out the sleeping shape of the house anymore. Then I squatted and dug with my hands in the soggy earth until I had a hole about a foot deep. And I buried the gun.

Sam was dead, all right. That eased my mind a little, as I walked out of the cold white room where they had him stashed in a kind of file drawer. A young woman deputy called T. Hodges, who was pretty, sort of, had an arm across my shoulders, in case I needed comforting. I needed it, but not about Sam. Somebody I loved, somebody who loved me, had killed him. He'd asked for it. It was past time. I wasn't the least bit sorry. But law enforcement wouldn't care that Sam deserved to die. They went by the book, didn't they? Their job was to find and punish the killer. Arlene, or Carlotta, or Garland. I'd done what I could to protect Carlotta. I could only pray they wouldn't find Arlene. But Garland I could protect. So after the patrol car dropped me and my book bag at school, instead of going straight in, I used a pay phone on the grounds to ring up Cap Willard.

"Cap, it's Jason," I said. "Please do me a favor."

"I'm sorry about Sam," Cap said. "That's terrible."

"Yeah, really," I said. Grownups are hypocrites. Cap didn't like Sam any better than I did, but he did need a book-keeper, and chose Sam so Arlene wouldn't have to support us all alone, on her waitress pay. And so I wouldn't starve. But they get pious when somebody dies. They can't help it, I guess. Maybe they figure if they tell sweet lies about the dead, people will do the same for them when they die.

"What's this favor you want?" Cap said.

"Nothing hard," I said. "Just, if the Sheriff comes around asking questions, don't tell him Garland came to see you yesterday, okay?"

"You don't think Garland shot Sam, do you?" Cap said.

"Of course not," I said, "but what I think doesn't matter. The thing is, not to put ideas in Lieutenant Gerard's head. He can't suspect Garland if he doesn't know Garland was around here yesterday. You and I are the only ones who saw him, so if we keep our mouths shut—"

The school bell rang for first period.

"I promise," Cap said.

Carlotta had been right—I shouldn't have gone to school.

The kids looked at me sideways and whispered. The teachers tried not to show it, but I could see they thought I was the most unfeeling little bastard that ever walked. I couldn't leave—I didn't have my bike. I had to stay until three, when Carlotta would come pick me up. So after second period, I went to the library. There were no kids in the library to look at me like I had AIDS. Busy at her desk, the librarian didn't even notice me. I went far back among the stacks and sat on the floor. In the quiet and the smell of old paper. To think.

I'd covered for Carlotta and Garland, now, but what about Arlene? Lt. Gerard might never even get around to suspecting Carlotta and Garland, but he sure as hell suspected Arlene. She shouldn't have run off. On the other hand, she must have known what the law would think. She'd gone to them when Sam had beaten her. More than once. That would make her the number one suspect. That's why she'd run. How scared she must have felt, how scared she must be right now, all alone out there in the world someplace. Nobody to talk to, nobody to hold on to. I had to find her. Only where?

I don't like to admit it, but I fell asleep. It didn't matter—in fact, it helped. Because I dreamed. Of summer days we'd shared, Arlene and Garland and me, back when things were still all right between the two of them, before Garland's boozing turned things sour. We always went back to this same place, Cluff Meadows in the high Sierras, and the times there were always good. And I thought while I was still asleep, *That's where she's gone.* Where we were all so happy together. That's where I can find her.

And I woke up smiling.

I came out the doors at three o'clock—into rain, but still smiling. It was a hell of a long way, clear across the San Joaquin valley, away beyond Fresno. How I'd ever get there I didn't know, but the more I thought about it, the surer I got that Cluff Meadows was where Arlene had gone. So that was where I was going. Now I lost my smile.

Carlotta was out here, all right, on the puddled parking tarmac with a lot of other parents and grandparents waiting to pick up their kids. But not in her Bronco. In a brown patrol car with a gold sheriff's badge painted on the door, and Lt. Gerard at the wheel. He tapped the horn, and feeling a lot of kids' eyes on me, I trotted over.

"What's wrong?" I said.

Gerard jerked his head to indicate the back seat. "Get in," he said. And when I did that, and slammed the door, he said, "Your friend T. Hodges checked gun registrations for me this morning." He started the car, and began backing and filling to drive out of the school grounds. "And she found that your grandmother bought a gun eighteen months ago. A handgun. A .357 magnum revolver." He glanced at Carlotta, who was fidgeting with her long red muffler. "She forgot to mention it last night."

"You didn't ask me," Carlotta said.

Gerard waited at the edge of the highway while cars raced past, their tires throwing up fans of water. When there was a break, he swung out across the highway and into the far lane. "It's the same type of gun that killed your—your stepfather." He held it up. "Recognize it?"

"Why would I?" I yelped. "I didn't shoot Sam."

"You had motive," Gerard said. He was kidding, wasn't he? "You had opportunity. You often visit your grandmother. You could have taken this gun out of the drawer where she keeps it without her noticing. When I went to ask her about it this morning, she hardly remembered where she put it after she bought it. You could have shot your stepfather, and put it back when you reached Sills canyon last night."

I could hardly speak. "You found it in some drawer?"

"The bottom drawer of my chiffonier," Carlotta said with a nod. "Under your great grandma's patchwork quilts."

Then whose was the gun she'd hidden in the car, the gun I'd buried last night in the rain? Where had that come from? I felt a chill that had nothing to do with the weather. She'd been out all yesterday afternoon. Had she gone back to the house on Old Bridge Road and found Sam dead and Arlene gone and the pistol lying there? Had she figured Arlene had got hold of a gun somehow and killed Sam with it? Had she been so sure of it that she snatched up the gun and stowed it under the car seat to protect Arlene?

"Are my fingerprints on that gun?" I said.

Gerard stopped for the winking red signal that hangs way up above the highway at the turnoff into Madrone. He shook his head. "Only Mrs. Wright's." He swung the car up toward the little town and drove past the phony Hollywood Western set they've turned the main street into. He turned again, and we were at the sand-color, flat-roof building of the County Sheriff sub-station, where they hadn't raised the flags today, because of the storm. Across the parking lot, that was girded by a stand of big old eucalyptus trees, he parked the patrol car next to Carlotta's Bronco, revved the engine once, and switched it off. He tossed me a brief smile over his shoulder. "I'm not serious, Jason. This gun has never been fired. I'm not arresting you for murder."

"You could have fooled me." I opened my door.

"May we go home, now?" Carlotta said coldly.

"I'm sorry for all the trouble," Gerard said.

She snorted and heaved herself out of the patrol car. "And so you should be. An old woman and a young boy." She rummaged in her big leather bag for the Bronco's keys. "How did a person with no better judgment than that get to be a lieutenant? Honestly. This generation!"

Gerard swung easily out of the patrol car and slammed the door. "A gun like this"—he came around the car to us, weighing the shiny thing in his hand thoughtfully— "can give an old woman or a young boy the same power as a man in his prime. And neither one of you can claim you didn't want Sam Dexter dead." When Carlotta started to protest, he held up a hand. "You threatened to kill him, ma'am. I heard you. In this very building, the last time we jailed him for assault on Arlene Dexter."

"I'd lost my temper," she said. "I didn't know what I was saying. Surely you know that much about human nature."

He handed her the revolver. "You can put this back with great grandma's quilts. We won't be needing it." After Carlotta had tucked it into that big shoulder bag of hers, he said, "You haven't heard from Mrs. Dexter? She hasn't telephoned? You still don't know where she is?"

"I'm frantic," Carlotta said.

"Me too," I said.

"Call me right away if you hear from her." He touched the brim of his hat politely to Carlotta, gave me another stiff little smile, and strolled off into the station house.

As she drove us up Sills canyon, the creek beside the winding road running hard and deep, Carlotta was very quiet, absorbed in her own thoughts. I said, as casually as I could, "I wonder what happened to the real gun."

"Real gun?" she glanced at me.

"The one that killed him," I said.

"Obviously," she said, fiddling with the switch of the windshield wipers, "whoever killed him took it away."

"Maybe not. Maybe that person heard somebody coming"—I was thinking of Garland—"and got rattled and forgot the gun. And whoever came next took it away."

She gave me a long look this time.

"Watch the road," I said.

She watched the road. "Why would this—hypothetical person do that, for heaven sake?"

"Maybe they thought they knew who the murderer was, and they wanted to protect that person."

"Jason," Carlotta said, "you found it in the car, didn't you? I thought I was losing my mind—but you took it."

"I buried it. In the orchard. Nobody will ever find it." I looked at her. And for the first time I saw an old woman. It was the worry, wasn't it, the strain? I said, "I'm sorry I kept it a secret, but you kept it a secret from me that you already knew Sam was dead, that you'd been to the house, and picked up that gun."

"You're too young to be burdened with such things."

"Yes, all right, and you shouldn't be burdened with lying—that's what I thought. If you didn't know where the gun was, you could say so when Gerard asked you, and it would be the truth."

"Thank you, Jason." She reached across and patted the side of my face. "Where did Arlene get that gun? When?"

"She didn't," I said. "Not that I ever knew of. Arlene didn't kill Sam, Grandma. She couldn't."

A deer bounded across the road. Carlotta jammed on the brakes and the Bronco's tires grabbed the pavement. It's times like that when you're glad for seat belts. The engine stalled, and Carlotta was shaky, getting it started again. When we were rolling once more, she said, "She had every reason, she had every excuse."

"But she wouldn't," I said.

"Then she should come home," Carlotta cried.

"She will," I said. "She will."

★ ★ ★ ★ ★

It was early, I admit that. Not even 6:00 yet. So it's no wonder Sean Touhy squinted at me through her screen door like I was crazy. Her hair was tousled, and she was clutching a bathrobe closed at her throat. She shivered. The day was going to be fine and clear but the sun hadn't had time to warm things up yet. She was barefoot. She stood on one foot, rubbing the other against the back of her leg.

"Jason Moore," she said. "What in the world?"

"I'm sorry," I said, "but it's an emergency."

"Dear God. Aren't you having more than your share?"

"Yes. I need your help."

"Come in." She pushed open the screen and turned away. "I'll get us some coffee."

"I already had coffee," I said.

"I didn't," she said, and went out of the room.

I called after her, "I need a ride to the Kaiser River."

"What?" She didn't mean she hadn't heard me. She meant the suggestion was goofy. She appeared with a glass pot in her hand. "That's clear across the state, Jason."

"I know, but I have to get there, and I haven't got a driver's license." I dug into my pocket. "Here's forty dollars. For gasoline and something to eat on the way."

She gave me a thin smile and with a wag of her head went back to the kitchen where I heard her rattling stuff. Then the kitchen went quiet. I sat down and picked up a copy of *American Artist* and looked through it while I waited for her to come back. I was fidgety. I couldn't spare the time. It would take hours to get there. We should be starting right now. I doubt she was gone ten minutes but it seemed much longer to me. Finally when I could smell coffee, the kitchen noises took up again, and soon she was there, washed, dressed, hair combed, with mugs of coffee and Danish pastries on a plate.

She set these things on a coffee table and sat on the floor opposite me. She'd heated the pastries in the microwave. Butter swam on them. Hungry, I picked one up.

She said, "Now, what's it all about?"

With my mouth full, I said, "It's private. I'm sorry."

"You want me to drive you two hundred miles to the high Sierras, but you won't tell me why?"

"If you don't know, you can't get into trouble." I licked my fingers. "Look, it's a matter of life and death."

She eyed me thoughtfully. "The radio's been saying the Sheriff is searching for your mother. They think she killed Sam Dexter, don't they?"

"Yes," I said, and washed the bite of Danish down with coffee. "But she didn't. I know she didn't."

"How do you know?" Sean Touhy said. "You weren't there."

"I know her. She wouldn't, she couldn't."

She said gravely, "He was very cruel to her, Jason."

"I know that," I shouted. "You think I don't know that?" I stood up. "Look, will you take me, or not?"

"Is that where she's hiding? In the high Sierras?"

"You could ski," I said. "There's good snow up there now, after the storm."

"So much snow, the roads are probably blocked." She got to her feet. "Jason, I'm your friend, but you know I can't do this. Whether she's guilty or not, she's a fugitive from justice, and I'd be breaking the law if I helped her."

"I'm not asking you to help her. Just get me to her."

"But what good can you do? You're not thinking."

"She needs somebody," I said, "she's all alone. She needs somebody who cares about her."

"Call the Sheriff. There's the telephone. Tell him where your mother is. He'll bring her home. Back to you. And your grandmother."

"He'll lock her up," I said. "For life."

"Not if she didn't do it," Sean Touhy said.

I gave a sour laugh, and headed for the door. "You believe that if you want to. Why do you think she ran and hid? She knows what they'll do to her, and so do I." I pulled open the door. "We'll go away together. We'll be all right." I gave her a smile. "Don't worry about us."

"Oh, Jason," she said sadly, "you are so very young."

"There'll be lots of skiers heading for the Sierras," I said. "Somebody will let me hitch a ride."

"Riding with strangers is dangerous," she said sharply.

"I'll be careful." I went out, then turned back. "Don't tell anybody about this, okay?"

"No one will ask me." She was in the doorway. "Jason, you're making a mistake. You have a good mind. Use it."

"No time," I said, and got on my bike.

Cap Willard didn't like traveling if it wasn't on the ocean. But the practical fact was, around here a person had to have wheels. His were attached to a rusty pickup truck, and he could drive it if he absolutely had to. If I couldn't get him to take me, I really would have to hitchhike, and to be honest, I was as scared of that as Miss Touhy was. So I headed up the coast road to talk to Cap.

Dressed in a yellow slicker and rubber boots, he was on the *Emily*, doing cleanup after the storm. Mainly hosing the salt water off her. It didn't surprise me that he was up early. His days, at least when there was business, began at dawn. What surprised me, so much I nearly fell off my bike, was who he was talking to. Lieutenant Gerard stood on the dock.

I braked hard, swung off my bike, and crouched down behind some old crates and barrels. They were shouting so their words crossed the distance between them, but I couldn't hear what they were talking about. They were too far away, the surf was too noisy, the crying of gulls. I could guess, though. Trying to locate Arlene Dexter, Gerard was looking up everybody who knew her, and of course Cap had known her since before I was born. He'd been good friends not just with Garland but with her. And me. I hoped he wouldn't mention those summers we spent at Cluff Meadows.

I squatted there, praying Gerard would leave, so I could talk to Cap, but instead, with a hand from Gerard, Cap climbed off the *Emily* onto the dock, the two men went into the office, and shut the door. I figured Cap would make coffee, and they'd sit there for hours, smoking and talking. Gerard would be less than human if he wasn't spellbound by the old man's stories. I was out of luck. I'd have to stand by the highway and stick out my thumb, and just pray I wasn't picked up by some maniac child molester.

I wasn't. It was a leathery old woman turkey rancher driving a big dirty stake truck full of empty crates. She got me as far as Fresno before she took the highway South to Kingsburg. On the way, I learned more about turkeys than I wanted to know. For one thing, they stampede. Like if there's thunder or something. Maybe a fighter plane from the Air Base flying over low. Or just a truck backfiring on the road. And they all run to one side of the enclosure in a panic and suffocate each other. Then there were lots of details about the diseases they get. I'd rather forget it.

Anyway, in Fresno I stopped to eat, and some students from Cal Poly, two women and a dude, got out of a car with skis poking out of the hatchback. They came in and ate, and when they were paying their bill, I got up my nerve and asked them if they'd take me up in the mountains with them, and they agreed. They were really decent. It wasn't on their way, but they checked their map, found the right route, and dropped me at the access road into Cluff Meadows.

I'd never seen it in the snow. It was still beautiful, but different from the summer when there was lush grass and wildflowers. And of course there was sound all the time, the creek running, insects buzzing, birds calling. Now once the car was out of hearing, the place was silent. Across on the far side, I saw the cabin, up among the big pines. I think it belonged to people Garland knew. But they only used it now and then, and because we were always broke, they let him and Arlene and me use it free for those summer weeks.

I started toward it, taking the trail I remembered through the trees edging the meadows. I went by guess, because the trail like everything else was deep in snow. The sky was clear, and the shadow that went with me was blue on the snow. My feet and legs got colder and colder until they went numb. I sat down on a stump, and rubbed my legs. My teeth chattered. I ought to have worn more clothes.

What if I'd been wrong? I'd wanted to find her. This was the only place I could think of. But that didn't make it the only place, did it? Hell, she could be in some motel, in any town, on any road the Wagoneer would take her, a no-name stranger nobody would pay any attention to. Why not? I was a dreamy kid. She'd told me that plenty of times. Miss Touhy had been right this morning—I hadn't used my brain. Why would Arlene come here in the cold and snow? Still—I was here. I'd better look. I climbed down from the stump.

I'd been slogging along with my head down so as not to lose my footing. Now I stopped, certain this was childish, ready to turn back, wondering how I was going to get home again—when I saw the Wagoneer. Just a corner of it. She'd parked it behind the cabin. I was so happy, I shouted. My voice echoed back to me in the white, empty, miles-wide silence. Then I began calling her name. "Arlene! Arlene! It's me. Jason." And I began to run. I stumbled and fell in the snow, and picked myself up laughing, and ran on, panting and gasping out, "Arlene, Arlene."

And when I was still a hundred yards off, the door of the cabin opened, and she was standing there in that lumpy old sweater and her corduroys, and holding up her hands against the sun glare on the snow, squinting, trying to see me. And then she did see me. And she came down the cabin steps and started running toward me with her arms out, laughing and crying. And then we were hugging, and we stayed out there knee deep in snow for I don't know how long, just hugging hell out of each other, and laughing and crying.

At last she stood me away from her. She studied me, worriedly. Her face was all bruised and swollen out of shape. One eye was closed completely. When she talked, she sounded different. Because of those missing teeth, right? She said, "You're all right. They told you not to go home. Sam didn't get you? Oh, Jason, how mad he was. Insane."

I stared. "You don't know?" I looked at the cabin. "You haven't got a radio?"

"Only in the car. And it would run down the battery."

"Sam's dead," I said. "He was dead when I got home from school. I had to go there. I needed clothes. Somebody killed him, Arlene. Shot him in the throat."

"Dead?" She was, like they say, stupefied. She didn't know. I was so happy, I burst out crying. She hugged me to her again. "Jason, what's the matter?"

"You ran away, so they think you killed him," I said. "I told them over and over you couldn't have, but they didn't believe me."

"Poor Jason." Arm still around me, she headed the two of us toward the cabin. "Come on, let's get you warm."

"You were just running away from him," I said. "So he wouldn't beat you up any more."

"I wanted to bring you with me." We went inside and she closed the door. Fire burned in a pot-bellied iron stove. She sat me down beside it and knelt to unlace my shoes and pry them off. "But I couldn't go to the school, not looking the way I did." She laughed a wobbly laugh. "I'd have made everyone sick."

"Never again," I said. "That's over. He's gone."

She pushed my shoes under the stove. "I can't believe it." She got snow from outside and rubbed my feet with it. They stung from the blood coming back into them. "It'll take me days to believe it."

"Grandma's worried sick," I said. "Couldn't you phone?"

"There's no phone here. And the service road's snowed in, so I couldn't drive to town." She went to the cook stove. "I'll fix us cocoa. I was lucky there was food here. I was in such a panic, I didn't think to stop off and buy any on my way. All I wanted was to hide." She fetched cold water in a dishpan. "How did you find me?"

"When I had time to think"—I put my feet into the water—"I knew it could only be here."

"It was brave of you to come," she said.

"I was lonely." I rubbed my feet. "I needed you."

"I was lonely too," she said.

And then there was a sharp, hard knock on the door, and the door opened, and there stood T. Hodges in her deputy sheriff uniform. It had begun to snow, so there was snow on her shoulders and the brim of her hat. She looked frozen. While we stared, she came inside. A uniformed muscle man followed her, and shut the door. He showed us a Fresno county sheriff's badge, and said:

"Arlene Dexter, you are under arrest for the murder of

42

Samuel Dexter in Madrone, California, in San Luis Obispo County."

Arlene shook her head. "I didn't," she said.

"She didn't," I said.

Muscles said, "You have the right to remain silent; if you give up that right, anything you say . . ." He droned on with it until the end. I'd heard it dozens of times on TV cop shows. It sounded different now.

I asked T. Hodges, "Who told you about this place? Miss Touhy? Cap Willard?"

"Nobody had to tell me." T. Hodges gave me the corner of a smile. "All I had to do was follow you."

Arlene wouldn't let Carlotta pay for a lawyer. So, after she'd spent seventy-two hours in jail, it was Fred May, a fat public defender in worn-out tennis shoes, a faded red sweatshirt, and jeans that kept slipping down below his belly, who went before a judge with her. I couldn't make up my mind which of them, poor, battered Arlene or Fat Freddy, with his mangy hair pony-tailed with a rubber band, looked the worst. Who'd believe either of them? But Fat Freddy did a good job, because the judge ruled there was insufficient evidence to hold Arlene for Sam's murder, and made the Sheriff release her. We felt good, we felt empty, we felt very tired, and we drove in Carlotta's car not those long miles up the canyon to the apple ranch, but to the house on Old Bridge Road. The first thing Carlotta did when we got there was drop her bag on the kitchen table and walk through the house and close the door to the den where Sam had worked and where he'd died. In the kitchen together we ate something Carlotta took out of the freezer and heated—I don't think any of us knew what it was or cared—then we went to bed. To be back in my own bed felt wonderful, but really it could have been stuffed with rocks, and I'd have gone to sleep anyway. I was dog-tired. For nights I'd lain awake worrying about Arlene locked up in a cell and maybe going to be locked up forever. Tonight, I didn't have to worry about anything anymore. It felt great.

Nobody thought I should go back to school the next day. I didn't like the idea of missing more classes and homework assignments than I already had. But I didn't want to face the sneers of the kids and teachers either, or the questions my friends would ask, not meaning any harm, but ready to get sore if I didn't answer and explain. I didn't want to lose any friends, but I didn't want to answer and explain either. Why should I? So I just stayed home.

After breakfast, Carlotta drove Arlene over to see old Dr. Belle Hesseltine, about her face. I was in my room, working on a drawing of Cluff Meadows in the snow. With me walking through the trees toward the cabin, and Arlene standing in the cabin door shielding her eyes the way she had. Like in Chinese art, I made the figures small, the trees and mountains tall, and tried to catch the snowy emptiness. After I got it sketched in pencil, I took out my bamboo pen. I really like my bamboo pen. And I'd just opened the India ink, when the door chime went.

It was Lt. Gerard. My heart sank. Because with him was Garland. In handcuffs. I'd thought my worries were over. I'd forgotten if the law couldn't have Arlene for killing Sam, it would have to have somebody else. "What?" I said.

"May we come in?" Gerard said.

"Garland," I said.

"I'm sorry about this," he said. "How are you?"

"You didn't kill him," I said.

"You know that," Garland said with a wan smile, "and I know that. Unluckily, the lieutenant has his doubts."

I was still standing in the doorway. I told Gerard, "He

hasn't been in Settlers Cove in years." I gave Garland the most reproachful look I could work up. "I kept phoning him in San Francisco, begging him to come. He never would."

"He did." Gerard backed me out of his way, and came inside, a big revolver holstered on his thigh. Garland came in too, and Gerard shut the door. "He came the day Sam Dexter died. He met you on your bike in the road. The two of you nearly collided."

I said, "I don't remember."

"You remembered when you went to Cap's Pier just after you discovered Sam Dexter's dead body"—he jerked his head to indicate the den—"on the floor in there. You didn't tell Cap about that, but you told him you'd seen your father."

"I didn't," I said. "I was pissed off about my boat, that's all. Cap had promised me the *Argo* when I grew up. I couldn't see why he'd let Sam go out drunk and sink her in the storm."

Lost in thought, Garland stood looking around the room, taking it all in, probably remembering old times when we all lived here together. I hoped some of the memories were happy. I hoped some of them had me in them. Then without looking at me, sort of absent-mindedly, he said, "Cap can get you another boat. With the insurance money."

I stared. "But he said—" I didn't finish.

"You saw your father, driving away from here in a panic," Gerard said. "And you figured, if he was in the area, he would have gone to see Cap too. You were afraid your father had shot Sam Dexter, and you went to ask Cap not to tell anyone he'd seen Garland Moore that day." He smiled wryly. "Especially not me."

I shook my head. "I didn't see him."

"The rubber from the skid marks down the trail . . ." Gerard gestured at the window, ". . . came from the tires on your father's silver Mercedes." He took a padlock from his pocket. "This is yours. It has your initials scratched on it. We found it where you fell off your bike."

Garland started to reach out to me, I guess to touch my hair, or to pat my shoulder, but both hands had to come at the same time on account of the handcuffs, and he drew them back. Still, the old gentleness was in his voice. "It's no use, son," he said. "I was here. I've admitted it. And you did see me. You may as well say so."

"You didn't kill Sam," I said.

"He was dead when I got here," Garland said. He glanced shame-faced at Gerard, and looked away again. "I ought to have called the Sheriff. But all I could think was Arlene had killed him. I still love her, you know, Jason. With all my heart. There'll never be anyone else for me." Tears were in his eyes. "That's why I don't come see you. It hurts too much." His face set, and he gave his head a quick shake. "I wasn't going to set the law on Arlene."

I turned on Gerard. "Where's the gun? If he killed Sam, where's the gun?"

"We'll find it," Gerard said. "All we need is time."

An hour later, at Carlotta's, I knelt in the orchard. In the dark and rain, I'd done a very poor job of concealment. Fallen apple tree leaves, blackened by the damp, lay thick on the ground everywhere except for where I'd buried the gun. In daylight like this, anyone could have found it. My heart thumped. What if they had? Maybe the gun wasn't there anymore. I dug with Carlotta's trowel. It clanked and I felt better. The gun was still there. I unwrapped it. The plastic had kept it dry. I hadn't even looked before. Now I checked. There were cartridges in the cylinder. Four of them. I stuffed the gun in at my waist and rode my bike back down the canyon. Coasting, mostly. I was grateful for that. My legs were really tired.

They probably wouldn't have taken me all the way to Cap's Pier, if I hadn't been so angry. I dropped my bike on the planks, ran to the bait shack, burst into the gloomy, tackle-hung room. Cap sat cross-legged on the floor, a sail spread out around him, mending a rip with a huge, curved needle. He looked up sharply.

"What are you doing here?" he said.

"Insurance," I said. "The next morning, after Sam lost the *Argo*, you called the insurance company, and they told you the insurance policy had expired. Isn't that right?"

Cap pushed the sail away and got stiffly to his feet. He wasn't looking at my face. His gaze was fixed on my waistband. "That's my gun. Where the hell did you get that?"

I took the gun out, pulled back the hammer, and pointed it at him. Very wobbly. My hand was shaking. "Answer me about the insurance."

"What do you know about insurance?" he snorted.

"I know you let Sam handle all your business stuff," I said. "He told me so. And you always said you hated bookkeeping, banking, bill paying. You used to groan over it."

"Put the gun down, Jason," he said. "Somebody's going to get hurt."

"You put it all in Sam's hands, let him look after everything," I said. "Including the insurance policies—right?"

He said, "You're in over your head, here, boy," and took a step toward me, reaching out. "Give me the gun, now."

"After you tell me the truth," I said. I was trying to sound tough, but I sounded like I was about to cry. "You murdered him because he was cheating you."

"He let me think he'd paid the insurance," Cap said. "But instead he'd written the checks to himself." He picked up papers from the desk. "I made him show me his bank statements. Here they are." He rattled them at me. He was angry now, remembering. His face got red. "He'd embezzled half the money I owed. No wonder I was failing, here. He was drowning me in debt."

"And when you found out," I said, "you killed him."

Cap nodded. "I sure as hell did." Then he gave a funny kind of gasp. His knees sagged. He dropped the papers, clutched his chest, leaned back against the desk. "Dead as mackerel." His eyes were angry, glaring at me. "And don't tell me you aren't glad. After what he did to you, sinking the *Argo*. Your boat, the boat I gave you. I'm your friend, Jason, aren't you forgetting?" He reached out again. "You should be thanking me, not waving a gun at me."

"What kind of friend?" I scoffed. "You promised not to tell anyone Garland had been here. You broke your promise. To save your own neck, you tried to put the blame on Garland. Don't ask me to thank you, Cap."

"Sam Dexter—stole—my life." Cap dropped to his knees. Heavily. Staring at me, begging with his eyes. For what? For me to say I forgave him? I guess I did, but I couldn't say it. He fell face forward on the floor. The weight of him made the old pier shake.

"All right, Jason," a voice said behind me. I turned. It was T. Hodges again. She put her hand out too. Exactly as Cap had done. Only for her, I handed over the gun.

"What are you going to do with your time," I said, "when you don't have to follow me around, anymore?"

But she didn't answer. She was kneeling beside Cap to see if he was alive.

I hoped for his own sake he wasn't.

Widower's Walk

The new kid has overslept and, being not much more than a teenager, could sleep till noon. Bohannon drags on Levis and boots, flaps into a shirt, steps over the windowsill onto the long porch of the ranch house, and heads for the stable building, clean low lines against the gray background of the drowsing mountains. Horses move restlessly, rumble and blow air through their big sinuses behind the closed doors of their box stalls. "Buck?" he says. "Seashell? Geranium?" And names the rest as he passes. His own horses, and horses he boards for folks in the little town of Madrone, at the foot of this canyon, beside the ocean.

He raps knuckles on the tackroom door, whitewashed planks. "Kelly? Time to get up." No reaction. He knocks again. Silence. He lifts the black metal tongue that serves as a latch, swings the door inward, pokes his head inside. "Kelly? Wake up." But the steel cot looks empty. He steps inside. It's empty all right. But slept in hard, sheets tangled, blankets half on the floor. He glances around in the weak morning light from the single window. Two of George Stubbs's horse drawings on the walls (shouldn't there be three?). No boots under the cot. He opens the drawers of the unpainted chest. Nothing. No clothes in the closet. He shuts his eyes and swears. Another one gone.

He walks back along the sheltered length of the stable

building, opening the top doors as he goes. He doesn't turn to see, but he knows heads are poking out to watch him. Hoofs move fidgety, hopefully. At the end stall he opens the whole door and takes Buck's bridle and leads him out. He loops the reins around a post and goes inside the building and gets his saddle.

"Come on," he says, throwing blanket and saddle over Buck's broad back. "Start you and me off with a ride today." He grunts, bending to cinch up the girth. Buck grunts, too. Bohannon puts boot into stirrup and swings heavily aboard. "Nice long ride." He nudges Buck's ample sides with his heels and they move out onto the gravel under the rustling trees. "Hell, maybe we'll just keep riding." Buck heads for the gate, that has a wooden arch over it, which holds the single name BOHANNON in cutout wooden letters. "Maybe we'll never come back." He leans from the saddle to unfasten the left leaf of the gate and when they're past it, leans and drags it closed again. Habit. This morning he wouldn't mind if somebody came and stole the place, horses and all. They'd be doing him a favor. Out on the pitted blacktop road, he reins Buck to the left up the canyon.

He can't remember how many stable hands he's lost since losing first Rivera—he'd expected that: Rivera had all along been training to be a priest—and then George Stubbs, the veteran rodeo rider who'd come to Bohannon already old, and whom arthritis at last has put into a nursing home. There'd followed drunks and itchy-footed men, green and lazy boys, even one girl, who worked hard but quit to get married. Bohannon promised himself when he hired young Kelly that he'd be the last. If Kelly walked out on him, it would be a signal to give up and sell the ranch to a land developer, the way everybody else in the canyons seemed to be doing. It was all work and no fun any more. Why prolong the misery?

He's a couple of miles up the canyon now and no longer on the main track. Buck is paying more attention than he is to his surroundings, and Buck shies. Now this is not the kind of shy that would unsettle any rider but the newest. Buck is, after all, no colt. He's got fifteen years on him, if not more. And he's heavy. So his shy only *almost* unseats Bohannon. For a second the man has to fight to keep upright. A hard-bitten fifty-two or three, his reflexes aren't what they used to be.

"Whoa, what's the matter?"

But before the words are quite out of his mouth he sees what's the matter. A man is lying face down in the road: half in the road, half on the shoulder. "Easy." Bohannon turns Buck's head, and they cross the road, where Bohannon swings down, and ties the reins to a tree. He gives Buck's trembling flank a couple of soothing strokes, then crosses the road to the man. He kneels and touches the man, lays fingers lightly on the man's neck below the ear. But there's no need to feel for a pulse: the man is cold. He's been dead for hours.

Bohannon was for a long time a deputy sheriff. He knows how to act in situations like this. From his crouch he looks around him, first at the whole wide scene, canyon, trees, rocks, dry streambed below, then up the slope that climbs to his right. Next he studies the immediate site. Close to the body. Spatters of blood. Then what's near his boot soles— dried leaves, sickle shaped eucalyptus, curled oak, pine needles, pebbles, no bullet, no shell casing. Nothing is stuck to the soles of the man's shoes.

The man is well dressed and not for a rustic place like this but for city life. The suit is dark. There's a necktie. The shirt is white. Where it isn't bloodstained. Somebody shot this man. From the front. Bohannon knows an exit wound when he sees one, and he sees one. Right between the shoulder blades.

51

He doesn't touch the body again, or the clothes. It was his job once, but no more. He stands, brushes grit off his hands, and looks to the right again. Some way up the slope, among trees, rocks, ferns and brush, he thought earlier he'd glimpsed metal. He had. He climbs towards it, and his heart sinks when his guess as to what it is turns out to be a fact. It is Steve Belcher's battered camper truck. Belcher is a bearded, longhaired Vietnam veteran who lives in the camper and leaves everybody else alone and wishes they would leave him alone. The best luck he has had in his four or five years here is since he took to the canyons. First he'd parked the camper different places in Madrone and the citizens had moved him on. "On" proved to be a leaky old fishing boat he'd anchored in Short's Inlet, a body of water nobody cared about except some migrating ducks now and then, but that everybody got protective about once Belcher had started to live there. Belcher was polluting, wasn't he? A beautiful natural wild-fowl habitat.

So Belcher gave up after making some ugly scenes at town council meetings—he had a rough mouth on him, did Belcher—and he'd taken to the canyons with this rusty camper. He never went into town except to pick up his disability check every month and buy supplies. The rest of the time he kept out of the way. Except for establishing his campsite once in the Mozart Bowl. Dr. Dolores Combs and the rest of the town's wealthy music lovers damn near had him hanged for that. Bohannon's boots crunch across strewn paper and crushed cans and plastic packaging. Coyotes or raccoons have broken open a trash bag, looking for a meal. He hears a noise and looks up, and Belcher is standing, buck-naked, in the camper's dented doorway, holding a Browning nine mm.

"It's me," Bohannon says. "Don't shoot."

"Fuckin' early," Belcher grunts. His dirty blond hair and beard are tousled from sleep. "What do you want? You never give me no trouble. Not you." He narrows mistrustful eyes. "Not yet."

"There's something down on the trail," Bohannon says, "that shouldn't be there. Put on some clothes. I want you to take a look at it."

Belcher tilts his head. "What do you mean—'something'?"

"A body," Bohannon says.

Belcher stares. "A dead body?"

"Shot through the chest. Middle of the night. You hear anything?"

"Jesus." Belcher scratches his beard. "Jesus."

"You want to answer me?" Bohannon says. "You want to hand me your gun to sniff at?"

Belcher jerks with surprise. He's forgotten the gun. "It ain't mine." He puts it down inside the camper. "It ain't been fired." His voice is hoarse and he has grown pale though his skin is like tanned leather. "And I didn't hear no shot."

"Not yours? It's the kind the Army issues, Steve."

"Banged against the truck. Middle of the night. Found it there by the front wheel." He kicks into ragged jeans. "Christ. Why here?"

"It's not your lucky day," Bohannon says. "Come on. Have a look at him."

"I don't see what for," Belcher says.

"So I can see your face when you say you don't know who he is. I've always trusted you. I want to see if I still can."

Belcher grunts and comes loose-limbed down the trailer's little metal stairs. His feet are dirty. "I don't want to see no more floppies. I seen enough. I told you that. Hell, Bohannon, I killed enough. Too many. Drives me crazy dreaming about it. I'd never kill again."

"You still keep your pistol," Bohannon says.

"I would," Belcher says, "if it would kill ghosts. It's not mine, Bohannon. I told you that. I hate the God damn things."

"Come on." Bohannon turns away and starts downhill. "You know Lieutenant Gerard is going to home in on you. You're the obvious suspect." He goes quickly, the underfoot is slippery with morning dew, he almost falls. "He and I were partners once, and if I tell him I'm sure it wasn't you, it might help." He looks over his shoulder.

The truck's cab door slams. The starter whinnies.

Bohannon turns back, loses his footing, falls to hands and knees. "Wait. Steve—don't do this."

The truck engine roars. Belcher looks out the window. "Forget it, Bohannon. You know what Gerard will do. I'm a homicidal maniac. He's been waiting years to prove that." He lets the parking brake go, the truck rolls backward about a foot, then springs forward. "So long." Its old gray tires kicking up duff, Belcher weaves the truck away fast, in and out among the trees.

Bohannon struggles to his feet. "You're only making it worse," he shouts.

But maybe not. Maybe there's no way Belcher could do that.

He sits on a stump, lights a cigarette, and waits. He can't leave the body. If instead of riding Buck up here, he'd come in the truck, he could radio the Sheriff station. He's just stuck, is all there is to it. Until somebody comes along. And Rodd Canyon is not known for heavy traffic. Whole damn day could pass without a single car. Sure as hell won't any horses be coming by. Not till he gets back down to his place.

It's the only rental stable around. He stands up. This is a hell of a note.

It remains that for forty minutes (he keeps checking his watch) and then he hears an engine, the loose tool rattle and spring squeak of a vehicle. It's a red pickup. Fire patrol. He steps into the road. The driver is Sorenson, whom he's known for years. Sorenson stops the truck. He stares through the windshield at the body on the road.

"What does that mean?" he asks Bohannon.

"Means you can use your two-way," Bohannon says, "to let them know down at Madrone, and they can come pick him up. Shooting victim."

"Get in." Sorenson stretches across and opens the door on the passenger side of the cab. "You know how to use the thing."

"Do it for me," Bohannon says. "And lie a little, will you? Tell T. Hodges you found him. Leave me out of it."

Sorenson, blond and sunburned, looking twenty years younger than his age, wrinkles his brow. "What for? You don't want her to know you were riding your horse up the canyon? Why not?"

"Just do it," Bohannon says.

"Hey." Sorenson half lies across the seat, craning to see up the slope. "Where's Steve Belcher? He had his camper up there."

"Did he?" Bohannon says. "Not here now."

"I wonder why?" Sorenson says. "You've protected him time and again, Hack. But for a shooting? A killing?"

"Don't drag Belcher into it," Bohannon says. "Just tell them about the body, okay?"

Sorenson takes the part of the two-way radio you talk into from its hook and puts it to his mouth. There are noises, cracklings, sandpaper voices, indistinct words. He switches those off and talks into the mike. "Sorenson, up here in Rodd Canyon, trail that drops off the main road at the stand of big old eucalyptus trees on the left? Dead body of an older man laying in the road. Shooting victim, looks like." An answer crackles, and Sorenson says, "Ten four" and hangs up the microphone.

"Thanks. Really appreciate it." Bohannon is already astraddle Buck and headed back for the main road. "Got to get home. Lost my stable hand again. Work enough for three men waiting for me."

For an answer, Sorenson gives a short hoot on his siren.

"As a licensed private investigator," Gerard says, "you can't encourage a suspect to flee. You can't aid and abet—"

"Shut up, Phil," Bohannon says, grinning. "This is my house and I don't have to listen to you rave. Not here. Sit down. Have a drink."

Red-faced, Gerard yanks a chair out from the round deal table that stands in the middle of Bohannon's big pine plank kitchen, and drops onto it. He bangs his helmet down on the table. "Naw, I'm serious, Hack. You just stood there and watched him take off. And you let us think you weren't even up there." Bohannon hands him a glass with Old Crow in it. "I can't understand you."

"Was the man shot with a nine millimeter Browning?"

"Nine millimeter something." Gerard takes a swallow from his glass and makes a face. "How can you drink this stuff?"

Bohannon chuckles. "I manage. You find any ID on the body?"

"Robbery," Gerard says. "That's what Belcher wanted it to look like. Anyway, no wallet. But that's a good suit, and the labels are in it. Expensive, maybe even tailor-made. We'll check the shop out tomorrow."

Bohannon grunts. He has his glasses on, and papers spread out in front of him. He pushes them into a raggedy stack and pokes the stack into a manila envelope. This was George Stubbs's job. Bohannon can't do paperwork and drink. Hell, he hates paperwork at the best of times. And this is not the best of times. He's worn out from rubbing down horses, picking gravel out of hoofs, mucking out stalls, raking gravel, hauling water, pitching hay, writing receipts, answering damn fool phone calls, trying to collect overdue board bills, walking little kid riders around the railed oval he had built for that back when Rivera was here.

"There was nothing on the soles of his shoes to indicate a hike. He drove there."

Gerard studies him. "No car around. One car brought him and his killer both? And the killer drove it away, afterward?"

Bohannon nods. "Which leaves out Steve Belcher."

"How?" Gerard says. "His camper was within yards of the victim. Why didn't Belcher bring him up from town for some kind of meeting? And it went sour, and Belcher lost his temper and shot him? He's got a mad dog temper, Hack. You've got to admit that."

"Maybe, but he's only a little bit crazy. He wouldn't leave the body lying there. He'd take it someplace else. Come on, Phil."

Gerard makes a skeptical sound, picks up his helmet, and gets to his feet. "We'll see what turns up in that camper."

Bohannon stares. "You've got it?"

"It's not hard to spot," Gerard says. "He hadn't got to Fresno yet when the CHP pulled him over. On our APB."

Bohannon switches on the lamp in the middle of the table. There's still some daylight outside, but the kitchen doesn't get a lot of it. The lamp is an old kerosene lantern fitted out for electricity and enameled red. Linda's idea—his wife, who is in a private mental home just over the ridge, has been for a long time, and looks like being there forever. Gerard walks to the open door.

Bohannon tells his back, "You're going to find the dead man's car up the canyon someplace. What? Mercedes? BMW? Jaguar? Abandoned in a ditch. Wiped clean of fingerprints."

"I know how to do my job," Gerard says, and pushes open the screen door.

Bohannon says, "Oh, and find a kid named Kelly. Hold on a second." He walks to the sideboard and takes a slip of paper from a drawer. He puts on the damn reading glasses again and peers at it. "Kelly Jeffers. No Social Security Number. Hails from San Bernardino. Jockey size, shaved head, tattoos. He'll likely be on foot, doesn't own a car. He was my stable boy till this morning very early. Maybe about the same time the man in the expensive suit got so fatally shot."

"We've got the nut who shot that man," Gerard says, "and you know it. Steve Belcher has been a disaster waiting to happen for years now. You always took his side. Don't make that mistake this time. You're already in deep, letting him get away this morning."

"What was I supposed to do? He had a gun, I didn't. He had a car, I didn't."

"Right. So why not admit right away that you were there? Way you handled it, anybody can think anything they want."

"They'll do that anyway." Bohannon walks to the door, steps out; watches Gerard go off along the porch to his brown Sheriff's patrol car. He calls after him, "Did you find the bullet up there? It went right through him."

"Not yet," Gerard calls, "but we'll find it. Don't get your hopes up." He starts the car, slams the door, and takes off.

★ ★ ★ ★ ★

Bohannon can't understand it. He comes from his bedroom down the hall to the kitchen, following bacon smells, coffee smells. Hair wet from the shower, he stands barefoot in jeans and T-shirt, blinking in the lamplight. It's not daylight yet. The old schoolroom clock on the kitchen wall reads 5:10. And beside the monster nickel and porcelain stove stands T. Hodges, the slim, dark young woman deputy who is Bohannon's prime friend. She is beating up eggs in a pottery bowl that has Indian designs on it. She throws him a smile. "Good morning."

"I'll say. What's the occasion?"

"The Lieutenant told me Kelly's left you," she says. A pitcher of orange juice is on the counter. She pours him a glass and holds it out for him. He limps to her and takes it. "That you're trying to do it all, here. Stubbs's work, Rivera's work, and yours."

Bohannon nods and swallows some orange juice. "True, but—"

"So, I thought at least I could fix breakfast for you," she says.

"Mighty nice. Pretty early for you to get up, though." He sets the orange juice glass on the table and goes to take the old speckled blue enamel pot off the back burner on the stove and pour himself a mug of coffee. He raises the pot to her. "Pour some for you?"

"Not yet, thanks. Go sit down and enjoy that." She examines an iron skillet, turning it in the light, finds it acceptably clean, sets it on the stove and cuts butter into it. "There's news. The dead man's name is Lubowitz. Cedric. A stockbroker. Beverly Hills. Age sixty-five. Newly a widower."

Bohannon lights a cigarette and squints at her, past the light of the table lamp. "How'd they come by all this?"

"His picture on the news," T. Hodges says. "Seems he used to appear now and then on Wall Street Week."

"Nobody in your department watches Wall Street Week?" She laughs. "Picture it if you can," she says.

"And what was he doing in Rodd Canyon? What did he want up this way at all? Only stock up this way is livestock."

"And commodities were not his line," T. Hodges says.

The coffee is hot and strong. He douses it with cream. "And Belcher. Did Belcher know him?"

"Belcher watches Wall Street Week even less than Gerard." She brings a plate of bacon, eggs, and hash browns and sets it in front of Bohannon. "Eat hearty."

"What about you?" he says.

"Coming up," she says, and it is. In another minute she has taken the pressed-wood chair opposite him. Now there's a stack of toast on the table too. She tucks in a gingham napkin, picks up her fork, then looks at him. Very seriously. "Hack, you can't let Gerard do this to Steve Belcher. He's the gentlest, sorriest creature in the world. But everybody is ready to believe the worst, you know that."

Bohannon piles guava jelly on a slab of toast. "So does Belcher. Nothing I can do about it. He'd been better off if he just hadn't—"

"He didn't kill that man!" T. Hodges says hotly.

"I guess not," Bohannon says. "But I'm not the jury."

"You mean you're going to let it happen? Just sit back and—"

"Teresa," Bohannon says gently. "You've already told me I'm trying to do three men's work around here. It's my living. I can't play detective anymore. Even if I had the energy, I haven't got the time."

"I'll do the leg work for you," she says. "You just tell me what needs to be done and I'll do it. Kelly. Gerard says you think Kelly might have done it. I'll find him and bring him here."

"You have a job, love," Bohannon says. "Eight hours a day and sometimes more. Anyway, Gerard wouldn't tolerate you working the case against him. Behind his back. Don't think about it." She opens her mouth to argue, and he says, "Eat your beautiful breakfast, kid, and listen to your old man. Things happen everyday that are at least as unjust as what's happening to Steve Belcher. All over the world. We can't stop them, no matter how much we'd like to."

"Oh, rubbish," she says. "Honestly, Hack. 'Old Man,' indeed. I repeat—you tell me where to go, what to look for, who to talk to, and I'll do it. Yes, I have a job, but I have a lot of time away from that. Besides, Gerard is sexist. He never lets me have a case. Closest I get is tracking down lost children. A case like this is Man's Work, right?"

"That's Phil," Bohannon grunts. "These are better hash browns than Stubbs ever made. What's your secret?"

"Don't boil the potatoes first. Grate them up raw." She gives her head an impatient shake. "Don't change the subject, damn it. Hack, Fred May says it's hopeless, he can't win without you."

May is the local Public Defender, those rare times when a Public Defender is needed around here. Fat and amiable, he devotes most of his time to his wife and kids, and to protecting the whale and the wolf and the wilderness. Bohannon has often acted as his investigator.

"Don't look at me that way," he says. "I can't do it, Teresa. I have horses to look after. They can't feed themselves and clean up after themselves. You know that. Be reasonable."

" 'Reasonable' won't save Steve Belcher." Tears are in her eyes. "The town can't wait to get rid of him. You know that."

"And I can't help it." Bohannon stands, picks up his plate and hers—she's hardly eaten—and carries them to the sink. He brings the coffeepot back and refills their mugs. When he sits down, it is a gesture of disgust. "What the hell was Cedric Lubowitz doing here, anyway?"

"I thought you'd want to know," a tart voice says from the doorway. Belle Hesseltine stands there backed by the first faint light of sunrise. She is a doctor who moved up to Madrone to retire many years ago now, and instead got busier than she'd ever been before. A lean, tough old gal, she's a mainstay of hope and courage and caring for many. For Bohannon too. "I went past the substation to tell the Lieutenant but he hasn't come in yet." She walks toward the table, pulls out a chair, seats herself, looks at T. Hodges. "You weren't there, either." She sets her shoulder bag on the floor. "So I thought the one to tell was you, Hack."

"Well, you're wrong about that," Bohannon says. "But I'm happy to see you, all the same. Coffee?"

"I'll get it," T. Hodges says and hops up and goes away into the shadows. "You persuade him he's got to help poor Steve Belcher."

Belle Hesseltine scowls at Bohannon. "Persuade? What's that mean? You aren't going to—? But the man's doomed unless somebody intervenes. He hasn't a chance. He can't rely on himself. He can't put his thoughts together. He can't fight back. Hack, I'm shocked."

"I'm stuck, Belle. I have to run this place alone. Time a day is over, all I'm good for is to sleep."

Belle watches T. Hodges set a coffee mug down for her. "What happened to my tattooed angel?"

"Kelly? Spread his wings yesterday morning and flew away. I told Gerard, it could have been the same time Lubowitz was shot. Phil doesn't see any connection. If I know him, he won't even bother to check." It is risky and he knows it but he lights a cigarette anyway. The old woman glares disapproval, but this time she doesn't bawl him out. And he asks, "So . . . what's Lubowitz's connection to our little township?"

"His sister-in-law," Belle says, and tries the coffee. "Aah!" She holds the steaming mug up for a moment, admiring it, then sets it down with a regretful shake of her head. "Why is it that everything that tastes so good is so bad for us?"

"Sister-in-law?" T. Hodges wonders.

"Mary Beth Madison." Belle Hesseltine leans toward the table's center, peering intently. "Is that some of George Stubbs's guava jelly? Hack, push that toast and butter over here. That wicked old man made the most sinfully delicious preserves!" She steals Hack's knife and goes after the toast and jelly as if the world had stopped for her convenience. When her mouth is jammed and her dentures are clacking happily away, when she is licking her fingers, slurping coffee, she notices their strained faces and makes an effort to swallow so she can speak. She sets down the coffee mug. "Very good Pasadena family. It was Mary Beth's older sister Rose that Cedric Lubowitz married. There was scandal and talk of disinheriting Rose for marrying a Jew, but that blew over."

A corner of the old woman's mouth twitches in a smile.

"The Lubowitzes were neighbors, after all, and their house was just as splendid. The girls and young Cedric had spent their childhoods together, very close. I also suspect some Lubowitz financial advice had helped stabilize the Madison fortune. It was shaky. Henry Madison III had not been clever with his inheritance. Among his lesser follies was buying land in Madrone and Settlers Cove. Worthless at the time. That's how it happens that Mary Beth settled here. And"—she looks at first one then the other—"the reason I retired here. My father, the Madison family doctor, had accepted a lot up here to settle a bill when times were bad."

"And that's how you know all this dishy stuff," T. Hodges marvels. "But doesn't Mary Beth Madison live with Dr. Dolores Combs? The Chamber Symphony? The Canyon Mozart Festival? The Gregorian Chant Week at the Mission?"

Belle Hesseltine nods. "And much else as well. Yes, that's Dolores. But the house and money are Mary Beth's. Hard to believe that as a child Dolores Combs was scarcely more than a foundling, isn't it?"

T. Hodge's jaw drops. "Are you serious?"

"The Madison girls took to her, brought her home from the park one summer with them, and after that she was in the Madison mansion almost constantly. The family soon accepted her. After all, what she lacked in breeding and background she made up for in brains and talent."

Bohannon says, "She cuts quite a figure these days."

Belle Hesseltine smiles. "Her people were poor, uneducated, the father drank. They had no idea they had a musical prodigy on their hands. It was the Madisons who bought her a piano, got her lessons, sent her to university."

"And so," T. Hodges says, "when it came time for Cedric Lubowitz to marry, and he chose Rose, Dolores Combs and Mary Beth Madison soldiered on alone together?"

Bohannon is laughing.

She frowns at him, startled. "What's so funny?"

"You never told me you liked love stories."

"Well—well, I don't," she protests. "But this is about a murder case, Hack. It's straight out of the training manual. The most important person in any murder case is the victim. And the most likely killer is someone the victim knew well. Right?"

"Sounds more like Agatha Christie to me," Bohannon says.

"Well—" Belle Hesseltine unfolds her tall, bony frame from the chair, and picks up her shoulder bag. "I have patients to see."

"Wait," Bohannon says. "Was Cedric Lubowitz up here to visit Mary Beth, is that what you're saying?"

"Oh, I don't suppose so, really. He owned one of those lots his father-in-law bought so long ago," the old doctor says. "He may have planned to build on it and settle down here to live out his sunset years in peace and quiet. Hah! I could have told him a few things about that, couldn't I?" She opens the screen door, and pauses to look back. At T. Hodges, really, so maybe she's teasing. "Then again, perhaps having lost dear pretty Rose, and feeling lonely, he came to renew acquaintance with Mary Beth, who is every bit as pretty. I suppose, if you like love stories, you're free to think that."

And with a bark of laughter, she marches off.

Tired as he is, he goes to see Stubbs. It's a long drive to San Luis, but he skipped last night, and it's not fair. The old man is lonesome as hell. Anyway, Bohannon misses him. If there's nothing to talk about, they play checkers or watch horse racing or bull riding on television. Tonight there is Steve Belcher to talk about, and Cedric Lubowitz. Stubbs regards Bohannon from his narrow bed with its shiny rails where he is propped up with his wooden drawing kit and drawing pad beside him on the wash-faded quilt. When the pain isn't too bad, he can still draw. He says reproachfully:

"You ain't gonna help him?"

"Stable boy left me. No time, George."

"Oh, Kelly," Stubbs grunts. "Yeah, I know. He come by here real early yesterday. Says will I tell you. Gotta go home. They're runnin' his ma out of the trailer park for fightin' with her boyfriend."

"He could have left a note," Bohannon says.

"Nothin' to write with," Stubbs says, "nothin' to write on."

"On the kitchen table," Bohannon says. "He knew that. Knew where I sleep, too. He could have wakened me and told me. He woke you."

Stubbs waves a gnarled hand. "Had to see me. Had one of my drawings. Took it down off the tack room wall. Wanted it for his room at home. Wouldn't steal it. Offered me five bucks for it. I give it to him."

"How did he get in here so early?"

"It was warm." Stubbs nods at the window. "Come in there."

Bohannon says, "Didn't say anything about the killing, did he?"

Stubbs frowns. "How would he know about it?"

"Just asking," Bohannon says.

Stubbs squints at him, surprised. "You don't think he'd of killed this Lubo—what's his name. Why?"

"I'd like to ask him," Bohannon says.

"He'd need a gun," Stubbs says. "Where would he get it?"

"A Browning automatic. I don't know. Someone got hold of one. Threw it away after the shooting."

"And Belcher just picked it up?" Stubbs says.

"That's his story. I doubt they'll find a record of it. Bought on the street, most likely. And the tattoos suggest Kelly knows the streets."

"Ballistics report in already?" Stubbs's white tufty eyebrows are raised. "They know it was the Browning?"

Bohannon shakes his head. "They can't find the bullet," he says. "But a paraffin test says Belcher shot the gun lately."

"Oh, hell," Stubbs says.

"He told Gerard it was to scare off a prowler," Bohannon

says, "but he told me earlier it hadn't been fired."

"You see why you have to pitch in and help him?" Stubbs says. "The fool's his own worst enemy. Always has been."

"Not always," Bohannon says. "Once it was Uncle Sam."

"Just a minute." Stubbs massages his white beard stubble thoughtfully. "Could the prowler have been Kelly?"

Bohannon blinks surprise. "Well, I'll be damned," he says. "Good thinking, George. Why not?"

He swings into the ranch yard and in the headlights sees a brown Sheriff's patrol car. Lights wink on top of it. Two doors stand open. Two people struggle beside it. He drives on hard towards them. One is T. Hodges, her helmet on the ground. The other is Kelly Jeffers. He pushes T. Hodges backward so she falls. He turns and comes running directly at Bohannon's truck. From one wrist dangles a pair of handcuffs, glinting in the light. His shirt is torn down the back and slipping off his shoulders, showing his tattoos. Bohannon jams on the Gemmy's brakes, jumps down with a yell and grabs the boy. Who twists and hits out with the handcuff-dangling fist. It knocks Bohannon's hat off.

"Stop it," he says. "Stand still, damn it, Kelly."

"Aw, let me go," the boy says. "I didn't do nothin'."

"Then don't fight," Bohannon says. "There. That's better." He calls to T. Hodges who stands in the headlight beams. "You all right?"

"Kelly . . ." she says in a menacing voice, and comes toward them.

"I'm sorry," the boy says, hangdog.

"I should think so." She is wiping dust off her helmet with her sleeve. "I was taking the cuffs off him. I told him I was sure I could trust him. And look what happened."

"We'll just put them back," Bohannon says, and clips the

cuffs on him again. "There." He picks up his hat. "Now, let's go into the kitchen, sit down, have some coffee, and talk this over civilized? All right?"

"I don't know anything to talk about," Kelly says, stumbling along, Bohannon holding his arm. "This is crazy."

They step up onto the long covered walkway that is the ranch house porch. Bohannon looks over Kelly's head at T. Hodges. "Is it crazy?"

"I don't think so," she says. "Not when you consider that his last name isn't Jeffers—"

"It could be," Kelly says. "It was my Mom's name."

Bohannon pulls open the kitchen screen door, they walk inside, he hangs up his hat. The lamp on the table glows. "It's Belcher, right?"

Kelly stares. "How did you know?"

"Sit down," Bohannon says, goes to the looming stove, picks up the speckled blue coffeepot. But T. Hodges comes and takes it out of his hand. "I'll do it," she says. "You talk to him."

"This is going to get you into a mess with Gerard," he says.

"We'll deal with Gerard later," she says.

Bohannon drops onto a chair at the table and as he lights a cigarette, studies the sulking boy. "You didn't happen in on me by chance, looking for work. You tracked down your father, and took this job to be near him, so you could see him, talk to him."

"He left when I was four," Kelly says. "Walked out on my mom and me. Beat her up, and walked out, and never came back."

"Which broke your mother's heart?" Bohannon asks.

"Not exactly. She couldn't take it anymore. He was so mixed up and half out of his gourd from the war, all that killing shit, those nightmares, the way he'd scream and hide . . ." Tears shine in Kelly's eyes and he hangs his head and sniffles hard and wipes his nose with the back of a cuffed hand. "It wasn't his fault. I knew that. She knew it too, but he wouldn't get help. The veterans, they're entitled to help, and he got some before they got married, but then he was happy and it was all right for a while, but the horrors came back, you know? It started all over again. He couldn't keep a job, he started boozing all the time, throwing stuff, smashing stuff, hitting her—" The boy's voice breaks and he shakes his head and looks at the floor.

"And you came to get him to come home?" Bohannon asks.

The boy nods, lifts his tear-shiny face. "It was years ago. And she needs him. She's always getting new men. And they're none of them any good. Highway trash. She's a waitress, works hard, they just take her money and lay around watching TV all day."

"You think he's cured now?" T. Hodges brings coffee mugs into the light and sets them down for the two men. "Kelly, he doesn't work, either. Lives off his disability check."

"Yeah." Kelly touches his coffee mug. "And hates everybody."

"You talked to him?" Bohannon says.

Kelly makes a face. "He wasn't happy to see me. It wasn't a good talk. Nothing like what I expected."

" 'Dreamed,' you mean." T. Hodges sits down with her own coffee in the circle of lamplight. "Kelly, some things just aren't meant to be."

Kelly blows steam off his coffee and gingerly tries it. "I wasn't giving up. I was going to take him back. I promised my mom. Take him back with me, and we'd be like we were in the seventies, a family. We had good times. He was okay then.

Steady. Cheerful, even. A good dad. I really have missed him. Twenty years is a long time."

"Granted," Bohannon says. "So you tried talking to him again?"

"Three, four times. He told me to leave him the hell alone."

T. Hodges hasn't done this for a long time, but now she reaches for Bohannon's Camels on the tabletop and lights one. In the slow-moving smoke that circles the lamp, she says, "And night before last?"

"I couldn't sleep. I kept arguing with him in my head. Yeah, I went up there." Kelly doesn't look at her or at Bohannon. His voice is almost too low to be heard. "He took a shot at me."

"You sure he saw you, knew who you were?"

"Well, hell, how do I know?" Kelly says. "Think I stayed around to find out? He had a gun. And I got my ass out of there. You don't know how fast you can run till somebody shoots at you."

"Uh-huh," Bohannon says. "And what did you stumble over?"

"What?" Kelly sits very straight, eyes wide. "What?"

"You were running scared, and you didn't watch where you were going, and you stumbled over the body of a man down on the road."

"Shit," Kelly says, "how did you know?"

"Your hands are scraped and scabby from falling on pavement," Bohannon says.

"And I'm afraid," T. Hodges says, "the thought that jumped into your mind was that your father had killed that man, and that he'd changed more than you'd thought in those twenty years, and you were suddenly very much afraid of him."

"And didn't want to stay anywhere near him," Bohannon says, "anymore. You were on your way. Which is why you didn't take time even to write me a note."

"I stopped to see Stubbs," Kelly says defensively.

"Sixty-five miles down the road," Bohannon agrees. "And George didn't describe it as a long visit."

"What will they do to my dad?" Kelly asks anxiously.

"You love him in spite of everything," T. Hodges marvels.

"Don't worry about him," Bohannon says. "I don't think he killed the man. But it would help if I knew who did."

T. Hodges puts out her cigarette. "You didn't see anyone around there? An expensive car, maybe?"

Kelly laughs, but there's no humor in it. "I was so scared I didn't see nothin'. Man, I was outta there, I mean, we're talkin' roadrunner here." They watch him without comment, and he pauses, and blinks to himself seriously. "Wait. No. You're right. There was a car. Other side of the road. Under big pepper trees. Mercedes. Parked wrong-way-to."

"No driver?" Bohannon says.

"Not that I saw." Kelly turns pale. "The killer, you mean?"

"The killer, I mean," Bohannon says.

For a long time, he didn't want and didn't keep a phone by the bed, but when Stubbs got to the wheelchair stage, it helped to have it there as an intercom in case of emergencies. After Stubbs went to the nursing home, Bohannon just kept the phone. And now it rings. Early morning. He's overslept. He groans, gropes out, gets the receiver, and mumbles "Bohannon" into it.

"The gun was the proud possession of the deceased," Gerard says, "Cedric Lubowitz. But the only fingerprints on it were Steve Belcher's."

"The good news," Bohannon croaks, "and the bad news all in one package?"

"No, the bad news is I know all about Teresa's activities last night, and she is on leave till this case is over with. I'm holding Kelly for at least seventy-two hours. The provenance of the gun suggests he could have been the killer. Motive, robbery. The vic's wallet hasn't turned up."

"Kelly got money on him?"

"Not very much," Gerard says. "You should pay your help better."

"I'd have thought a man like Lubowitz would keep a couple hundred bucks cash on him." Bohannon throws off the blankets and sits on the edge of the bed. "Well, since you haven't got the wallet, that means it wasn't in the camper. And that clears Steve, anyway." He reaches to get a cigarette from his shirt that hangs on a painted straw-bottom Mexican chair. "Of course you checked to see whether the killer threw the wallet away along the roadside."

"That's what the citizens pay me for," Gerard says. "Me, not you, Hack. Will you stay out of this, now?"

"I keep trying," Bohannon says. "Don't worry. I haven't got time. Not with my stable hand in jail." And he hangs up.

"He didn't tell you about Lubowitz's car?" T. Hodges says. She is at the stove cooking breakfast for him again. Earlier, she cleaned out the box stalls, fed, watered and groomed the horses while he slept. Now she puts plates of ham and eggs and fried mush on the table. "They found it at the Tides motel on the beach where he was staying."

Bohannon raises his eyebrows. "Not in the guest room at the beautiful home of his sister-in-law and her eternal friend Dr. Combs?" Bohannon pitches into his breakfast. Mouth full, he says, "So much for the love story motive."

T. Hodges quietly pours syrup on her slabs of fried mush. "Don't jump to conclusions," she says. "His first night, they all had dinner together at the Brambles. Very pleasant. Fresh salmon, champagne. Lots of laughter and jokes about him sweeping Mary Beth off to Paris on the Concorde. The check went on his credit card."

Bohannon chews a chunk of ham. "And afterward—?"

"The waiter at the Brambles said they took Mr. Lubowitz home with them afterward, for dessert, and to listen to some new Mozart CDs on the stereo. The motel says he didn't get back there until midnight."

"Mozart. You remember when Steve Belcher camped up in the Mozart Bowl?" It's a little natural amphitheater among the pines in Sills Canyon. "Dr. Combs got on his case hot and heavy for that."

T. Hodges laughs. "She'd taken some possible large contributors to the Canyon Mozart Festival up to see the place in all its unspoiled loveliness. Sasquatch was not what she'd expected to find. She could have killed him."

"You don't mean that," Bohannon says.

She wags her fork in denial. "Figure of speech. When our team examined the Lubowitz Mercedes," she says, "it had no fingerprints on it. Inside or out. Not the victim's, not anyone's."

"A careful murderer," Bohannon says and tries his coffee. "A schemer, a planner-ahead. Wore gloves. Nothing spontaneous about this killing, Teresa." He sets his cup down and lights a cigarette. "Nobody at the motel saw who returned the Mercedes?"

She shakes her head. "Not the day man, not the night man. None of the guests Vern could find to question."

"Yup," Bohannon says, looking across at the sunlit kitchen windows which are open. Smells of sage and eucalyptus drift in on a cool breeze. The sky is clear blue above the ridges. "Craftily plotted. An organizing mind, used to managing people and events."

"But insane," she says. "Cedric Lubowitz was a gentle old man."

"Yup." Bohannon scrapes back his chair, and goes to stand looking out the door. "Nobody's given me the medical examiner's findings. No, don't say it. Let me guess. He was shot at close range, right? Only a few feet. And through the chest. He was facing his killer. His killer was a friend."

"He must have thought so." T. Hodges gathers up the plates and carries them to the sink. "What a horrible way to die."

"Sure as hell too late to learn anything from it."

Water splashes in the sink. "You go along and find out what you want to find out," she calls. "I'll look after things here."

"On a day like this," he says, "there'll be lots of people wanting to go horseback riding. You'll be run off your feet."

"Be careful," is all she says.

And he takes down his hat and goes.

Steve Belcher sits on the bunk in his cell and glowers. Outside the windows towering old eucalyptus trees creak in the breeze. Fat Freddie May stands leaning against the sand color cinderblock wall. Bohannon leans back against the bars. Down the way, someone is softly playing a harmonica. Not an easy song. *"I'm comin' back, if I go ten thousand miles . . ."* A dime-store mouth organ can't handle it, but the player keeps trying. Bohannon repeats his question:

"You said there was a prowler and you shot the gun to scare the prowler off. What did the prowler look like, Steve?"

"How the fuck do I know? It was midnight. It was pitch dark."

"Tall, short?" Bohannon says. "Thin, fat? Wearing what?"

"I only heard him tramping around," Belcher says.

May says gently, "It was Kelly, wasn't it? Your son, Kelly?"

"Oh, shit," Belcher says, and runs a hand down over his face. "Is he messed up in this too, now?"

"Since last night," Bohannon says. "He went up there in the dark to tell you he was leaving, and you shot the gun off. Which makes it after Lubowitz was dead, after his killer threw the gun your way, right?"

But Belcher is shaking his shaggy head. "It wasn't him. This one was bigger. Taller. Heavier. Kelly's head is shaved. This one had hair."

"That's all?" Bohannon asks. "Clothes? Voice? Anything?"

"Went crashing down through the trees." Belcher grins. His teeth are in poor shape. "Maybe it was a bear."

"You don't want to help us get you off the hook? Okay." Bohannon sighs, straightens, peers through the bars. "Vern?"

Fred May says, "And Kelly. You don't want to help him?"

Vern comes, a gangly blond deputy, the gun on his hip looking heavier than he is. He unlocks the cell door. Bohannon goes out, May after him. The door closes. They follow Vern along the hallway.

And Belcher calls, "It could have been a woman."

Bohannon doesn't break stride but he smiles and says, "Ah!"

He noses the green pickup truck into a diagonal slot in front of the drugstore. A pair of sleepy old huskies with pale

75

eyes looks at him as he passes. One of them sniffs his boots. He pushes into the gleaming shop and stands looking for Mrs. Vanderhoop. There she is, at the back, by the prescription counter. When he nears he sees she is talking with a bald little man who plays cello in local music ensembles. Mrs. Vanderhoop, wife of the pharmacist who owns the sole and only drugstore in Madrone, is a busy part-time musician herself. Piano. Though Bohannon seems to remember she once sang. She sees him and gives him a smile, excuses herself to Mr. Cello, and comes to him, gray haired, thin, running to homespun skirts, Navajo blouses, Indian jewelry.

"Mr. Bohannon?" Her expression is concerned. "Isn't it terrible about that poor man. Liebowitz?"

"Lubowitz," Bohannon says. "Listen. You can correct something I heard. That he came up here to see his sister-in-law, Mary Beth? Wouldn't he have seen her at her sister's funeral, his wife's funeral?"

"Oh, no." Mrs. Vanderhoop shakes her head firmly. "Not that Mary Beth did not love her sister. But Dolores wouldn't allow it. They had a terrible argument about it. I came back for a shawl I'd forgotten after a rehearsal. Mary Beth was in tears."

"I don't understand." Bohannon pushes back his hat. "I heard they were all close friends together when they were young."

Mrs. Vanderhoops's smile is bleak. "Yes, well, for some of us, young was rather a long time ago. No, there was no love lost—"

"But they had dinner with Mr. Lubowitz only the night before he was killed," Bohannon says. "Very friendly and good-humored, I'm told. Laughing over old times."

Mrs. Vanderhoop stares. "Do you know, if it wasn't you telling me, Mr. Bohannon, I wouldn't believe that. Dolores

76

Combs despised Mr. Liebowitz. She wouldn't let Mary Beth near him."

Bohannon circles the house, a sprawling redwood place with windows that stare at the ocean. It's isolated on its hill, land once owned by Henry Madison III. Big pines shelter it. Nobody is around. Cars? The garage doors are closed. He parks the green pickup truck, gets out and looks down the road. Only a short walk to the beach, only another short walk to Cedric Lubowitz's motel room. You could do it in ten minutes. He hikes up through the trees around back of the house, where he spots the structure he wants and goes toward it, waiting for some reaction if he's been seen. He doesn't hear or see any. The enclosure of redwood plank fencing he has had his eye on has a gate but it isn't locked. He works the latch quietly, opens the gate, and sees inside what he expected. Trash barrels. Two are filled with yard trimmings and their lids are propped against the enclosure, but the third has its lid in place. Heart beginning to beat fast, he pries the lid off. Inside is a large green plastic bag. He undoes the wire twist that closes it, pulls the bag open, reaches inside, and a voice behind him says:

"What the hell do you think you're doing?"

He turns. It's Gerard. He looks stern.

Bohannon says, "Collecting trash. Is that against the law?"

"You haven't got a license to collect trash," Gerard says. "What you are doing is breaking and entering, conducting a search of private property without a warrant."

Bohannon pulls a white cable-knit sweater out of the bag and holds it up. It has bloodstains on it. And next, a brand new pair of women's jeans, also splashed with blood. "Hundred to one," he says to Gerard, "those will match Cedric

77

Lubowitz's blood type. And his DNA." He brings out a pair of expensive low-heeled women's walking shoes. Turns the soles up. "More of same off the road." With a fingernail he pries out scraps of oak and eucalyptus leaves, pine needles. "Stuff like this lay all around the body." He looks at Gerard, whose face is expressionless. "What you're saying is that I've made this inadmissible evidence."

"It would be," Gerard answers, "except when I learned you were out and around, talking to prisoners behind my back, checking out the tires on Lubowitz's car at the impound, generally acting your usual hotdog self, I got a warrant." He pulls the folded paper from inside his uniform jacket. He edges Bohannon aside and rummages in the trash bag for himself. "The wallet," he says, and holds it up.

"Isn't it disgusting," Bohannon says, "how right I always am?" Gerard starts off. "Bring that stuff. Let's go arrest her."

He presses a bell button on the wide, redwood-beamed porch. Handsome stained glass frames the doorway. The motif is California wildflowers. Yellow poppies, blue lupine, white yucca. Suddenly the door flies open and Dolores Combs stands there angry, a big-boned woman, white hair cropped handsomely. Arty women in Settlers Cove run to sweatshirts, but not she. A shirtwaist of brown shantung. Tailored slacks. A jade necklace. From Gump's probably. "I warned you—" she begins. "Oh, it's you, Lieutenant Gerard. Forgive me. I thought it was more news people. They've been pestering the life out of us."

"Morning," Gerard says. "We're here about the death of your friend Cedric Lubowitz. This is Hack Bohannon, investigator for the Public Defender's office."

She glares at Bohannon. "You're defending that animal Belcher?"

Bohannon tugs his hat-brim. "Ma'am."

"These things belong to you?" Gerard takes sweater, jeans, and shoes from Bohannon and holds them out to her.

She blinks at them and turns pale. "N-no. Certainly not. Where did you get them?"

"Out of your trash barrels back of the house," Bohannon says.

She acts indignant. "You had no right to—"

"We have a search warrant." Gerard hands her the sweater, jeans and shoes, and produces the paper again, unfolding it, holding it up for her to read. "It covers the grounds, the house, and all outbuildings."

She eyes it and seems to shrink a little. But she braves up in a second. "I have no idea how these got there. No idea." She drops the clothes and snatches the paper, reading it closely. Her head jerks up. "Harold Willard? Why—why— Judge Willard is a close personal friend. He's one of the principal contributors to—" She thrusts the paper back at Gerard. "Why would he sign such a warrant? What lies did you tell him about me?"

"It's not going to be hard to prove those are your clothes, Dr. Combs, your shoes. And they have bloodstains on them. We can trace the clothes to where you bought them. We can trace the bloodstains to Mr. Lubowitz. And"—he flashes it— "Mr. Lubowitz's wallet."

"Dolly? What's wrong?" A dainty pink and white woman appears behind the doctor of music. Fluffy would describe her. Curvaceous once, now pudgy. Her voice is little-girlish. "Who are these men?" Her blue eyes widen, looking at them. "What do they want? Is it about poor, dear Cedric?"

"Go away, Mary Beth. Let me handle this."

Mary Beth Madison sees the clothes. She stoops and picks up the sweater. "Why, where did you find this? I've been looking all over for it. I was going to take it to the cleaners days ago." She draws in her breath. "Why, just look at those stains. Now, those were not on it when I—"

Dr. Combs tries to kill her with a look. "Will you be quiet?" she says. "Do you have to rattle on and on constantly?"

The plump little woman is amazed. "But, Dolly, I only—"

"Shut up, can't you?" The Combs woman is trembling. "Mary Beth, please go away, now. You're only making things worse." But Mary Beth simply stands, holding the sweater, totally bewildered.

Gerard asks her: "Is that Dr. Combs's sweater?"

"Oh, yes," Mary Beth nods. "Hand knitted. From Ireland. We were there two years ago." She looks adoringly at her big friend. "Dolly played an organ recital in Dublin. Beautiful old church." Her small hands are stroking the sweater. She looks at it again. "Dolly, what are these awful splotches? Will they ever come out?"

Her lifelong friend lets out a snarl and strikes Mary Beth Madison hard across the face. The little woman staggers backward, appalled, holding her bruised cheek.

"Dolly," she gasps. "You hit me. What's happened to you?"

Gerard steps forward, taking handcuffs off his belt. "Dolores Combs, you are under arrest for the murder of Cedric Martin Lubowitz." He reaches to turn her around, but she swings at him. He dodges the blow, but she is running away, down a long living room where a Bosendorfer grand stands glossy in stained-glass gloom. Bohannon takes after her. Oriental carpets slide under his boots. She has reached French doors at the end of the room, and is tugging at the latches before he can grab her. She is strong, and flails and kicks, but he gets her arms behind her finally, and swings her—she's a good weight, Dr. Combs—back toward Gerard, who now manages to cuff her wrists. Behind her, as if she were some L.A. street tough.

He half nudges, half lifts her down the room, toward the front door, droning the Miranda warning, grunting with the effort she is costing him. Bohannon goes ahead to gather up the jeans and shoes from the floor. He reaches out to Mary Beth for the sweater. She hands it to him, but she is listening to the outraged Dr. Combs.

"This is grotesque," the big woman says. "Why would I kill Cedric Lubowitz? Why would I kill anyone? No jury in the world will believe Dr. Dolores Combs is a murderer. When Judge Willard hears—aah! Let me go. You're hurting me."

Mary Beth begins beating on Gerard with her little fists. "Stop it," she says, "stop hurting Dolly." Bohannon pulls her off the Lieutenant. She clutches his arms. "Where are you taking her?"

"Just down to the Sheriff station," Gerard grunts, wrestling the large woman through the doorway, out onto the porch. "For a nice talk."

"I'll come too," Mary Beth says. "Dolly, what shall I wear?"

"No, dearest," the handcuffed woman says. "You stay here, and feed the cats." And she goes with Gerard down the plank steps to the path, no longer resisting, lumpish, defeated.

The little pink and white girl of sixty gazes wanly after her. "When will you come home, Dolly?" Her question drifts off into the noon silence of the woods, as sad a sound as Bohannon ever heard.

It is sundown. T. Hodges is washing down Twilight, while Mousie stands by, reins loosely knotted to a post of the long stable walkway. Before Bohannon has fully stopped the truck, Kelly is out of it, running to help the deputy. She smiles at him, hands him the sponge, walks toward Bohannon, wearily brushing a strand of hair off her face.

"Boy, am I glad to see you." She gives him a hug.

"You okay?" he says.

"I think," she says thoughtfully, taking his hand and walking toward the ranch house, "you work much too hard for a living."

"I'm sorry I stranded you here." They go along the house porch and in at the kitchen screen door. "I didn't know so much would happen so soon. And Gerard wanted me there for the interrogation."

"It was Dolores Combs, then?" She drops onto a chair. "Oh, am I going to be sore tomorrow."

"It was Dolores Combs." Bohannon fetches Old Crow and glasses, and sits down opposite her at the table. "She thought we'd never guess, so she didn't bother to hide her bloodstained clothes." He pours whisky into the glasses and hands her one. "She just threw them in the trash."

"How did she get him to drive her up the canyon?"

"Some romance about Mary Beth being stranded up there. I don't know why he believed her. But he did. And took along his gun."

"Odd." She frowns. "A man like that carrying a gun."

"One of his fellow stockbrokers got mugged and badly beaten recently. It upset the firm and Cedric Lubowitz not least. Another lesson for society. Leave the guns to law enforcement. But they won't learn."

She tastes the whiskey and again reaches for Bohannon's cigarettes on the table. "And the prowler Steve Belcher shot at?"

"Combs. After she'd driven halfway home, she guessed planting the gun might not work, and she went back for it.

But it wasn't there, was it?" He gives his head a wondering shake. "She and Kelly must have missed each other by inches, running away from that shot in the dark."

She laughs briefly, grows somber again. "We know why she hated Steve. Why did she hate Cedric Lubowitz?"

" 'Fear' is the word you want." Bohannon stretches to switch on the lamp. "Mrs. Madison, the girls' mother, believed the scheming Jew only married Rose for her money, and Dolores thought the same."

"Hack! The Lubowitzes were rich. Belle Hesseltine told us that."

"If you want to hate Jews, sweet reason is meaningless, deputy."

She sighs. "I guess so. So . . . Dolores believed when Rose died and Cedric came up here, and immediately started wining and dining Mary Beth, that he meant to marry her? For her money?"

Bohannon nods. "And put Dolores Combs out to starve and freeze in the cruel world. And she didn't want to give up the beautiful house, the antiques, the jewelry, the Cadillac, the parties and banquets. And most of all the power. Money is power, deputy. Ever hear that before?"

"Mary Beth's love didn't count for anything?"

Bohannon shrugs, sighs. "Who knows? Maybe once long ago. But Dolores learned how nice being rich was and, face it, she didn't do much with all that talent she kept raving about this afternoon." He adopts a plummy elocutionary voice. " 'I could have been an international star. But I gave that up for Mary Beth. Stayed here in this backwater . . . et cetera, et cetera.' " He resumes his normal voice. "Hell, a backwater was what she needed. Organizing her little ensembles, festivals, concerts. She swayed around here like a duchess. You've seen her."

"And she thought Cedric Lubowitz would end all that?"

"Not if she killed him first," Bohannon says.

T. Hodges sits studying her hands around the glass for a long minute. "It's pitiful," she says, raises her head, looks into his face. "And Mary Beth? Mary Beth worshipped her. What will she do now?"

"Wait for her to come home," Bohannon says.

Confessional

Bohannon ran the green pickup to the side of the road where the tires crunched dry brush. He pulled on the parking brake, switched off the engine. Up through the pines, among the hulking yellow machines, backhoes, graders, dump trucks, he saw men clustered, men in blue hardhats and orange vests. A brown sheriff's patrol car had pushed its way up there too. He got down out of the pickup and started in his worn boots up to where the excitement was. Excitement was in the first voice he heard when he came into earshot.

"You got to tell me first that these ain't Indian bones, old Indian bones, the bones of my ancestors." The speaker was Jimmy Schortz, a leathery broad-chested, middle-aged man, in a faded, plaid flannel shirt. He was spokesman for the ragtag remnant of Indians in the area, spokesman maybe self-appointed, maybe not: opinions differed. "If these here are Indian bones, then this is sacred ground, a burial place, and you got to cover it up again and leave it alone forever."

Someone had fallen in beside Bohannon, now, a tall, raw-boned figure in Levis and a leather jacket. It was the doctor, Belle Hesseltine, white-haired, in her eighties, and still going strong. These days she was acting medical examiner in these parts. "How does he know a dead body's been unearthed before I do? It's uncanny."

"A lot of Indians in road building," Bohannon said.

85

"Maybe they sent him smoke signals."

"Hold on." She caught Bohannon's arm, and peered at him. "You're short of breath." She looked back the way they'd come. "Hack, this is no grade at all. Do you hear me puffing and blowing? I'm thirty years older than you." She tapped the pocket of his shirt. "Cigarettes. If I've told you once—"

"You've told me a hundred times." Bohannon walked on. "And I've told you, Belle—cigarettes don't kill people, death kills people."

"Man that stables horses," she said, "ought never to smoke at all."

"I never do," he said, "not in the stable."

"Until the time you absent-mindedly light up out there, drop the match in the straw, and suddenly your whole livelihood is up in flames. To say nothing of a dozen beautiful animals you were supposed to be protecting."

"Doctor, ma'am," Bohannon said, "you're turning into an old nag."

But she wasn't listening. The workmen had made way for her, and she was standing over a scattering of human bones a grader blade had turned up. Settlers Cove was growing. They were putting a road through a piece of woodland that had been wild from the beginning of time. The old doctor dug latex gloves out of a pocket in her leather jacket, pulled these on over bony, freckled hands, and knelt for a closer look. With a snort, she turned her gaze up to Jimmy Schortz. "These bones aren't five years old, yet, Jimmy. And they never belonged to anybody who could be your ancestor. One of your offspring, maybe—you lose any of them lately?"

"No," Schortz said. "What are you talking about?"

"These are the bones of a young person." She poked among them for a minute. They rattled softly together. She picked up a pelvis. "A young woman."

"Wait a minute." Lt. Phil Gerard crouched and pulled out of the loosened soil a thin gold chain with a pendant. He thumbed dirt off the pendant. It was a drop-shaped gem-stone, green. He looked up at Bohannon. "Remember? He said she was wearing it."

"So this is Cressy Garner." Bohannon said. "What's left of her."

Gerard stood up. "After three years in the ground in a damp climate."

Bohannon nodded. "February, wasn't it? Ninety-four?"

Belle Hesseltine got to her feet. "There's a body bag in the back of my Cherokee," she told a lanky blond deputy, standing beside Gerard. "Fetch it for me, will you, Vern, please?"

"Yes, ma'am," Vern said and went gangly down the hill.

"Brent lied, it appears," Gerard said. "She didn't run off."

"You always thought he killed her," Bohannon said.

"Would I brag?" Gerard said. "*I told you so* is bad man-ners."

He and Bohannon had once been deputies together. Four-teen, fifteen years ago Bohannon had taken against sheriffing, bought stables up Rodd canyon, and kept away from crime as best he could. But that wasn't easy, and he had to take out a private investigator's license finally. Sometimes he worked for the district attorney, sometimes for the public defender, sometimes for just plain citizens who couldn't figure ways out of their troubles. Gerard had called him in on the Cressy Garner disappearance, because there was something off about it. Brent, her husband, forty years her senior, had beaten her a few times and been locked up for it once or twice. It was popularly agreed she, a poor girl, had married him for his house, car, a few thousand in bonds and mutual funds. And some said that she was no better than she should be. When she had been gone a week, Brent had reported her missing. After big hard fights between them, she'd usually de- camped for her mother's place in Fresno, but her mother hadn't seen her this time. Still, there was nothing to show any harm had come to her. Not until this fine, brisk March morning.

"They probably got into one of those knockdown drag- outs of theirs," Gerard said, "and this time he overdid it and she died on him, and he dumped her in the trunk, drove the body out here and buried it." Bohannon looked around him. "This was a popular place to bring your girl after dark if you were a high school kid and you had a car. Maybe somebody saw something."

"Nobody came forward at the time," Gerard said.

Bohannon shrugged. "You can still ask."

"They'll have graduated by now. Scattered all to hell."

Vern came with the body bag, and Belle Hesseltine, brushing the dirt off the bones, dropped them into the bag, while everyone stood around and watched. When the bones were all in the bag, she zipped it up, got creakily to her feet, and pulled off the latex gloves. Vern picked up the bag and carried it down the hill between the trees.

Looking after him, Schortz asked, "You sure it ain't no an- cient Indian?"

"I'll bet you a body bag full of wampum," the doctor said.

"Don't patronize me, old woman," Schortz said.

"I apologize," Belle said. "Forgive me, Mr. Schortz."

It was the first time Bohannon had ever seen her put in her place. He almost laughed aloud.

Brent Garner had once owned his own contracting business, painting new apartment complexes, shopping malls. Maybe in Los Angeles, maybe not. Bohannon didn't remember. In any case, he'd sold it, retired early, and built a place up here in the woods across the Coast Highway from Madrone. That had been a dozen years ago. His wife had died. Cressy Troupe had come in to clean house for him. One day a week. Later, full time, cooking his meals as well. Then they'd married. He stood now in his doorway, staring at Gerard and Bohannon, looking grouchy. It had been a while since his trousers had been to the cleaners. His shirt looked slept-in. He needed a shave. And his gray hair, a wreath around his pate, stood out uncombed.

"I don't have any outstanding tickets," he said. "What is it?"

"It's about Cressy," Gerard said.

"She's never coming back." The old man turned away, turned back. He squinted. "Whoa. You saying you found her?"

"We think so." Gerard took out the chain and pendant and held it up for him to see. "Was this the one you described to me?"

"Where is she?" Garner craned to peer past them. Hope like a young man's was in his voice. "Did you bring her home?"

"I'm sorry, no," Gerard said, "I'm afraid she's dead, Mr. Garner."

"Oh, my God." Garner's knees gave and Bohannon caught his arm to steady him. "Dead. Who told you that?"

Gerard explained. "We'd like you to come with us."

"I don't want to see her that way," Garner cried.

"You don't have to. We just need to talk to you."

"What about? You asked me forty-eleven questions when she ran off. You got your answers then."

"But now we have a whole new set of questions," Gerard said.

"I didn't kill her," Garner said. "She was the most precious thing in the world to me. I've been a dead man since she ran off."

"You got pretty rough with her sometimes," Bohannon said.

"That was because I loved her so much. I couldn't stand it when she'd get all—the way she got. Making me jealous. On purpose. Just so she could laugh at me. Nothing in it, of course. She was true to me, but she liked to get me all worked up. It proved I loved her, she said."

"When you knocked her around?" Gerard asked.

"I didn't want to," Garner muttered, looking away. "I never wanted to do anything but touch her gentle. She drove me to it."

"She kept on cleaning other peoples' houses," Bohannon said.

"No need for that," Garner said. "That was her, that was Cressy. Knew it embarrassed me, made me furious, so she kept on with it. 'Mad money,' she said. A woman needed money of her own in case of emergencies, something she wasn't beholden to a husband for. Women!" Shaking his head, he went back into the house and picked up a jacket. "All right," he sighed. "Let's go." He pulled the door shut, not bothering to lock it: few householders did in Settlers Cove. Flapping into the jacket, taking the porch steps heavily, he said, "I didn't kill her. So I've got nothing to be afraid of. Might's well talk my time away with you as sit home and stare at the TV."

It was pleasant to walk into the big, plank-walled kitchen of the ranch house and find George Stubbs at the table.

Stubbs had come to work for Bohannon already an old man, the bunged-up veteran of a lifetime of rodeos. He was better than good at handling horses. He knew them inside and out, understood them, loved them as Bohannon did. How Bohannon would have made a go of these stables, where he kept a half dozen mounts to rent out to riders who wanted to explore the canyons, and where he boarded another half dozen horses for people who owned them but had no place to stable them in town—how he'd have made a go of it without Stubbs, he didn't know. Likely he'd have failed.

Stubbs was good with people too, including little kids wanting to learn to ride. And maybe best of all, Stubbs was a demon bookkeeper, bill payer, supply orderer, good at paperwork, which Bohannon had no tolerance for. A year or two ago, Stubbs's arthritis had grown so bad, and Bohannon had found himself so short-handed, he had to put the old man into a nursing home. He'd gone to visit him there pretty near every evening, but sometimes that was impossible. And Stubbs was deteriorating, that became plain. He lost interest in life. Lost his appetite. Was listless over their nightly checker games, the bull riding shows on TV, the old Westerns.

And at last Bohannon couldn't watch him fading away anymore, and had brought him back home, with a male nurse to look after him. There was room enough in the ranch house. And Stubbs's presence made Bohannon feel as if things with the stables were going to be all right again. They weren't. He couldn't get decent help, not that would hang on. And he didn't see that situation changing in the future. The new generation of horse-centered kids wanted better pay, shorter hours, and softer work than he could offer. Once he'd been able to depend on a postulant priest called Manuel Rivera to look after the horses conscientiously, religiously, if you liked the word. Even after he'd become a priest, he'd been assistant to the Monsignor up at the seminary on the ridge for several years, and so within Bohannon's call, or at least hope, for a time. But Rivera had moved on, first to a local church, then to parishes elsewhere. No, once Stubbs left for the rodeo in the sky, Bohannon bleakly foresaw the end of this place, and thought about that grimly all too often.

"George," he said now, fetched the white-specked tall blue pot from the stove, and filled a couple of mugs from it. "How you feeling?"

"Would I be out here with these accounts if I was feeling bad?" His gnarled and twisted fingers lifted and let drop a sheaf of papers. "How the hell did you manage to tie everything in such crazy knots?"

"I have a gift for it," Bohannon said, and lit a cigarette. "Smoke?"

"Maybe a drag or two," Stubbs said. He looked over his shoulder. "Before Mister Clean walks in and starts bawling me out."

Bohannon held the cigarette for the old man to inhale from. He did it gratefully, sighing as he blew the smoke away. "Say, that is a treat. Oh-oh! Sit down. Here he comes."

Mister Clean was Otis Jackson, a big, powerfully built black youth, good-natured, but dead serious about his business. Like Rivera. Only Jackson was saving his money to finish medical school and become a surgeon. He studied late into the night. His room was heaped with books and papers. What was there about Bohannon that attracted these single-minded youngsters?

"Mr. Stubbs," he said, "haven't you been sitting up long enough?" Stubbs was in a wheelchair, a power one Bohannon had bought him. "Shouldn't you rest before dinner?"

"Long time till dinner," Stubbs said. "I'll keep on here till I finish."

Jackson studied his watch. "Only if that doesn't take more than twenty-seven minutes. All right?"

"Maybe with you," Stubbs grumbled.

"Temper," Jackson said with a grin. "You do need a nap. I will return." And with a cheerful nod and a quick smile for Bohannon, he was gone.

"What did Gerard want with you?" Stubbs asked, and Bohannon told him all about it, and Stubbs said, "It had to be Brent Garner. I said that from the start. They going to try him now?"

"On what grounds? Gerard thinks the way you do, that Brent killed her and took her out in the woods and buried her. But where's the evidence? Gone, if it ever existed. Gone with the wind and the rain and the weather and three years of fallen pine needles and dead ferns and gone-to-seed poison oak. Generations of dead squirrels and blue jays, possums and raccoons. A thousand spider webs built in hope and shredded by the wind."

"Easy on the poetry," Stubbs said. "His record's enough. He was a wife-beater. What about the bones? What'd that old scarecrow Belle Hesseltine report? Any of 'em broken?"

"As a matter of fact," Bohannon said, "yes. Skull bashed in. By what, though? Vern and Lundquist combed Garner's house while we were talking to him at the station. No traces of old blood on floors or rugs or tiles, inside, none on the front deck, none on the rear deck. No murder weapon. No blood on any of the tools. Anyway, the skull break, according to Belle, suggests something wide, a baseball bat at least, and Garner didn't own a baseball bat."

"What about the car?"

"He had it up at the Mobil station," Bohannon said. "Fuel

line on the fritz. Gerard and company will be checking it out right about now."

Stubbs finished off his coffee and set down the mug. Clumsily, loudly because he couldn't help it. "All right." He slowly, painfully got a grip on the ballpoint pen and picked it up and poised it over the mess of papers. "Let me see if I can untangle you from the spider web you wove here. I was only gone eighteen months. Any longer, you'd be up to your ears in lawsuits."

Bohannon laughed. "Did I ever say I could get along without you?"

"Don't try it again," Stubbs warned him.

Bohannon scraped his chair back and rose. "I've got horses to look after. That I can do."

"More or less," Stubbs grunted, bent over his work. "But Young Father Rivera was better at it. What ever became of him?"

"I've sometimes got so desperate"—Bohannon took down his sweat-stained old Stetson from a hook by the door—"that I've asked God to let him go and come back to work here." Bohannon put on the hat. "So far I've been ignored. Not surprising. God probably doesn't remember me. Why should he?"

"Keep praying," Stubbs said. "These kids you're getting now—"

"Times change." Bohannon pushed open the screen door. "Attitudes change with them." He stepped out onto the long, covered, wooden walkway that fronted the ranch house. "Horses are already a hundred years out of date, George. And you and I—well, I'll let you fill in the blanks."

It was nothing like a miracle, really. It wasn't even like an answer to a prayer. But to those who think that way, it could easily seem like either or both. Rivera turned up. Mid-morning, the next day. Bohannon was out in the white-fenced oval across from the green-trimmed stable building, watching a pair of twelve-year-old girls from over Atascadero way take first stabs at low-jumping. Their horses were re-spectable standard breeds and knew their part. The girls were uncertain, tomboys in manner and brag, but actually a little timid about jumping. Bohannon was sweet-talking them and easing them into trying and trying again. The sound of Rivera's car coming through the gate made him turn and look. It wasn't a distinctive car. Japanese. Clerical gray. It parked with an assertion that it belonged here, between the stake truck and horse van. But it wasn't until Rivera in tweeds and a turned-around collar got out of it that Bohannon thought about that answered prayer. He told the girls:

"Holly? Kimberly? Just walk them around for a few min-utes, all right? Just step over the jumps. Okay? I'll be back."

He went out the gate and closed and fastened it behind him. He called to Rivera, "Manuel. This is a surprise." They shook hands in the cool, long, morning shadows of euca-lyptus. "It's wonderful to see you."

"Yes." Rivera looked worried, but he managed a smile. "It is wonderful to see you too." He looked around him, at the practice oval, at the ranch house, the rustling trees, the hills, meadows, blue sky, the stables, where the newest boy (nose-ring, green hair in a ponytail) was saddling up Geranium and Seashell for a young couple. "I miss this place." Rivera gave a sad little laugh. "At times like this, I wish I had never left."

"I feel that way all the time," Bohannon said. "What's the matter?"

"They have arrested the wrong man," Rivera said.

The news had been on Stubbs's radio this morning. The old man had talked about it at breakfast. A shovel had been found in the trunk of Brent Garner's car. There was dried blood on the shovel. The lab had typed it. It was Cressy's blood. It made no sense to Bohannon. The man had three years to get rid of that shovel. Hell, he hauled groceries in that trunk all the time. Bohannon had often seen him load it up at the market parking lot in Madrone. He wouldn't want to look at that shovel every time he opened the trunk. Guilty, he'd have ditched the shovel long ago.

"I'd like to think you're right," Bohannon said to Rivera. "But it looks bad for him."

"They have to let him go," Rivera said. "It was not Brent Garner. I know that, Hack, I know it. We must talk."

Bohannon didn't remember another time when Rivera was so serious, so urgent. "Of course." He glanced back at the girls, who were not riding, just slumping in their saddles, gazing at him resentfully. "Go on inside. Get yourself some coffee. Stubbs will be happy to see you." Bohannon started back to the oval. "I'll join you as soon as I can."

Rivera said, "I have not much time."

"In that case," Bohannon said, "why didn't you phone?"

"Phones are not private. This is a private matter. Face to face. One on one, as they say."

"I'll be right with you," Bohannon said.

And Rivera went up the wheelchair ramp, and along the porch. The screen door twanged, and Bohannon heard Stubbs's shout of startled delight as Rivera stepped inside.

"I know Brent Garner's voice," Rivera said. "He came to confession at least once a month."

He sat beside Bohannon on rocks and looked at rocks out in the kelp-matted tide. On them cormorants perched black, holding out their ragged wings to dry in the sun. Out farther in the kelp sea otters showed dark, sleek heads now and then.

One lay on his back, feeding. You could tell from the quarrelsome gulls flapping above him, and darting down for scraps. The sails of little pleasure boats shone in the sunshine farther out on the sparkling water.

Rivera went on, "He has an old man's voice."

"And the one who told you he killed her?" Bohannon fastened a cigarette in his mouth, and cupped a hand around a flame to light it. The wind off the water blew the flame out quickly. But he got the light. The wind blew the smoke away. "What kind of a voice did he have?"

"He was a boy," Rivera said. "It had that light, flat quality of a boy who is not yet used to the deep sound. And something about the speech is still imitating the mother, you know?"

Bohannon grinned. "I know exactly. I also know Father Manuel's flock don't stand a chance at anonymity. You know who confesses and what they confess to. They must squirm when you preach the sermon."

"Maybe." Rivera was in no mood for joking. He picked up a rock and threw it into the tide, which washed up only ten feet off, all manner of greens and blues, swirling together in this small inlet. "But once I had urged him solemnly to go straight to the police and tell them what he had done, I did a forbidden thing. When he left, I ran to get a look at him." He glanced wryly at Bohannon. "It was your influence. My training is that a priest assigns acts of contrition. The church is concerned with man's immortal soul. You, as an officer of the law, are concerned with the mortal man, with evening the score on earth. No man must be allowed to get away with murder. Courts, juries decide this. And in this society, in this state, he must be put to death."

"Right," Bohannon said impatiently. "But you wanted a look at him. I don't call that unpriestly."

"What you call it, forgive me, Hack, and what I call it are totally different. God has given us all free will. I overstepped my limits."

"Maybe." Bohannon shrugged. "But you're not going to let Brent Garner go to the gas chamber for a killing he didn't do. You came to me because, priest or not, you can't let that happen."

Gazing away at the glittering waves, Rivera nodded slowly, regretfully. "He was average height, thin. It was foggy that morning. The light was poor. He left at a run, slammed out of the confessional, and ran up the aisle—frightened, oh, yes, very frightened. So he was some distance off by the time I got to the church door. Trees and shrubs. He was no more than a silhouette. He wore glasses. That is all I can be sure of. Had he ever confessed to me before? Boys' voices change. Had I ever seen him before? Boys grow."

"And you expect me to find him?" Bohannon asked. "Without any help from Gerard and his troops? It's a tall order, Manuel."

"I am breaking my vows telling even you about it," Rivera said. "But you were like a father to me for many years, Hack. I trust you."

"Not to work miracles." Bohannon stood up, stiff in his joints.

"No, but you are the best." Rivera followed him, climbing toward the highway, where the green pickup waited. "You will find a way. You always do."

At lunch in the screen-porched cottage cafe where they often ate, T. Hodges laid a book in his hand. She was a deputy, and down the years a close friendship had developed between them that somehow along the way, and against his will, had turned into love. Not physical love. He had a wife,

Linda, in a mental home over the other side of the mountains, her mind and spirit demolished by a night of terror years ago at the hands of smugglers running drugs up the coast on an old fishing boat from Mexico. It wouldn't have happened if he hadn't been a law officer, and he'd punished himself for a long time about that. But he'd got his balance back after a few years. He used to visit her once a week, faithfully, though she never spoke to him, and when she did look at him, seemed not to know him. There had come a remission, once, but it hadn't lasted. He'd let them treat her with electro-shock after that. But it had done no good. It saddened him terribly, but he still forced himself to drive over to see her at Easter and Christmas. Thin, and pale, wasting away, mostly now when he came to her room she lay in bed, interested in nothing, dying of no cause but the memory of shock and horror from which no one and nothing could free her. So . . .

T. Hodges, neat and trim in her uniform, handed him this book across the table. He'd expected a little dime store notebook. Cressy Garner kept a record of her clients, the families she cleaned house for, the amounts they paid her, and when. Brent Garner had said so. He hadn't added that the notebook was an artist's sketch pad. Spiral bound, stiff covers, thick, grainy paper. But that's what it was. Inside the cover was hand-printed, *Cressida Troupe, Art 101, Mr. Winslow*. The next pages were taken up with drawings, cones, cubes, cylinders, then still lifes of fruit and baskets, bowls and vases. Class assignments. Then some outdoor stuff, mostly seaside, boats, the rickety pier with Cap's bait shack on it, gulls, sandpipers, a diving pelican, a mother with two toddlers on a beach towel under an umbrella. Then, it looked to him like later, boys—surfers. Not a school assignment. Then began the list of her customers with addresses and phone numbers and rates paid and the dates. Of course, Brent Garner's name was here, along with others known and unknown to him.

"She was pretty good, wasn't she?" T. Hodges asked. "Oh, look—she made drawings of some of her clients."

"That's old Brent to the life," Bohannon said, and turned a page. "Wait a minute." He held the open book up for her to see. "Who's that?"

"Some skinny boy in swim-trunks with glasses." She raised her eyes to Bohannon's. "Why?"

"Nothing." He closed the book, and slid it into his Levis jacket pocket.

"Something," she said. "Why did you ask me to bring you that book?"

"Brent didn't kill her," Bohannon said. "Gerard's making a mistake."

"Didn't—" She tilted her head, frowning. "Are you sure? How sure?"

"Your enchiladas." He nodded at her plate. "They're getting cold."

"Oh, this isn't like you," she said. "Hack, what's going on?"

He grabbed his fork and dug into his own food. "Delicious," he said. "Go ahead, eat. It's great."

She didn't. She continued to study him. "It's got something to do with Manuel Rivera, hasn't it?"

"Who?" Bohannon chewed, swallowed, tasted his beer. "What gave you that idea?"

"Stubbs," she said. "When I phoned the stables for you. He answered. It's wonderful having him back, isn't it?"

"Like the old days." Bohannon nodded and filled his mouth again.

"He told me Rivera had cropped up," T. Hodges said. "And the two of you had gone off to the beach for a very private talk. His nose is out of joint, of course. He feels left out, insulted and abused."

Bohannon chuckled. "And so do you, right?"

"And so do I," she said. "You've never kept secrets from me, Hack."

"I've never broken a promise, either," he said gravely. "And I made a promise to Manuel, and you aren't going to ask me to break it, are you?"

"He knows something about Cressy Garner's death, doesn't he?"

"I can't stop you from guessing," Bohannon said.

"Something important," she said, "something conclusive."

"If I do my job," Bohannon said grimly. "And do it right."

"All alone?" Her eyes begged him to let her help.

He nodded. "And very much on the quiet. There's no way to stop Stubbs gossiping. He'll set Heaven to buzzing with it when he gets there. But you, you I can depend on to tell nobody that Rivera is in any way involved with what I'm doing — nobody, all right? Most of all not the Lieutenant."

"You're going to start asking questions around," she said. "As you always do. The people you ask will speculate on why. You can't hush them all up. Gerard is bound to find out."

"But not about Rivera, and not from you." He loaded his fork again. "Now, Teresa, will you please eat? It's a sin to waste good food."

She laughed. "You *have* been talking to Rivera." But she did begin to eat.

Hall Winslow was fiftyish. Plainly he didn't like it: he was suntanned, and brushed color into his thinning hair each morning, and dressed young, chinos, polo shirt, but he was putting on pounds around the middle, and the line of his jaw was puffy. Bohannon found him in a classroom with water-

101

colors tacked all over the walls. The little benches art students straddle with drawing boards propped between their knees were scattered around. Sheets of paper with abandoned sketches on them strewed a floor splashed and dribbled with paint of every color. A large bouquet of calla lilies stood on a small table in the middle of the room. Winslow leaned above a teenage student, reaching across her shoulder presumably to point out something on a drawing. No one else was present. The door had squeaked when Bohannon pushed inside and at that Winslow had straightened up guiltily.

"Yes?" His tone was sharp. "What do you want?"

Bohannon gave his name and said he was a private investigator looking into the matter of Cressy Garner's death.

"Oh, yes, of course." Winslow said to the student, "That's all for now, Jen. You see how to get that white effect behind the white lily?"

"Yeah." She rolled the drawing up. She stood. Her cheeks were very flushed. Her mouth curled in a little sly smile at the art instructor. Her pale hazel eyes looked Bohannon up and down. Then swaying hips that were too narrow yet for swaying, she breezed out the door into a hall noisy with high schoolers finished for the day. Winslow came to Bohannon.

"I was only her art teacher," he said, "and only for one term."

"It's a place for me to start." Bohannon dropped onto a steel and plastic chair beside the desk, pushed back his hat. "Your one term took with her. She kept right on drawing. Did you know that?"

"She had talent." Winslow warily sat down. "She ought to have gone on taking art classes. But—" He lifted and let fall a hand, and sighed. "What are you going to do? Teenage girls. They can keep their minds on a single subject, all right—boys. But that's it." He worked up a grin and made a gesture as if wiping sweat from his brow. "They make me glad I'm not a father."

Bohannon glanced toward the bench where Jen had sat. "Jen? She talented too?"

"Nothing like Cressy. What a shame. I was shocked when I heard."

Bohannon took out the sketchbook. "Speaking of boys, any of these mean anything to you?" He leafed over pages till he came to the surfers, and handed the book over to Winslow. He examined the drawings. "Even on her own," he murmured, "her skills improved. Clever portraits. Yes. She could have had a career. Maybe only commercial art, advertising art, but—" He closed the book and passed it back. "No, none of those boys do I know."

"Not the skinny one in glasses?" Bohannon said.

Winslow half smiled and shook his head. "Sorry. But did you notice? Some pages have been torn out around that drawing."

Bohannon rose, sliding the book back into his pocket. "I noticed. I wondered why. Any suggestions?"

"If as a kid you develop a facility," Winslow said, "sometimes finding you can draw anything can carry you away."

Bohannon narrowed his eyes. "Meaning, you might draw something you shouldn't. What?"

"Adolescence takes us all differently," Winslow said, "and all the same."

"And some of us never outlive it." Bohannon studied Winslow for a moment, pulled his hat forward, headed for the door. "You're right. Thanks for your time."

A very young man opened the door for Bohannon at the McNally house. But he was stocky and he didn't wear glasses. "I'm Hack Bohannon." He showed the boy his license. "Investigating the death of Cressida Garner. She used to clean house here. Your mother in?"

"She's at the market in San Luis." Something hit the stocky boy in the back. He turned. "Okay," he called to someone inside. "I'm zapped. Don't zap me anymore, okay?" He stooped, picked up the missile that had struck him, and tossed it back to the assailant. A small-boy voice jeered an answer Bohannon couldn't make out. "Yeah, Cressy did used to clean here. I remember her. She was okay. Really sexy, too." Young McNally wiggled his eyebrows. "Me and my brother used to make up sex stuff about her. Really dumb, you know? What did we know about sex?" His expression sobered. "Jesus, and now she's dead. Somebody killed her. Life sucks, right?"

"Your brother here?" Bohannon asked.

"He works at the lumberyard in Los Ossos," the boy said.

Bohannon took out the sketchbook and showed him the drawing of the thin kid with glasses. "This him?"

The McNally boy laughed. "That wimp? Shit, no."

"Your brother built like you?" Bohannon said.

"Built like Arnold Schwartzenegger," the boy said.

Nobody answered the door at the Lister place but Bohannon heard sounds from out back and went around there. Ken Lister was brick laying, building a barbecue at the far end of the yard. Bohannon called out to him and trudged on down to him. Bohannon looked at the sky.

"You sure it's not going to rain?" he said. "It's only March."

"Bohannon," Lister said. He sometimes drove up Rodd Canyon on Saturdays or Sundays and rode Bohannon's horses, he and his wife. "What brings you around?"

104

"It's the mortar I'm talking about," Bohannon said. "Will it ever dry?"

Lister gave a short laugh. "It'll have to. This is my week off, before tax time sets in." He was a CPA who manned the H&R Block office in Madrone.

"It's the Cressy Garner business," Bohannon said.

"Ah. Tragic. So young." Lister laid down his trowel, pulled off canvas work gloves and dropped them beside a green plastic bin of mortar. "You like some coffee? Come on in the house."

Bohannon followed him. "She used to clean house for you."

It seemed to him Lister flinched slightly. "Yes, she did."

"What, finished already?" Nora Lister said. She had gained weight. Bohannon wouldn't put her on Seashell if she came for a ride now. Bearcat, more likely. Bowls and pans stood on counters around her. Celebrated for her cooking skills, she was preparing some elaborate recipe. When she turned and saw Bohannon, she gave him a smile. "Hack. What a surprise. Sit down."

He took a rush-bottom chair at a table with fresh flowers in its middle. Snapdragons. Dark red. "When did Cressy Garner stop working for you?"

"Oh, that poor child," she said. "What a fate." Nora Lister frowned at him, drying her hands. "When did she stop?" She filled cheery mugs from a glass coffee maker and set them on the table for Bohannon and her husband. "I don't know for sure. Well before she disappeared, though. Months before that. I still needed her. She was a whiz in the kitchen, you know. Helped me a whole lot. Then she quit. It was quite sudden." Nora went back to her onions and celery and cilantro and tomato. "Her husband didn't like it, she said. Didn't like her working, you know."

"So he says." Bohannon dug out Cressy's workbook again

and consulted numbers in it. "Says here the last time she collected pay from you was January of 1994."

"That's about right," Ken Lister said quickly.

"Oh, no, Ken," Nora said. "That's away off. I remember I was planning a Mother's Day party at the church. Thirty, forty people to cook for. And I was counting on her. And then she tells me she's leaving." Nora laughed. "Believe me, I'll never forget that. May. 1993."

"I wonder why she wrote in here you paid her a hundred dollars a week from June till the following January," Bohannon said.

"Let me see that." Drying her hands again, Nora came and leaned over his shoulder, peering at the book. "Oh, look, Ken. She's drawn your picture here." Dutifully, Ken looked, and said something about how well the girl could draw, but he appeared uncomfortable as hell. "You could be misremembering that Mother's Day thing. It could have been the next year."

"No, that was exactly when she quit," Nora said.

"Then what were you paying her for?" Bohannon said.

"I wasn't," Nora said. "Why would I? Anyway, she never got a hundred dollars a week from us. We don't have that kind of money, Hack. Forty was the most I ever paid her. She only came in twice a week. I paid her twenty dollars a time."

Back in the green pickup at the roadside, Bohannon lit a cigarette and studied Cressy's accounts in a new light now. He wasn't going to bother with the clients on her list who'd stopped paying long before her disappearance. He laid the book on the seat, started the truck, and headed for the nearest who was paying right up to the end. Again, a hundred a week. Hohenzee. It was a big, comfortable looking place on a lot that dropped away from the road. There wasn't room for a backyard, he calculated, but in the front a swing and slide and seesaw set were gathering corrosion among unmanaged underbrush. A nurse in white uniform answered the door. And took him to see Olga Hohenzee who was probably no more than forty-five but sat like an old woman, with an afghan wrapped around her shoulders in a chair beside a hospital bed. An oxygen tank stood nearby. She gave Bohannon a fine brave smile, but plainly she was sick, had been that way for a long time, and wasn't about to get better.

"Mr. Bohannon," she said. "How can I help you?"

"I won't take a lot of your time," he said. "I just wonder if you can answer a question for me about Cressy Garner."

"Oh, yes. Poor Cressy. So full of life." The smile this time might mean anything. "Just a little bit too full, I'm afraid."

"Really?" Bohannon said. "How's that?"

"Oh, she was good at house cleaning," Olga Hohenzee said. "Quick and tidy and never had to be scolded or reminded of oversights. But the clothes she wore! Short shorts, tiny little halters she was almost popping out of—"

"She cleaned for you right up until the time she disappeared?"

A surprised look. "Why, no. Her husband didn't like it, she said. And I suppose not. He was well-off, or so people said. How did it look for her to be cleaning people's houses? As if he couldn't support her."

"So when did she stop working for you?"

"I'm not sure exactly," Olga Hohenzee said. "But at least a year before she disappeared. At least a year."

"Your husband home?" Bohannon said.

"He's an attorney," she said. "He works very long hours."

"The children?" Bohannon said.

"They're scattered," she said. "They come visit me pretty regularly."

107

"Your sons become lawyers too?" Bohannon asked.

"Sons?" she said. "There were no sons, Mr. Bohannon. Only daughters. And in this day and age, of course, on principle, unmarried."

"Just one last thing, and I'll stop bothering you." He showed her the drawing of the skinny kid in glasses. "Cast your mind back. That boy ever come courting any of them?"

She gave a little laugh that turned to a cough. A serious cough. The nurse looked in, but her patient waved her away. She recovered, sat for a moment panting to get her breath back, then said, "Goodness, no. Poor starveling." She fumbled for eyeglasses on the table beside her, a table crowded with pill bottles and books. She put on the glasses, took the sketchbook and studied the drawing. "Who drew this? It's really quite good."

"Cressy," Bohannon said, and reached to take the book back.

But she wasn't ready to give it up. "I'd no idea she was so gifted." She turned pages this way and that, then stopped with a little gasp. "Why, look at this. It's Thorvald." She turned the book to show him. "My husband." She seemed not just surprised but pleased and proud. "Imagine that. It's perfect. Oh, Mr. Bohannon, is there some way I could have this? I want to show it to him. He never mentioned it to me. I'll bet he didn't even know. How surprised he'll be."

"I expect he will." Bohannon took the book from under her marveling gaze. "I'll see if I can't get a copy made for you."

Vern sat on the front steps of the Garner house. In uniform. On duty. But playing a game on some electronic gadget he could hold in one hand. It beeped and burred in the silence of the pines. Bohannon trudged up to him. "Unruly crowds of curiosity seekers been throwing rocks at you to get you to let them in?" he asked. "Reporters and TV cameras making your life a hell?"

Vern laughed. "Not so you'd notice. This is dumb duty, ask me."

"I need a photo of Cressy," Bohannon said. "Can I go in and get it?"

Vern gave his head a shake. "Can't do that. Lieutenant's orders. He said to watch out for you. Says you're trying to wreck his case against Garner."

"Now, where did he get that idea?" Bohannon said.

Vern shrugged. "Darned if I know."

Bohannon pretended to tense up, shifted his eyes this way and that. He whispered, "Got me under surveillance, has he?"

"Your every move." Vern laid down the video game and got to his feet and stretched. "A photo of Cressy? That's all you want?"

"Absolutely all," Bohannon said. "Name your price—gold, diamonds, eternal youth."

"Yeah, sure." Vern climbed the steps, went indoors, and in no time at all was handing Bohannon a five-by-seven color portrait of Cressy. Vern sat down on the steps, picked up the game and went to making it beep and burr again.

"You're not curious about what I want with it?" Bohannon asked.

"I'm curious"—Vern stopped to look at his watch—"about when I get relieved here and I can go home to supper."

Motels stood along the beach below the pines of Settlers Cove in numbers everybody spoke about counting but no one ever did. These Bohannon didn't even consider. Not in this case. He drove northward up the Coast Road and found motels out of the ken of such inquiring minds and gimlet eyes as peopled Settlers Cove and Madrone. Stopping at each one, getting down from the pickup, he would pause to look at the sunset. Sunsets were often spectacular on the Central Coast. Tonight's certainly was. He prayed none of the local painters was trying to get it on canvas. Then he strode into the offices of each place in turn, showed them the drawings of her men that Cressy had made in her sketchbook, and Cressy's photo. But an hour later, when the sun had disappeared in a red blaze at the far edge of the Pacific, he had learned nothing.

Where he learned something was at the third or fourth motel to the south, on the road to San Luis. A man with brown skin and black hair who was about the height and weight of a ten-year-old boy looked at the drawings across the reception counter at the SleepTight Inn, and said, "Yes, these gentlemen have been here. But not recently."

"No," Bohannon said, "not for about three years, right?"

Singh was the man's name. "Yes, I believe that is correct." His smile was as tidy as the rest of him. His teeth were beautifully neat and white. "My father had only recently bought this motel and installed my wife and me to run it. And we were astonished soon by the brief time some guests stayed. Only for an hour or two. We were naive."

"What about this girl?" Bohannon showed him Cressy's picture.

Singh paled a little. He looked up from the picture to Bohannon's face and his eyes were wide. "It is her," he said. "I told my wife when her picture was shown on the television news. I told my wife, 'She used to come here, that girl did.' "

"And my wife was terribly upset. 'Murdered,' she said. 'Oh, no.' "

"Sometimes stopping with too many different men,"

Bohannon said, "too often at motels where guests stay only an hour or two can lead to trouble."

Singh's brown eyes were wide. "The murder might have happened here. Oh, what a scandal, what a disgrace."

"It might have," Bohannon said. He leafed over Cressy's sketchbook. "What about this boy? Was he ever here?"

"Dear God," Singh gasped. "Where did you get this book?"

"The boy?" Bohannon said. "Did she ever bring him here?"

Singh opened his mouth to speak, but then thought better of it. He shook his head hard. "No, she did not." He pushed the sketchbook away.

"But you have seen him," Bohannon pressed. "He did show up here."

The door opened. A woman with a flower print scarf tied over her head came in with a young girl. Singh hurried to check them in. Bohannon waited for a minute, then interrupted. "Excuse me, Mr. Singh. One more question, then I'll clear off. What was his name?"

"He did not register, so I do not know," Singh said, "but I hope you find him. He broke a window in a fit of temper and ran away without paying for it." A small brown finger pointed. "A large window. That one, right there. Plate glass. Hugely expensive."

"What was the fit of temper about?"

"Please," Singh said, "I am busy here, can't you see?"

"Sorry." Bohannon went and sat down on a hard couch that faced a coffee table with artificial flowers and a stack of magazines. He leafed over an old copy of *Arizona Highways* until Singh had outfitted the woman with a key to unit 107, and she had bought sandwiches, cookies, and sodas from vending machines along the end wall of the office and gone off with the whimpering, whining little girl. Then he stood up.

"Why are you still here, sir?" Singh said dismally.

"Because I need to know the date when the boy had his fit of temper. You must have the bill for the plate glass repair. Can I see that bill please? Or a cancelled check?"

"Impossible," Singh said. "Who knows how long ago it was?"

"I'd bet on February eleventh, 1994. The date Cressy Garner disappeared. You do keep records, don't you?"

"Certainly," Singh said. "My father would—" But he let that go. "If I find the receipt for you, then will you leave me alone?"

"Swear to God," Bohannon said.

Singh opened a door to rooms behind the office. Sitar music drifted out. Singh stepped into it, and a fine strong smell of curry. Singh closed the door. Bohannon sat on the couch again, opened another magazine, but soon Singh was back with a large manila envelope. *1994* was scrawled on it in red marker pen. The delicate little man laid the envelope on the counter, pulled papers from it, and sorted through them while Bohannon stood and watched. "There." Singh slapped a pink printed form down in front of him. It was rumpled, creased, thumb-smeared, and a corner had been torn off. But it had what Bohannon needed to see. The scribbled date was *2-12-94.*

"Good," Bohannon said. "Thank you. Now, the boy came looking for Cressy, didn't he? Had she been here that day with one of these men?"

"Oh, sir, you are really upsetting me very much," Singh said.

"It will stop hurting in a minute," Bohannon said, and held out the book again. "Show me which man."

Singh sighed with vexation, and flipped over the pages angrily. But he found the sketch of the last man ever to visit his motel with Cressy Garner, stabbed the sketch with a finger, and thrust it under Bohannon's nose. "That one," he said. "Now, will you please, sir, go away?"

"Promptly." Bohannon shut the book, slipped it into his pocket, and smiled. "Thank you for your patience." And he pushed out into the night.

It was quite a house. Bohannon remembered when it was built and the excitement it had caused, the shock, the indignation. The owner was an industrial architect and had made the plans himself and nobody had ever seen a house like it. White, piled-up boxes, tall ones, short ones, sprawling six different ways, on a grassy ridge where horses used to graze, right above the town, not a tree around it. Now, nobody groused anymore. And some people, architects, students, and the like came to Madrone only to look at it, people who wouldn't be caught dead sightseeing Hearst Castle a few miles up the Coast Road. Jasperson was the architect's name.

Dogs barked indoors when Bohannon rang the bell. The door was opened by the skinny boy with glasses in Cressy Garner's sketch. Bohannon was so shocked, he almost fell down. The dogs were Rottweilers. They stood flanking the boy, looking up at Bohannon, but not barking now, not whining, not moving, just panting slightly. Bohannon thought if he reached out, they would kill him. He had no intention of reaching out. He in fact did not know what to do. He was too surprised. He showed his license with a shaky hand.

"Like to talk to Adam Jasperson, please? He at home?"

"He's in Taiwan," the boy said. "Business trip. He's away a lot."

"Your mother?"

The boy twitched a wry smile. "I'm between mothers right now. I'm Wright Jasperson. I'm twenty-one. Is there something I can do?"

"I'm looking into the death of Cressy Garner." Bohannon put away his wallet. "I believe she used to clean house for you?"

"That was years ago," the boy said. "She quit long before she was—before what happened to her." He frowned, tilted his head. "Looking into it why? It said on the news they arrested her husband."

"Just routine," Bohannon said. "Checking out loose ends."

"Well, I'm sorry, but we wouldn't know anything about it." Wright Jasperson stepped back and the dogs with him. He started to close the door.

"One more thing," Bohannon said. "Mr. Nanda Singh at the SleepTight Motel? He'd like you to pay him for the window you broke three years ago."

"What?" The boy lost color. "What the hell is this? You're no Sheriff. Who are you?"

Bohannon held up his hands. "Don't kill the messenger."

"You're crazy," the boy said, and slammed the door.

"Good night." Bohannon said, and made his way through the dark back to his truck. Climbing inside, starting the engine, switching on the lights, he smiled grimly at his words: this would be anything but a good night for Wright Jasperson. Not the worst one of his life. That had been three years ago. Bohannon released the parking brake, put the truck into gear, and took it down the road. No. Wrong. The worst one was still to come.

Back in the ranch house kitchen, he dug from his wallet a slip of paper with the number on it of a church out in the San

Joaquin Valley and, at the old pine sideboard where the phone rested, punched the buttons to get the number. The message on the church answering machine gave answers to all sorts of questions about hours and services, bingo games, prayer breakfasts, sports events, and outreach programs, it gave many numbers a caller might ring to get more information. It went on this way for quite some time. But finally it admitted the caller might want to leave a message, there was a beep, and Bohannon left a message for Father Rivera. He hung up the phone and headed for the cupboard where he kept his Old Crow. With a glass in hand he turned for the round table where the lamp glowed, and George Stubbs rolled into the room in his wheelchair.

"Well, what happened? You been gone all day and half the night. On that tip Rivera gave you. Accomplish anything?"

"Found Cressy Garner's killer." Bohannon pulled out a chair and sat down at the table. He lifted the bottle toward the old man. "Care to join me?"

"Thought you'd never ask." The motor of the wheelchair whined and Stubbs was at the table. "You mean they got him locked up?"

"Not yet." Bohannon fetched him a glass, sat down again, watched the whiskey trickle into both glasses, set the bottle down, re-capped it. He sipped his whiskey, and lit a cigarette. "But I hope he's a little bit frightened."

Stubbs needed both gnarled hands to manage the glass, but he managed it, and said, "You want to light me one of them weeds?"

Bohannon did that.

Smoke wreathing his bald head, Stubbs said, "So it's not open and shut."

"I can't shut it," Bohannon said. "Only Gerard can shut it. And I'm not free to ask him. Not free to ask anybody. So

I'll have to make do, won't I?"

"You phoned somebody just now," Stubbs said. "You won't be alone."

"You're a sneaky old coot," Bohannon said.

"Wish I could help you," Stubbs said. "Damn, I hate this old man stuff." He squinted. "It's really not Brent Garner that killed her?"

"Knowing what I learned today," Bohannon said with a short laugh, "I'm surprised it wasn't. But it wasn't. He never caught on."

"What do you mean?"

"She was sleeping with three or four other men she'd cleaned house for."

"Well, I'll be doggoned," Stubbs said.

"The pay was better," Bohannon said. "Much better."

Stubbs managed the glass again, set it down noisily, shook his head. "So the gossip was right. I heard rumors. And I seen her, of course. Market, drugstore, laundromat. She was pretty and showed it off a lot. Made eyes at pret' near anybody who wore pants."

"There are safer games to play," Bohannon said.

"Looks like it," Stubbs said. "You gonna tell me who it was?"

"A teenage boy who thought she was his alone," Bohannon said. "Until he found out she was sleeping with his father."

"Oh, my." Stubbs's jaw dropped. "You don't mean it."

"Like some old Greek play." Bohannon tilted whiskey into the glasses again. "Big surprise. Mankind doesn't change."

And then Otis Jackson stormed in and raised hell with them both.

It was 4:50 in the morning, not yet daylight. Ahead of

Bohannon, Rivera parked across the street from the Jasperson house, which loomed up against a black sky white and ghostly. Rivera got out of the gray Honda and walked back to the green truck. In his black clerical suit, he shivered. "I had forgotten how cold it gets by the ocean."

"You sure you want to do this?" Bohannon said.

"What option do I have?" Rivera said.

"Drive down to the Sheriff's station and tell Gerard."

"You still do not understand." Rivera turned away. "I will be back."

"Let me come with you." Bohannon opened the truck door.

"No, please." Rivera raised his hand. "I will be all right." And he crossed the street and climbed the long winding pathway to the house. He looked fragile. Bohannon lost track of him in the shadows. The door chimes must have sounded because a light went on in the house. Upstairs. The dogs barked. Briefly. There was a wait. Then the door opened, a rectangle of light. Wright Jasperson stood there. Rivera's form stepped into the frame. Bohannon took his Winchester down from its rack behind the seat. He raised it. Then the boy backed up, Rivera stepped inside, and the door closed.

Bohannon sat taut, edgy, gripping the rifle hard, squinting into the darkness, straining to hear. There was nothing to see. Nothing to hear. He put the rifle back. Not steadily. He was shaky. His heart was pounding. He reached for the door handle. But he didn't move it. Rivera had the guts to do this dangerous thing: Bohannon must have the guts to wait. He lit a cigarette. When he had smoked it down, he lit another from the butt. When that was gone, he opened the door quietly and got out of the truck and stood in the road, breathing deeply to try to calm himself. Watching the house all the time, of course. Then he couldn't bear to do that any more, and he began to pace.

The sky slowly lightened. One by one the stars faded out. He got back into the truck, pulled his hat down over his eyes, tried to sleep. And maybe he did. For a few minutes, anyway. Then the sound of the door closing across the street woke him. He sat up straight. Down the long twisting path Rivera came. Wright Jasperson was beside him. In gray sweats. And a baseball cap. When they got near the truck, Bohannon could read CAL POLY on the cap. Rivera opened the door on the passenger side, and the boy climbed in. He was pale, and behind his glasses, his eyes were swollen. From crying? He said nothing to Bohannon. Bohannon couldn't think what to say.

"Now it is Lieutenant Gerard's turn," Rivera said. "Goodbye, Hack. Thank you." He slammed the truck door, walked to his own car, got into it, and drove away. Bohannon started the truck's engine.

"You know what he said?" Wright Jasperson asked. Bohannon grunted, put the truck in gear, let the brake go. The boy said, "He said sometimes God asks the impossible of us."

"He sure as hell asked it of Father Rivera." Bohannon began to drive. The boy said, "He asked it of His own Son. This is Good Friday, did you know that?"

"I didn't know that," Bohannon said.

"I'd forgotten," the boy said. "Father Rivera reminded me."

At the big round table in the plank kitchen, crankily letting Otis help him with his breakfast, Stubbs said, "What about the damn shovel?"

"She drove the car to meet him where he asked her to on

the phone," Bohannon said. He had stayed at the substation while Gerard interrogated Wright Jasperson. "The shovel was in the trunk. He smashed her head in with it. Buried her with it. Put it back in the trunk. Drove the car back to the Garner place and left it there."

"Pretty cool and calculating," Stubbs said. Otis wiped egg yolk off the old man's newly-shaved chin with a napkin. Stubbs scowled and brushed his hand away. To Bohannon he said, "I thought you says the boy was half-crazy with what she done to him."

"He was." Bohannon lit a cigarette. "His prints are on the handle of the shovel. They couldn't identify them until I brought him in."

"You still ain't said how you done that," Stubbs said.

Bohannon drank coffee, smiled. "And I never will," he said.

Survival

It was a long drive north, half of California, all of Oregon, most of Washington, and then inland to George Stubbs's sister's house in Norton's Mill, Idaho, thirty miles from the Canadian border. And all the way, Stubbs's trophy cups had rattled in their carton behind the seat. Bohannon had wrapped and cushioned them in newspaper but somehow they'd managed to rattle anyway.

He hadn't known what to do with them exactly. They had stood on the mantel of the boulder-built fireplace in his ranch house for the eighteen or twenty years Stubbs had worked for him, lived side by side with him, been an interwoven part of his days. Those rodeo trophies for roping and bulldogging, for bronco busting and bull riding, had belonged on that mantel.

And it sure as hell had looked strange and naked once he'd taken them down and packed them for the trip along with Stubbs's body in its coffin to where the old man had said he wanted to be buried. In the same graveyard as his mother (God knew where his father's body lay), his brothers who'd still been boys when they died, and his sister when her time came.

Norton's Mill had proved no different from what Bohannon had pictured it, a sleepy little town among towering white pines. More mid-western than western, its houses

were mainly wood frame, and two-storied, and getting on for a hundred years old. The house where Ada Tanner lived was one of these, white, foursquare, with a wide, comfortable front porch, but no fancy architectural furbelows. A wire mesh fence enclosed the yard, and fruit trees in the yard, and flowerbeds.

Ada Tanner looked like her brother, talked like him, was straightforward and homey. Bohannon hadn't known of her existence till Stubbs gave in to the idea that he was going to die. Then he told Bohannon about her and the man she had married. Stubbs and Luke Tanner could not agree on whether it was raining. That was why he'd stayed away from his boyhood town even at the height of his rodeo fame and money. When Luke died, he'd thought about a trip to see Ada, but there was always so much to do at Bohannon's stables, he'd put it off. And then he had become too arthritic, "stove up," as he put it, to travel.

So he did his traveling this October week in a pine box in the steel bed of Bohannon's green pickup truck. His trip home. Bohannon stayed for the funeral, of course, and the burial in the cemetery with its tilted headstones and lawns going brown for the winter. Nobody much came. Stubbs's glory days had gained him renown in Norton's Mill, but those glory days were the 1930s and 1940s, and the graveyard had claimed most of the people who'd remembered George Stubbs as a boy, before he'd left for more exciting places.

Women outlive men, so it was mostly white-haired neighbor ladies who came for lunch to Ada Tanner's house following the ceremonies. There was one man, a skinny old geezer, who cornered Bohannon and talked about lunatics living in the woods up here, survivalists, anti-taxers, anti-blacks (there wasn't but one or two blacks in the whole county), trying to live on forage, starving their children,

sometimes freezing in the winters.

At last an old woman led him away. When they'd all gone, Bohannon told Ada Tanner goodbye, and she handed him a Bible, with red page edges and floppy covers, plastic meant to look like leather. Stocky, ruddy-cheeked, hair freshly set for the funeral, she smelled of lavender soap and starch, "I want you to have this," she said. "I wish it was a fine one, but I live on Social Security, and it's what's inside that counts. It's been my guide and mainstay all my life so it's the gift I want to give you for being so good to George all those long years when he was past being able to do the strong, wild, crazy things he was so proud of."

"He didn't owe me," Bohannon said. "I owed him. I'd never have been able to make it without him. I'm going to miss him."

"I guess you don't call yourself one," she said, "but you're a Christian. Never mind"—she patted his hands as they held the Bible—"you have that, and keep it near you. It won't re-place an old friend. But there's comfort in it."

"Thank you." Bohannon put on his sweat-stained Stetson and stepped out the screen door, an old one, with a long black spring to pull it closed. The spring twanged. The door swung loosely shut. He crossed the porch. "Take care of yourself, Miz Tanner."

"Don't grieve," she said through the screen. "He's in a happy place, now."

"If they have rodeos there," Bohannon said, and crossed over to the driveway where the green pickup waited.

Nothing was wrong with the motel room that wasn't wrong with all motel rooms but he slept badly and was up and showered and dressed by 4:30 and on his way home. In the dark. He had good sense and most of the time he used it. But

Stubbs's death had shaken him. And he began fretting and making bad decisions. Leaving Deputy T. Hodges in charge of the stables was asking too much of her. He'd rung her up every day of this trip, and she'd always sounded cheerful and on top of things and teased him for worrying. There was a hired hand. She wasn't alone, and she was young and strong, but she wasn't very big, and accidents could happen. Horses were unpredictable. No harm must come to T. Hodges. Not now. He couldn't take it.

So, instead of returning to the coast and following the route that had brought him here, he took a state highway heading straight south, telling himself it would save time. Maybe it would have, but he wasn't going to find out. The highway wasn't much and it soon entered a stand of giant Douglas firs that promised no end to itself. It was quiet, dim and cold on that road. A little bit eerie. Soundless. He would have welcomed the rattling of those rodeo trophies now. He tried the radio but reception was fitful and anyway he never much liked country and even less did he like gospel and that was all the music there was. The trip grew stranger by the hour. Where was everybody? Not another car, not another truck. The world could have ended for all he knew.

Then, he had to stop. That famous tree we all have heard about, the one that falls in a forest where there's no one to hear, and therefore can it be said for sure that it made a sound when it fell?—that tree had fallen across the road. A tremendous tree. As thick through as his truck. He couldn't drive around it. The ditches beside the road were too deep. He got stiffly out of the truck, stretched, lit a cigarette, studied the tree, finished the cigarette, dropped it, put it out carefully under his worn boot, climbed back into the truck and after some backing and filling, pointed it north again. He'd seen a turn-off a few miles back. It had no signboard. But it would take hours to get back to Nolan's Mill and start the trip over. He'd try the side-road, see where it led.

It was narrow, went crookedly through the trees that grew denser here and were even older and thicker and taller than any he'd so far seen. Maybe the road had been graveled once. His tires threw up gravel now and then that rattled under the fenders. But before mankind had taken it over, he figured animals had laid it out and used it from the ancient start, deer, bear, puma. And when they came along, the Indians had seen no call to improve on it, and the Europeans when they got here hadn't wasted much energy on it. Why they'd wasted even one load of gravel Bohannon couldn't see. He saw no signs of human settlement.

Then he came around a bend and sawhorses stood across the road, and beyond them a parked van. He braked the green pickup and stared. The sawhorses were old, unpainted. Unlike his truck, with its horse-head logo on the door, the van had no markings. Oh, a sign had sometime been lettered on its side, but then painted over. Maybe it had been white once, but it was gray now, mud-stained below, rain spotted and dusty above, and crusty on its roof with bird-droppings and brown pine needles. Its slide door opened and two young men jumped out of it, wearing army camouflage fatigues and floppy camouflage hats. Each had a gun. One was a .357 Magnum. The other was an AK-47.

Bohannon had not brought his Winchester. In California he was licensed to keep it on its rack over the back window of the truck. But for getting without hassle from state to state he figured he'd better leave it home. He jammed the truck into reverse and began backing off as fast as he could. But not fast enough. The man with the AK-47 fired shots. Not at him. Not at the truck. Over the truck roof. Warning shots. Bohannon braked, one rear wheel in the ditch. They came jogging up the road. He put up his hands.

"Just a mistake," he said. "I got lost."

"You shoulda picked someplace else." Both boys had beard-stubble and blue eyes, and hair too long for their hats to conceal. "Get out of there."

"He don't look like no FBI," the boy with the handgun said.

"He looks like a Goddam Indian," the other one said. "Get out."

Bohannon got out. "My folks were Irish, if that's any help."

"You say," the AK-47 boy said. "Turn around. Hands on the hood there. Spread your legs."

"Who are you? What gives you the right to—?"

"You're in Ninth Amendment America, now." The boy held onto the gun but patted Bohannon down with his free hand. "We don't go by Jew York D.C. laws here. We got Christian laws, God's laws. Question isn't who we are." He straightened up and looked through the wallet he had taken from Bohannon's hip pocket. "It's who you are and what you're doing here. Oh, my!" He turned to his partner. "Lookee here, Hadley. This man is a Private Investigator." He grabbed Bohannon's arm and swung him around. "Who sent you? Who you working for? FBI? Alcohol, Tobacco and Firearms? Who tipped you off to find us here? Nobody knows. Nobody."

"Including me," Bohannon said. "I just stumbled in here. The State road is blocked. A fallen tree. I was looking for a way to keep going south without—"

"You're lying." The boy slapped him.

"Don't be nervous," Bohannon said, "I'm not going to hurt you."

The boy slapped him again, and Bohannon punched him

in the face, and he fell on his butt on the road and the gun went off. A chatter of fire into the air. He scrambled up. "Hell, it don't really matter who you are or why you come." He wiped his bloody mouth with a hand, looked at the hand, glared at Bohannon. "I'm going to shoot you dead one way or the other. Cause I can't let you go back and tell where we are." He jerked the gun barrel. "Go on. Walk into the trees. I'll be right behind you."

Bohannon didn't move. He heard footsteps. Someone was coming through the trees opposite. The boy took hold of him again, yanked him, shoved him toward the ditch, and a man appeared on the other side of the road. A middle-aged man, camouflage pants and jacket, also with long hair with a camouflage cap on it. Only his hair was gray. He wore Desert Storm dark glasses and a big old .45 revolver in a holster.

"Ford, Hadley?" he said. "What's all the ruckus? Anybody could have heard that gunfire. The whole damned U.S. Army could be down on us."

"Niggers," Ford jeered. "Mud people. Who cares?"

The middle-aged man walked up to Bohannon. "Who are you?"

"Bohannon is my name." Close up, he recognized the man. His picture was in the files at the Sheriff's substation in Madrone. Bohannon checked those files out now and then. Cunningham? Yes, Chester Cunningham. U.S. Marine Corps, retired. Something about stockpiling firearms, altering firearms, transporting firearms across state borders. "What's yours?"

Cunningham ignored that. "What are you doing here?"

"He's an investigator licensed by the State of California," Ford said. "You think he's going to tell us what he's doing here?"

"I think you should remember who you're talking to,"

Cunningham said, "and correct your tone." And to Bohannon, "Where did you learn I was here?"

Bohannon told his story again.

"I guess not," the man said.

"Captain?" The Hadley boy had been rummaging in the truck. "He might not be lying."

Cunningham and Ford looked at him. Bohannon looked too. Hadley came bringing Ada Tanner's Bible. He said, "This man's a Christian."

"That right?" Cunningham held out a hand for the book and the boy gave it to him. He looked at it thoughtfully for a minute, lifting it a little, weighing it in his hand. He blinked at Bohannon, "That a fact?"

Bohannon didn't answer.

Cunningham opened the truck door, laid the Bible on the seat, and turned on the radio. Staticky music played. A lush orchestra backed a sincere-sounding baritone who crooned, "I am satis-fied with Je-sus, He has meant so much to me-e-e . . ." The music ceased. Cunningham slammed the door of the truck and said to Bohannon, "Come with me," motioned with the revolver for Bohannon to go ahead of him across the road and into the trees. Bohannon went.

"Don't mean nothing," Ford called. "About all you can get on the radio up here."

Cunningham stopped and looked back. "What do you want, Ford—rock and roll? Rap? Hip-hop?"

"No, sir," Ford said quickly, turning red. " 'Course not."

Cunningham grunted. "Bring that truck to the compound." Then he nodded Bohannon into the trees. The walk was a long one. Then there was a small settlement of rough shacks set at odd angles to one another, a large open space between. At a guess, the planks and two-by-fours had been sawn up here out of trees felled illegally. With gas-powered saws: there were no power lines. He glimpsed crude out-houses set back in the brush. That meant no running water, didn't it? What then: a well, or maybe a spring or stream near enough to walk to with buckets? The old geezer at Ada Tanner's had been right: life here was primitive. Vehicles stood around, a sad assortment of rusty pickup trucks, vans, RVs, a once-racy red sports car layered with dead pine needles, its cloth top hanging in tatters.

Two buildings rose up bigger than the rest, one living quarters, the other for storage, a warehouse. Or was it a barn? The pine smell that dropped from the huge trees was strong in the growing warmth of the day, but still he detected a whiff of horse. Cunningham pushed open the plank door into the dwelling house and motioned Bohannon through, came in after him, and closed the door.

Inside, in a wash of greenish daylight through dirty win-dowpanes, sagged sorry old furniture, not much of it, a sofa, a greasy overstuffed armchair, side chairs with seats worn threadbare. On the mantel a row of smoky kerosene lanterns. Over them a big American flag. A case to hold rifles, the pane of one of its glass doors cracked. A round dining room table from fifty years ago or better. Some rickety unmatched chairs. A battered library table along one wall was heaped with papers, magazines, typewritten stuff. Tacked to the wall above it was a map of the eleven Western States, with colored pushpins stuck into it. A marked-up street map of some town was held by one of these.

At the far end of the room, a kitchen housed a cast-iron cook stove, shelves holding unmatched china, battered pots and pans hanging up, sooty skillets. Stacked on the floor were supplies, sacks of flour and rice, restaurant-size cans of baked beans, vegetable soup, sliced peaches, applesauce. Boxes of crackers and cold cereals, dehydrated milk and mashed potatoes. Great big cans of coffee. COFFEE. No brand name. Stairs fashioned of half logs climbed to a loft that bracketed the room below. He glimpsed tousled bedding.

"Sit down," Cunningham said. "Care for some coffee?"

"I'd like to buy it at a diner in the next town," Bohannon said.

"We can't always have what we'd like," Cunningham said with a thin smile. "Sit down." He raised his voice. "Selina?" It was a name. The kitchen door opened. A thin woman in her mid-thirties came in, shut the door, set down a bucket of coal. Blond hair combed out long and straight. No makeup, but good features, good bones. She wore glasses, jeans, an unbuttoned lumberjack shirt, under it a black T-shirt with *9th Amendment* stenciled on it, old work boots. But something about her said breeding, education. "Coffee," Cunningham told her, and sat down himself. In the overstuffed chair.

"Who's that?" she said, staring.

"Name's Bohannon."

"Do we know him?" She tilted her head. Then she gave it a shake. "No. We don't know him. So what's he doing here?"

Bohannon took off his hat and nodded to her. "I strayed in by accident."

"Bad luck," she said, as if she sympathized. "And bad timing."

"Will you just get the coffee?" Cunningham said.

Her expression of alertness changed to one of wooden obedience. "Yes, sir," she said, and turned to the stove.

"Do you know who I am?" Cunningham asked Bohannon.

"Is that Captain a real rank or honorary?"

"Real. Vietnam. Actually"—the thin smile came back—"I'm the General. Field Marshal, Chief of Staff."

"President," the woman said and set down coffee mugs, one beside the Captain's chair, one beside Bohannon's. "Of Ninth Amendment America."

"You know what that means?" Cunningham asked.

"I get the feeling you're going to tell me," Bohannon said.

" *'The enumeration in the Constitution of certain rights shall not be construed to deny or disparage others retained by the people.'* "

"What others?" Bohannon said.

"Those are the words the Founding Fathers wrote. That is the whole sum and substance of the Ninth Amendment. Every word of it." He gave a patronizing smile. "Good question, though. Gets to the heart of it. Most of the laws the overlords have passed since it was written deny and disparage the rights of the people. Taxes, licenses, building regulations, zoning regulations, speed limits, fishing rights, grazing rights, hunting rights, compulsory insurance, can't do this, can't do that, can't do the other thing . . . Those elected so-called Representatives over in D.C. say 'What Ninth Amendment? What unnamed rights? We're the ones who make the laws. Can't run a country without laws. Can't run a country without taxes. You paid yours?' "

"I see." Bohannon had put his hat on the floor. He picked it up and got out of the chair. Cunningham with surprising quickness pulled the .45 from its holster and pointed it at him. He didn't say anything, he just looked mean. Bohannon asked, "What about my rights? I'd like to leave here. I have horses to look after, a business to run. I have to get back to California."

"Sit down." The man waited, with the gun pointed, and Bohannon sat down again. "You don't know my face? You never heard of Chester Cunningham?"

"In what connection?" Bohannon looked out the window

beside the fireplace. "Politics? Run for office on the Ninth Amendment ticket, did you?"

"Don't play games," Cunningham said. "TV, radio, the newspapers. You're not a monk. Of course you've heard of me."

Bohannon judged the man needed for him to say yes, to light up with excitement if possible, even better, to fall down and worship. "I stable horses up in a canyon where TV doesn't reach any better than it probably reaches here." He looked around pointedly. "I don't see any TV set here. As to the radio, I check the weather reports. In my line of work, you get up before sunrise, work all day, and you're ready for bed directly after supper. No, I don't read newspapers. No time."

"Well said." Cunningham nodded, holstered the gun, stood up. "I guess they school you in your identity so you've got a background all ready to spill when you get questioned."

"You can check it out. Phone down there. The San Luis Obispo County Sheriff's substation in Madrone. They'll back it up."

"I don't have a phone, but I expect they would. They're standing by waiting for me to call. With all the answers." He watched out the window as Ford and Hadley brought the green pickup into the compound and parked it. He turned back and said almost pleadingly, "Look, if you hadn't carried that Private Investigator's license I wouldn't keep you. I mean, Ford and Hadley aren't out there to take prisoners, just to keep strangers off, and without that darn license, I'd have let you go. But you're law enforcement. And law enforcement means only one thing to me: trouble, and worse than trouble." He glanced toward the map on the wall. "The end of all my plans for America." He wagged his head sorrowfully. "No, I can't take a chance with you."

"If I was here on government assignment, do you think I'd

have carried that license? I left my gun at home. Why wouldn't I have left the license?"

"Don't know, but it would have been prudent."

"And would I have come alone?"

That got Cunningham's attention. He took off the dark glasses, and narrowed his eyes. "Somebody out there, counting the minutes you're here, waiting to move in?"

Bohannon gave a small laugh. "Would I say so, if there were?"

Cunningham sighed and pulled the gun again. He motioned with it, meaning Bohannon was supposed to go out the door. Bohannon went out the door. Cunningham came after him and closed the door and pointed with the gun at one of the small buildings. "Keep you there," he said, "until I can decide what to do with you. Move."

Bohannon moved. Another blond youngster in camouflage pants and jacket and combat boots came out of the storage building. He stopped, saluted Cunningham, and stared at Bohannon. "Who the hell is that?"

"Don't curse, Elroy, remember?"

"Forgot, Captain, sir." He frowned hard at Bohannon. "He from the bank? I thought you said no prisoners."

"I don't know what you're talking about," Cunningham said. "And neither do you. Shut up, Elroy. You finished that mimeographing yet?"

"Yes, sir," Elroy said, not looking away from Bohannon, plainly puzzled and worried by him. "But that fuck—I mean, that lousy Addressograph. That's real old, sir. Them cardboard stencils—they jam all the time. Can't we get a new one?"

"Get a rifle," Cunningham said, "see that it's loaded, and stand guard over this man until you're relieved. K building." And to Bohannon, "Over there, in the corner. March."

Elroy saluted and went back into the storage building, and out of the woods and into the open hardpan between the shacks came a teenage girl riding a tall elegant sorrel mare. The girl had long straight blond hair, wore a camouflage coverall too big for her, and a floppy-brimmed camouflage hat. The mare was pregnant. On sighting the girl, Cunningham holstered the gun again and looked at his watch.

"Liberty," he said, "you've been gone too long. That means too far. That means you could have been seen. You want me to ground you?"

"No, Daddy," she said, patting the horse's neck, "we didn't go far."

"I doubt you know where you went," he said. "All right, you sponge her down, now, clean her hoofs, give her some oats, be sure she has water. Having your own horse means responsibility, hard work."

"I love looking after her." The girl tilted her head at Bohannon. "Who are you? Is that your truck? With the horse head on it?"

Bohannon said it was. "I keep a dozen horses on my place. She's about ready to foal, you know. You don't want to go too far with her. She could need help when her time comes."

"Help?" Cunningham snorted. "She's an animal. Instinct will—"

"She's not a cayuse," Bohannon said. "She's a thoroughbred. Centuries of breeding. They can't survive without human help."

The girl said, "I know what to do. My horse book has got a whole chapter about it."

"Just the same," Bohannon said. "I'd keep her in her stall from here on out. With plenty of fresh dry straw."

"I know what to do," the girl repeated sulkily, reached down from the saddle, swung open a wide door, and rode the mare into the storage building. Looking after her, Bohannon glimpsed 50-pound sacks of fertilizer, a truckload of them. Not to grow food. Not around here. They were labeled *Ammonium Nitrate*. He got a cold feeling in the pit of his stomach. There must be a ton of it. What was Cunningham going to blow up? The entire state?

"How did you come by a horse like that?" he said.

"Liberty wanted a horse, wouldn't leave me alone about it. You know how they nag." Cunningham grunted. "I took her in payment for a debt. No bargain. She'd never won a race."

Bohannon shrugged. "Maybe her foal will be a winner."

Cunningham's laugh was brief. "Another mouth to feed. Move."

The K building held a cot with a rolled-up sleeping bag on it, a tubular patio chair whose web seat and back sun in a different climate had long ago bleached to gray, and whose metal time and weather had pitted. A set of battered veneer bookshelves had new-looking books on them. *The Turner Diaries, The Anarchist Cookbook, Christian Identity, Edible Wild Plants of the West, The Improvised Munitions Handbook*. Multiple copies. And brown-wrapped parcels, probably of the same books. A kerosene lantern with a smoke-smudged chimney, a single window with a huge tree trunk right up against it. No way out. Bohannon stood studying the room. Cunningham from the open doorway, studied him.

"Think I ought to chain you up?" he said.

Bohannon smiled. "Save yourself the trouble. Let me go."

Cunningham ignored that. "No, I don't think, with Elroy outside with his Uzi, you'll try to make a break. Anyway, the woods are full of my troops. You wouldn't get far."

"All night?" Bohannon said.

"All night, all day. Don't give it another thought. Read."

Cunningham nodded at the bookcase. "*The Turner Diaries*. It will open your mind." He backed down the two short steps that led up to the door, began to close the door, and then said, "Anyway, you won't be here long. Just till I see if you're useful. If not, you won't be here at all."

Bohannon's brows went up. "In what way useful?"

"As a bargaining chip," Cunningham said, and closed the door. It had a heavy slide bolt on the outside. Bohannon heard him rattle it into place. Cunningham said through the door, "If nature calls, just ask Elroy to take you. Elroy?"

"Sir," Elroy said.

Lunch when Elroy brought it was a wiener sandwich and a glass of milk. He wasn't sure what the milk tasted like but not milk. Powdered milk. He remembered the boxes stacked on the kitchen floor. The meat tasted like a hot dog, any hot dog. Mustard. Ketchup. Sweet relish. And the bread itself was good, fresh-baked, still a little warm. A treat. And he was damned hungry and finished the sandwich off in gulps, and the chocolate bar that lay beside it on the plate. A half-hour afterward, when the bolt slid and the door opened, it was Cunningham's woman, Selina, who came to collect the plate and glass.

"That was good." Bohannon stood to hand them to her.

"You'll get damn tired of hot dogs," she said.

"Don't you mean 'darn'?" he said with a little smile.

"Yes, I mean 'darn,' " she said and smiled back.

"And what did you mean when you said, 'Bad timing'?"

"I meant sometimes we're busy around here." She wasn't going to stay and chat. She opened the door. "Tomorrow will be one of those times."

"All the more reason to let me go my way," Bohannon said.

"A sane person would think so." She went out and bolted the door.

And Bohannon lay on his bunk and read *The Turner Diaries*, which made clear on page after sneering, blustering, bloodthirsty page, what the woman had meant. No admirer of this book could possibly be sane. If she knew that, why did she stay?

Elroy knocked at 5:00 and woke him. While reading, he had drifted into a troubled sleep filled with murder, mayhem, bombings, and by contrast the quiet of the compound under its enormous trees was almost welcome. The blond kid brought in a battered old cafeteria tray. On it was a plate with beans and franks, a ketchup bottle, two slices of buttered bread on a side plate, another glass of milk, and a bowl of red Jell-O. Bohannon sat up on the edge of the bed, and Elroy handed him the tray. He studied him.

"You all right?"

"Nightmares." Bohannon set the tray on his knees and ran his fingers through his hair. "You know what the psychology books say about nightmares?"

"No, sir," Elroy said.

"The only ones who have them are children and artists."

"That right? I never did hear that. Which one are you?"

Elroy was brighter than Bohannon had expected. "Neither one, so I guess that makes the psychology books wrong, doesn't it?" He was hungry again, and tilted ketchup over the beans and franks and filled his mouth. "What's this mimeographing you're doing for the Captain?"

"*Ninth Amendment Bulletin*," Elroy said. "The Captain writes it, Miz Cunnningham, she types the stencils, and I make the copies."

"And address the envelopes?" Bohannon took a bite of the

bread. It was good again. "You complained about the Addressograph."

"I address 'em and stuff 'em," Elroy said wearily. "Takes forever."

"Big mailing list, is it?" Bohannon took a swallow of milk.

"I guess I better not tell you that." The boy wandered to the open door and, rifle cradled in his arms, stood there gazing out at the dying daylight through the trees. "Even if they are going to kill you."

Bohannon blinked. "I thought they were going to trade me off."

"Trade you off?" Elroy turned around. "For what? For who?"

Bohannon shrugged. "A bargaining chip, that's what the Captain called me. Where do you mail all these copies of your bulletin? Coeur d'Alene?"

"Hell, no. That would give away where we're at, here."

"I guess it might, at that." Bohannon continued to down the beans and franks and bread. "So what do you do about that?"

"Pack 'em all in a carton and truck 'em to Tacoma, and they forward the carton to Omaha or maybe El Paso or Enid, Oklahoma, and they take the envelopes out of the carton and mail 'em from there. Except sometimes it's Columbus, Georgia. Or San Diego."

"Must make getting contributions a little chancy," Bohannon said.

"I don't know. The Captain—he's the one worries about the mail. I just follow orders." He sat down in the doorway, the rifle across his knees. Bohannon wondered if he could take the necessary six or eight steps to him silently enough to catch Elroy's thin neck in the crook of his arm and render him unconscious, but guessed that even if he could, there might be someone in the compound, or looking out a window, who would see him, and shoot him for his trouble. He finished off the Jell-O, the last inch of milk, set aside the tray, slipped the spoon into his boot, and lit a cigarette.

Elroy turned. "Say, how did you get to keep those? The Captain don't allow smoking. No tobacco, no beer, no swearing . . ."

Bohannon held out the pack. "You want one?"

"I'm dyin' for one." Elroy came and got a cigarette and leaned for Bohannon to light it with a plastic throwaway lighter. "Oh, good," the boy said, blowing smoke away with a deep, grateful sigh. "Oh, yes."

"Not even rock and roll," Bohannon said. "What does the Ninth Amendment Militia do for fun?"

"Fun?" Elroy stared at him with an odd half smile. "Oh, mister. We're gonna have our fun tomorrow." He went back to the doorway and stood leaning there, looking out, enjoying the cigarette and chuckling to himself. "Oh, yeah. We're gonna have real fun tomorrow."

"You mentioned a bank," Bohannon said.

"Bank?" The boy turned, scowling. "Oh, you are for sure gonna be killed. You know way too much."

Bohannon put out his cigarette on the floor. "You going to rob a bank? Is that your idea of fun?"

"You got it backward, like most everybody," Elroy said. "It's the banks that are the robbers." He threw away his cigarette and turned. "Anyways, we ain't about money. We're about takin' this country back from the Jews and lawyers and niggers and immigrant trash from Mexico and China and all them and givin' it back to the white people the way God meant in the first place. And we ain't a militia, either. We're a family."

139

Bohannon smiled thinly. "That just happens to carry guns at all times."

"We're embattled," Elroy said. "We tell the people of this country how things really are, and the rich and powerful don't like it. They'll kill us if they can. Them and their bought-and-paid-for Army and FBI and all. We got to defend ourself, we got to defend the truth." He reached out. "I'll take that tray, now. You need to go to the outhouse?"

"I thought you'd never ask," Bohannon said.

He lit the lamp and read about and looked at pictures of wild plants you could eat without poisoning yourself. It was more cheerful reading than *The Turner Diaries* and he thought it might be useful if he could get away from here and past Cunningham's circle of fire and make his way by shank's mare to civilization, if there was civilization anywhere. He wasn't going to be able to memorize all this stuff, so he guessed he would take the book along. It was not going to be that hard to get out of here after all. The floor planks were indifferently nailed down. Using the spoon, with patience, main strength, and persistence he could pry up one plank with difficulty and another without difficulty. There was two feet of crawlspace under the shack. From there under cover of darkness he could creep into the ferns and brush beneath the trees, and if he went carefully get back to the main road. Then he—

The bolt on the door rattled, the door opened, Selina came in. She pointed a Browning 9mm pistol at him. In a worn and weary way, she was beautiful in the lamplight. "I'd like the spoon back," she said.

"Shucks," he said, and reached into his boot for it. He stood up to hand it over to her. "A feller can't have any fun around here."

She took the spoon and put it into a pocket of her jeans. She assumed a Colonel Klink accent. "No vun escapes from Stalag Thirteen."

"No one ever got shot at Stalag Thirteen, either," he said.

"Life is not television." She backed to the door. Hand on the knob, she asked, "You need anything? Other than a crowbar?"

"How is Liberty's mare?" he said. "Liberty your daughter?"

She gave a short laugh. "She was, when I carried her in my belly. Since then, she has had only one parent. Strange but true. And he has had only one true love. If anything happened to me, I doubt he'd notice. If anything happens to Liberty— God help us all."

"And if anything happens to him?" Bohannon asked.

Alarm flickered across her face, but she said stoutly, "He's not the kind of man things happen to. He makes things happen."

"That can be dangerous. Especially if you can't think straight."

"You're not talking about Chet Cunningham," she said.

"He's crazy, and you know it," Bohannon said.

"He's the sanest man in America." She pulled open the door.

"That's not an answer, that's a slogan. You're too bright for that."

"It's the truth," she said.

"He plans to shoot me," Bohannon said. "You going to let him do that?"

"You're not afraid," she said scornfully. "You were never afraid in your life. I know your kind. I married one."

"So you are going to let him shoot me?"

She took one step down. "That's between the two of you."

"Only if we both have guns." Bohannon held out his hand for the 9mm.

She smiled faintly and shook her head. "Do you want him to shoot me, too? How would that help?"

Bohannon sat on the cot. "What about the horse?"

"Still pregnant." She took the second step down, pulled the door shut, and bolted it.

Clattering and banging woke him. Through the cracks in the siding of K building he saw light. He smelled gasoline. Young male voices called to each other. A starter mechanism whinnied, an engine clattered to life, died out, started up again. Another. The tailgate of a pickup truck banged shut, its chains rattling. More engines started. Cunningham barked orders and admonitions. There was a chorus of "Yessirs," and there was also laughter. Everybody sounded keyed up. The large door of the storage building slammed shut. The cars, trucks, vans began driving out of the compound. Right past him. He crawled out of the sleeping bag and through the crack between door and frame, caught glimpses of jittering headlights, red taillights. He peered at his watch. 2:30 a.m. That busy tomorrow he'd heard about from Leroy and Selina started early, didn't it? A car braked, its door opened, someone came to his door, rattled the bolt, pushed the door open.

"You're awake," Cunningham said.

"It's nice of you to invite me out," Bohannon said, "but I'll need time to choose a frock. What do you suggest?"

"I suggest you read this." Cunningham held out Ada Tanner's Bible. "And meditate on it. Try the twenty-third psalm. That's the one the padre usually reads to condemned men. That and the part about 'I am the resurrection and the life.' "

Bohannon took the book. "Thoughtful of you," he said.

"Appreciate it." He peered past the Captain. "You taking my truck?"

"Spoils of war," Cunningham said.

"As Mrs. Napoleon said before Waterloo, when will you be back?"

"Forget it," Cunningham said. "This won't be Waterloo."

"If you were sure of that," Bohannon said, "you'd shoot me now."

Cunningham drew a breath to answer and didn't answer. He pulled the door shut, bolted it, and Bohannon listened to his footsteps cross the hardpan, heard the springs of the truck squeak slightly as the man climbed into it, heard the door slam, the parking brake let go, heard the gears grind because Cunningham didn't know this vehicle, and heard it drive away.

After that the silence of the forest night came and settled on the place, and he felt the high mountain cold, laid the Bible on the bookcase, crawled back into the sleeping bag, and when he had stopped shivering, went to sleep. In a dream, George Stubbs sat at the round kitchen table in the ranch house with his big drawing pad. He drew well for a man with no training. But he rarely drew anything but horses, and Bohannon took his hobby for granted and wasn't watching. "Here it is," Stubbs said. "This is what you want." And he held up the pad for Bohannon to see. A horse's head in silhouette. "Now, ain't that just the ticket?"

And then Bohannon was awake in K building of Cunningham's compound, hundreds of miles from that kitchen, wondering what woke him.

"The ticket to what, George?" he said, and worked his way out of the sleeping bag again and went to the door. He stood by the door listening. It was unnaturally quiet. If a guard was out there, he wasn't breathing. "Leroy?" he said. No answer.

Then he realized what he had heard that woke him. The bolt. He turned the knob and very gently pulled the door. It came open. His heart began thumping. He peered out. No Leroy. No light showed in the house across the way. She'd come in the dark, hadn't she, and gone back in the dark, and if she was watching from over there, she was watching from the dark. He smiled to himself. He'd had her figured right, after all. She wasn't going to let Cunningham kill him. Now, with all the long-haired boys with guns and grenades gone off with the sanest man in America, she was letting Bohannon walk away.

He put on his boots, jacket, hat, returned to the door, opened it and stood with it open for a wary moment in the darkness and the silence and the cold. Then he took a step down. And waited. And another step. And waited. He wished to hell his truck was still here. He wished for a compass. For a map. For a flashlight. He made his way to the rear of K building and into the brooding, ancient darkness of the giant trees. He wanted to run. There wasn't much in the way of undergrowth to impede that. Only ferns. But there was no safe way to go fast. Hands held out in the hope of not running into low branches he started off. Was he heading for the state highway? Did it matter? He was putting Cunningham's camp behind him. Bark and sharp twigs kept scraping his hands. They'd be bloody before the night was out. Then they met something else. Fabric, and under the fabric, flesh and bone.

"Who the hell?" a voice said. A gun barrel poked his belly. A flashlight beam glared in his eyes. "Jesus Christ," the voice said. "How did you get out?"

"Don't you mean 'Judas Priest'?" Bohannon said. "The door was open. I figured that meant I'd overstayed my welcome."

"Turn around." The gun barrel jabbed him again. "Go back."

And he went back, and was pushed into K building so hard he lost his footing and fell. And the door slammed. And the boy bolted the door. Disgusted, Bohannon clambered to his feet. She'd miscounted, hadn't she? Hadley had been left behind, cut out of the fun. Poor Hadley would have to hear about Armageddon, second-hand, over breakfast.

But no one was back for breakfast. At six in the morning, the camp remained vacant and still. He heard the hoofs of Liberty's horse pass. Dimly from across the way he heard coal dumped into the black old cook stove. Hadley was red-eyed when he came with an M-16 to escort Bohannon to the outhouse.

Bohannon told him, "You should get some sleep."

"If I'd slept last night," Hadley said, "you'd be in Coeur d'Alene by now."

"I don't understand how the Captain could have left my door unbolted."

"He had a lot on his mind," Hadley said.

Back at K building, Bohannon said, "You can sleep now."

"Not me," Hadley said sourly. "Gotta watch you. You're tricky."

"Not if you remember the bolt," Bohannon said.

Hadley closed the door and rammed the bolt to. "I got nothing on my mind. Just you."

Selina brought his breakfast on another of those battered cafeteria trays. It was scrambled eggs and Spam, toast and jam, a mug of coffee. "You tried to leave us last night," she said. "I thought you'd get tired of hot dogs. But not so soon." She held out the tray. "In contrition, I've brought you something different. Not better, just different."

He took the tray from her. "Appreciate the thought."

"The eggs are powdered," she said. "How did you get out?"

He looked at her. "You don't know? Somebody forgot to bolt the door."

"Hadley had stepped into the trees to relieve himself," she said. "It's lucky you happened to meet up with him."

"Not for me." Bohannon sat on the bed with the tray on his lap, and began eating. The eggs had no taste at all, but they were hot and there was a good heap of them. The Spam tasted like salt. The jelly tasted like no known fruit or berry, but the bread was good and so was the coffee. She was still standing there. The Browning was tucked into her belt. He wiped his mouth on a paper napkin. "I ought to have chosen a different way out, right?"

Her smile was bleak. "So it seems."

"Hadley the only man left in camp?"

"That would be telling," she said. "Anyway, I saw you leave. I'm a very light sleeper when Chet's away."

"Meaning you're worried." Bohannon held out his pack of cigarettes, and saw her eyes light up. "When's he due back?"

She took a cigarette. "First, I am not worried. Chet knows what he's doing and just how to do it. Second, he'll be back when he's done it."

"And did you take aim at me from your window?" Bohannon held out his lighter, hoping she would bend close to take the light, and he could get the Browning away from her. She didn't bend. She took the lighter, backed off a couple of steps, lit her cigarette, tossed the lighter back to him.

"Thank you. That's good. A luxury we can't afford. Among many." She blew smoke away gratefully, watched

Bohannon light his cigarette, and said, "No. I scrambled down from the loft, got my gun"—she touched the butt of the gun now—"and opened the front door. I was furious that Hadley had left his post. I wanted to run after you but"—she laughed at herself grimly—"I'd forgotten my boots. And while I dithered about that, Hadley brought you back."

"To your enormous relief," Bohannon said, watching her steadily.

She nodded. "Of course," she said, but she flushed a little.

"I suggested to Liberty she keep the mare in her stall until she foals, but I heard her ride out earlier."

"Liberty takes suggestions only from her father," Selina said.

"I hope she's back before the colt decides to arrive." Bohannon stood up to pass the tray over.

Selina took it one-handed and backed off, her other hand on the butt of the Browning. "Why not 'the filly'?"

"No reason," Bohannon smiled. "What's the dam's name?"

"Paprika. For her color. She raced as Nonstopshopper."

Bohannon grunted. "Racing people drink too much."

Selina shrugged. "She never did stop. She just didn't run very fast."

"Why should she?" Bohannon said. "Every horse is not a fool."

The compound was still empty at noon. "Bohannon," Selina called. "Sit on the cot and stay there." Her boots knocked the steps. She slid back the bolt and pushed open the door. She set the tray on the floor to one side. "Wait," she said, "until you hear me bolt the door before you come for that."

"Where's Hadley?" Bohannon asked.

147

She shut the door and bolted it. "Don't worry. You're under guard."

Bohannon went and picked up the tray. "You mean by you? Where did Hadley go? Why did Hadley go?"

Maybe she stood there in the pine-splintered sunlight, thinking about answering, but she didn't answer. In a moment, he heard her boots crossing the compound away from him.

"They're late, aren't they?" he shouted. "Something went wrong."

It didn't provoke her. Not to speech. And he sat on the cot and ate canned chili not quite heated through. No fresh home-baked bread this time. A few stale soda crackers, that was all. And the usual glass of watery milk. He didn't hear the door to the dwelling house. He heard the door to the warehouse-cum-stable. And then in the hush, the start-up of an automobile engine. Muffled. He had noticed on his brief escape attempt last night that all the junkyard vans, pickups, RVs had gone off with Cunningham's expeditionary forces. Except for the red runabout, of course. That would never go anywhere again. So the car he was hearing had been stored out of sight, indoors, hadn't it? He knocked with the handle of the spoon hard on a knothole. The knot fell out. He knelt and put his eye to the hole. And saw a van roll out of the warehouse. It looked new. Then it was out of his line of vision.

But his ears told him it had come this way. Moving too fast. It braked hard, the tires squealing on the hardpan. They kicked up dust. He smelled the dust. The horn blared. "Liberty!" Selina shouted. "Liberty! Come home." The horn blared again. "Damn," she said, and leaving the motor idling, got out of the car, and he knew from the sound of her steps she was running. Into the house, out again, sliding open the doors of the van, throwing things into the van, stopping for a moment with each load, to lean on the horn. It trumpeted into the somber forest and echoed back. She shouted each time, "Liberty! Come home." And her voice echoed also, and sounded lonely.

He called, "Shall I go fetch her?"

"I can't trust you," she said. But she came and opened the door and looked at him. She was holding the Browning. "You're the enemy."

He shrugged. "Hostilities are over. Aren't they?"

"Never," she said. "I'll find her myself, thanks."

But it wasn't necessary. Liberty had heard. And Liberty had come. Not riding her beloved Paprika. Leading her. And Bohannon saw why. The foal had shifted inside her. She looked twice as pregnant as before. Her bag was swollen. "She's going to foal, mama." Liberty was pale. "Any minute now."

Bohannon asked, "Is her stall cleaned out? No junk on the floor? How big is it? She'll need room to walk around. No cracks the baby can put his legs through? Plenty of fresh straw?" He stepped forward. "I'd better look it over."

"Stay where you are," Selina said. And to Liberty, "Take her inside. I'll be along in a minute." Jerking the pistol at him, she told Bohannon, "Back off. Away back. That's it." And she pulled the door shut and bolted it.

He called: "How many foals have you delivered?"

She didn't answer. The engine of the van quit. The huge, primeval silence of the place was back. He stretched out on the cot. A brood mare could drop her young before you could catch your breath. Or could keep you waiting for hours. He closed his eyes.

What woke him was so unexpected he didn't open his eyes. He lay and held his breath, straining to hear because the sound was far off. The beat of helicopter rotors. He opened his eyes, lunged at the bookcase, and pawed the load of books off the first shelf. As he had thought, the shelf lay on pegs. It fit tightly, though, and he had to bang it with a fist from underneath to get it loose. He rammed with the end of it hard at the siding planks in the corner. The builders hadn't spared nails. With all his strength, he banged at them again. The whole of K building shuddered. But the planks didn't give. He kept ramming at them with the bookshelf, in a sweat to get out where that chopper could see him.

"What are you doing?" Selina stood in the open doorway. With the Browning leveled at him. "Drop the board," she said.

He laid the board on the cot. "I was getting worried about the foal."

"The man who loves horses," she said with a thin smile, "better than he loves freedom."

"What's happening?" he said.

"Nothing, but Liberty's too stressed to be out there alone with her, and I have packing to do."

Bohannon sat and put on his boots. "I noticed. Once she's through delivery, you plan to leave the horse and colt?"

"Maybe before," Selina said. "There are bigger issues at stake here than one little girl and her pet race horse."

"We won't tell Elizabeth Taylor," Bohannon said.

He stood with Liberty outside the box stall. He was relieved that it was roomy, and clean, and that good daylight came from overhead. At times like this, you had to be able to see clearly. "She gets up," Liberty said, "then she walks around. Then she lies down again. Now look. See her shudder? Look. She never holds her tail straight out like that. Look, Bohannon. She's kicking at her belly." The girl was trembling. He gave her a quick hug.

"It's all right. It's perfectly natural."

With a heavy thump and a heavy sigh, the breedy mother lay down again, then scrambled up, rolling her eyes, and there was a rush of amniotic fluid, gallons of it. From out in the compound, Selina shouted, "What was that?"

"She broke her water," Bohannon called. "Now the serious stuff begins."

"I think I'm going to throw up," Liberty said. But instead, she cried.

One of the Captain's favorite amenities, a wood and canvas collapsing cot was in this cubby beside the horse's stall and Bohannon picked the weeping girl up and laid her on it. Whimpering, she curled tight, her face to the board wall. He covered her with an army blanket. "Everything's going to be fine," he told her.

Everything was fine. Eight or ten minutes later the mare was on her feet again and a long slim leg stuck out beneath her tail and the blunt head of the foal with it. He breathed easier. The newborn's hoof had pierced the amniotic sack. The rest of the sack would slip away with the mare's contractions as they came. Or should. If not, he'd have to step in there and pull it off the nostrils so it could begin to breathe. An instant later, the mare contracted again, the foal's nostrils were free, and it began to struggle.

"Liberty, come on," Bohannon turned, threw the blanket off, shook the girl awake. "You don't want to miss this. It may be the only miracle you'll ever see." He got her to her feet. She was numb as a child is, roughly roused from sleep. He steered her by the shoulders. "Here. Stand here. Look. Look."

The foal struggled. The mare slowly, a little stunned,

bending her graceful neck, reached around to help. The foal wriggled mightily, then dropped with a thump into the straw, legs sprawling. It was always a shock, the unbelievable length of a newborn foal's legs. Those were what a horse was all about, and this was the moment when that showed itself to the veriest fool. A horse was born for one thing only. A horse was born to run. The mare turned and bent to lick her newborn dry.

"She did it all herself," Liberty looked up at Bohannon, wonder in her eyes. "Just like Daddy said."

"Whatever happened to Daddy?" Bohannon said.

Liberty didn't hear. "I have clean towels to help her clean him up and dry him off." She turned away.

"She's doing fine," Bohannon said. "Let her do it. Come back. Watch."

Cleanup over, the mare began nudging the gangly little horse to urge it to its feet. It put those stick-like legs out, this way, that way, and trembling, teetering, began to stand. The dam put her elegant nose under to help.

"Wonderful!" Liberty clapped in delight.

And the little creature collapsed. It took two more tries, then he was firmly footed, and his mother was nudging his butt with its damp whisk of tail to point him along to where her milk was waiting for him.

"Excuse me." Bohannon stepped out the big door into the golden sunlight slanting through the pines and, away from the hazards of straw and ammonium nitrate manure, lit a cigarette. Selina was across the way, setting a heavy cardboard storage file in the van. "You lose," he shouted. "It's a colt."

"This is not a woman's world." Selina slammed the van doors, climbed in behind the wheel, started the engine. "Come on, Liberty. Time to leave. Your father will be frantic." She brought the van around in a quick circle to

where Bohannon stood. Panic edged her voice. "Liberty, we have to go."

Bohannon raised his eyes. The helicopter was back. From high up, its jittery shadow flickered across the compound. "Forget it," he told her.

"What are you talking about? Liberty! Come out here. Right now."

Liberty appeared in her floppy camouflage coverall and hat. "I'm not going. You go on without me. Mama—he's just born. He can hardly walk. Anything could happen. And Paprika? After what she's been through?" Liberty waved her arms. "I'm her friend. I can't leave her. She trusts me."

"There's feed, there's water." Selina jumped down and came for the girl. "They'll be all right till we can send for them. A day, two days. What can happen?" She grabbed Liberty's wrist. "Come on, now. Before it's too late."

Bohannon touched her, jerked his chin up. "It's already too late."

"Let me go!" Then she saw, and the starch went out of her. "Oh, no."

Bohannon opened his mouth to speak, and a pickup truck banged noisily into the compound, and slurred to a halt on the hardpan, kicking up a cloud of dust. The green pickup with the horse head on the door. Bohannon's pickup. Ford jumped out of it, clutching his AK-47. He came running toward them, wild with excitement and fear. "Where's the Captain?"

"That's dried blood," Selina said. "Are you hurt?"

"No, but a lot of other people are. Hell, they're dead. I killed a lot of people, Miz Cunningham." He began to cry. "I wasn't supposed to. Nobody was supposed to kill anybody, just like hold them real quiet." He shook his head in agony. "I didn't mean it. But this nigger, this big security guard, he

153

wouldn't stand still like I said, and he ran at me and I shot him and the gun kept on running and everybody in the place fell down, and, oh—" He dropped to his knees in the dust, head bowed, sobbing. "God forgive me for what I done." Then he was on his feet again, half crouched, and staring all around. "Where's the Captain? Where's everybody?"

"Not here," Selina said. She was very pale, and she was hanging onto Liberty, frightened by this maniac, but her voice stayed calm, the voice of the Captain's lady. "You know what the orders were. If anything went wrong no one was to return here. What's the matter with you, Ford?"

"He said he'd protect me," Ford said, "wouldn't let nothin' happen to me. Always promised us that. He'd look after us, all of us. And now look." He waved upward wildly at the helicopter. "They're after me, and they're going to get me and where is he? Where's the Captain?"

"You stupid boy," she cried, "don't you understand? You've finished the Captain. You've finished us all."

He stared at her, slack-jawed. Then he saw Bohannon, and his eyes lit up. "Oh, no. Not all. Not me." Bohannon saw it coming, but he wasn't quick enough. He was past fifty. He could no longer move with the speed of the boy, and the boy caught him. "They can't take me. Not with a hostage. Come on." And he yanked and booted and hoisted Bohannon toward the truck, the rifle-barrel at Bohannon's ear. It was awkward. He probably couldn't fire it if he tried, but Bohannon remembered the other morning on that lost roadway. The gun had gone off on its own. He didn't resist. The boy slammed him against the cab.

"Open the door. Get in there."

And Bohannon did these things, and the next moment the boy was on the seat beside him, still clutching the AK-47. The engine revved. He clashed the gears. The pickup backed,

and slued, going too fast. It braked and the dust rose around them, blocking off the anxious faces of the two women. Then the truck raced ahead, moving off through the great trees, heading along the crooked little access trail, back to that dismal road. But not all the way. An official car came ambling along to meet them. It stopped with its bumper against the bumper of the green pickup and Ford said, "Shit," and two men in starchy tan uniforms got out of the car. It was a Highway Patrol car. They wore dark glasses, had their hair cropped tight around the ears, and looked about fifteen years old. Service revolvers were holstered on their hips but they didn't seem about to draw these. They came ambling forward looking as if they meant no harm. One of them called:

"Mr. Bohannon, is it? Mr. Hack Bohannon? Green pickup with the horse head on it? We been looking for you. Your friends down in California. They haven't heard from you. They're worried about you. Sheriff's department?"

"He don't count." Ford put his head out the window. "He's just my hostage. Corporal Ford, Ninth Amendment Militia? I got a gun here." He stuck it out the window and waved it. "See that? That's what counts. Now you get back in that gov'mint car and get it the hell out of my way."

The patrolmen stopped. One of them looked skyward. "Whatever you say, but they're watching all this from up there. You won't get far."

"This thing can blow them right out of the sky," Ford said, "after it blows you into the ground. I already killed twenty people. What have I got to lose?"

The men put their hands up and backed submissively toward the patrol car. Hanging out the truck window, Ford watched them, grinning. "Way to go," he said. He had forgotten Bohannon. And Bohannon laced his fingers together and raised his fists high and brought them down on the nape of the thin boy's neck. There was a crack of vertebra. Ford's head drooped and his cap fell off and the AK-47 dropped to the roadway. He didn't move. Bohannon got down out of the truck. His knees were weak and he figured his smile must look a little anemic but he smiled it anyway.

"Good to see you," he said.

Home Is the Place

The light was poor. It was early morning and fog hung in the pines of Settlers Cove. But as he rounded a bend in the road, Hack Bohannon saw the gray shapes of three men cross up ahead. The hats told him two were sheriff's deputies. The lumbering prisoner was Clay Gilmore, a coach at the high school. The deputies opened a rear door for him and he folded into the car. The officers got in, doors slammed, and the car came toward Bohannon and passed, heading for the Coast Highway. Lieutenant Phil Gerard drove. The deputy in the back seat was named Vern. Bohannon lifted a hand to them. Gerard touched his hat and looked grim.

Bohannon parked his battered green pickup in front of the Gilmore house, a hulking dark box in the fog. He climbed a slope among ferns and poison oak under trees with rags of fog caught in their branches, nodded to the bulky young deputy, Lundquist, stationed at the front door, and went along the side of the house to the rear where he found a tall plank gate half open, and stepped into a patio with a large swimming pool that was empty except for dry brown pine needles. They'd piled up. The pool hadn't held water in a long time.

There was a story to that. He knew part of the story. Everybody did. But nobody knew the end of it. Or hadn't until this morning, about 3:30, 4:00. One panel of a sliding glass door at the back of the house stood open, and fog had crept into the room, but he knew whose the trim figure was that stood there—deputy T. Hodges. "Morning," he said, stepped inside, twitched her a half smile and looked at what lay at her feet. If he hadn't been told different, Bohannon would have thought the body sprawled there was that of an old man. He crouched beside it. In spite of ugly dark splotches on forehead, cheek, jaw-line, the face was a very young man's. Bohannon touched the thin black leather of the jacket. The shoulder and arm inside were wasted like those of an old man sick and dying. A bullet had gone through the leather right at the sternum. A little blood had seeped from the entry wound, but not much. Death had been quick: when the heart stops, so does the bleeding.

He looked up at T. Hodges, who had jangled the alarm-bell phone in his stables before sun-up, as he was making the horses ready for the day, and asked him to come here. Though young, T. Hodges had been in law enforcement for years, and wasn't as a rule shaken up by murder, though it was far from common in her bailiwick, here on California's picture-postcard central coast. But her eyes glistened now with what he figured to be tears.

"Belle still not here?" He meant the wry old woman doctor who grudgingly served as district medical examiner. "It's been hours."

"Maybe she had horses to look after too." T. Hodges tried for a smile but failed. She gazed again at the boy. "His name is Charles Gilmore—Chico, his father calls him. Called him. Age twenty-six. Last known place of residence, San Francisco. He wasn't expected home."

"No?" With a grunt, Bohannon got to his feet. "Well, the shooter didn't let surprise spoil his aim. Right through the heart. Find the weapon?"

She shook her head. "We'll search the woods once it's light."

"No bullet?"

"It could be under him," she said. "Or in him."

"Right." Bohannon looked around the floor, wanting the glint of a shell casing. There was ample dust, but no shell casing. The room had a pair of raveled green wicker chairs and a green wicker couch. An old white enameled chest of drawers with flaking Donald Duck decals. No books, magazines, no pictures on the walls, just faded rectangles where they'd once been. No one cared about this room now, any more than they cared about the swimming pool.

The door of a closet was ajar. He looked in. A lumpy blue canvas backpack hunched on the floor. A zipper was open on one of its pouches and little white-capped amber plastic vials, the kind that hold prescription medications, had tumbled out. Bohannon didn't touch it. He had long ago quit sheriffing. He had a Private Investigator's license, but no status here. She had asked him to come. He loved her, and he had come. "Anyone search this bag?"

"I left it for you. You'll read it better. I cleared it with the Lieutenant."

With a grunt, he picked it up, set it on the bed, opened the zippers one by one and took everything out. It was pathetic. The sexy bikini briefs were ragged, the elastic gone, the bright dyes too. Same for the net skivvy shirts. All of it was very clean and smelled of Clorox. Cheap white dime store socks. Two pairs of jeans. Three shirts. Shapeless sweaters that had cost a lot once long ago.

In one pocket of the backpack were papers that showed Charles Gilmore had sold his life insurance to a company that had then doled money out to him, on the odds that he would soon die, a company pretty sure it could not lose, a company of such compassion it made you want to weep.

There were sad receipts. He had sold his car, a late model Lexus, a pair of Mapplethorpe photographs, his sound system, his 40-inch television set, his part-ownership in a sailboat. A bundle of paycheck stubs showed he had left his job at a brokerage eight months ago. They'd given him big separation pay, but his medical bills—hospitals, laboratories, pharmacies—had been bigger.

He poked around. There was a scuffed and faded children's picture book, *Fletcher & Zenobia*, but there were no personal letters. Stranger still, no snapshots. Not from here, not from San Francisco. He was leaving a big part of his life behind, friends, events, yet he hadn't brought reminders of any of it. Why not? Bohannon sighed, and stuffed everything back. Except the book. The book he handed to T. Hodges. "What do you make of that?"

"I'll read it," she said.

Bohannon said, "He wasn't just sick, he was broke."

T. Hodges gave him a crooked little smile. "And 'home is the place where, if you have to go there, they have to take you in.' "

"Robert Frost," Bohannon said. "Well, not even he was right all the time." Another door showed him a dusty little bathroom with a toilet, basin, shower-stall. No towels on the racks. Nothing in the rust-flecked medicine cabinet but a long-ago toothbrush. He came out again.

Charles Gilmore's worn Nikes lay on the floor beside the couch. The faded cushions on the couch showed he had been lying there, but not at the time he was shot. When he was shot, he had been standing. That was plain from where he lay now, how he lay.

Bohannon lit a cigarette. "Gerard arrested the father, right? Clay?"

"Did he have a choice? There were only two people in the house, Hack, the dead one and the living one. As the lieutenant sees it, if it wasn't deliberate murder, then Clay heard a noise, grabbed a gun, ran out here, and in the dark shot what he thought was an intruder."

"And what's Clay's version?"

"He didn't know Chico was here. Assumes he arrived late, very late, found the house dark, didn't want to wake his parents and just sacked out here. Clay's sleep was broken by shouts and a shot. He stumbled out of bed, ran back here, found Chico dead, went to the phone in the kitchen, and dialed nine-one-one. Didn't shoot anybody, doesn't even own a gun."

Bohannon said, "His son's been gone must be eight, nine years. What was he, seventeen? It was about swimming. The kid was going to be on the Olympic team. It was in all the papers. His father was his trainer and he was proud. Then all of a sudden the boy quit. Left town, and never came back."

T. Hodges made a brief, bleak sound. "He should have stuck with that."

Fingerprint powder was around the lock on the patio door. Bohannon squinted at the lock. "This hasn't been forced."

"Coach Gilmore says it's never locked. Anybody could just walk in."

"Could and presumably did," Bohannon said. "Who? And why? Was it a mugging? Did they take anything?"

"His wallet was in his jacket. Twenty-nine dollars in it."

"That so?" Bohannon pushed back his old Stetson and peered upward. The fog still hung in the pines. The ocean was downhill a short way through the woods. Waves thudded. A sea lion barked. Bohannon took a last drag on the cigarette, stepped outside, dropped it, ground it out under a straw-caked boot. He turned back. "And Clay claims nobody knew he was coming?"

"It could be true. We searched the house for letters. Didn't find any. And there's no computer."

"Phone records being checked?" Bohannon said.

"Here and in San Francisco," she said. "The coach also claims he didn't know anything about his son's life since he left home, how he lived, where he lived, who his friends were." She made a face. "He didn't want to know, Hack. He didn't say that, but it was obvious."

Belle Hesseltine banged in at the patio gate, tall and gaunt and grumpy, in jeans, sheepskin jacket, cowboy hat. "Sorry. Triplets. In a shack. Mexican illegals. They didn't send for help. Scared to." She marched toward them, soldier straight and grim of face. "Neighbor finally ran to the gas station and phoned."

"Triplets," T. Hodges said. "Did you drive her to the hospital?"

"Too late for that. But mother and young are doing well. Three brand new American citizens." She laughed. "I filled out the birth certificates. That made the parents happy. Whole reason they came, poor things." She stopped short and scowled down at the dead youngster. "AIDS," she said, and looked at T. Hodges. "Those lesions on his face. Kaposi's sarcoma. You didn't tell me he had AIDS."

"It's not what killed him," Bohannon said.

The old woman set down her kit. "I hope you didn't touch the body."

Bohannon ignored that, and asked T. Hodges, "Isn't there a mother? Real estate agent? Celia, that her name? Where is she in all this?"

"At her sister's in Santa Barbara. There's a sick child, and the sister is divorced, and has to work. So Celia is down there keeping things together for a few days. I've called her; told her there's been an accident. She's coming home."

"You didn't let on who the accident happened to?"

She tightened her mouth. "Hack, I didn't just fall off the turnip truck."

"Sorry," he said.

"She thought it was Clay," T. Hodges said. "She thought he was dead."

Belle Hesseltine pulled on latex gloves and dropped to her bony old knees beside the body. "Get out of here, you two," she said. "Let me do my work."

"When you roll him over," Bohannon said, "look for a bullet."

The old woman zipped open the black jacket, apologetically, as if it were an intrusion. "If it had gone through him, there'd be blood and tissue splashed around." She unbuttoned the boy's shirt. His chest was parchment stretched over a rack of bones. The entry wound was small and neat. The neatness made it obscene. She touched it. "Poor child," she murmured.

Bohannon raised his eyebrows. "The doctor has a heart."

"I thought I asked you to get out of here," she snapped.

They got out and met a skinny bespectacled boy and a hefty Latina girl in green coveralls, coming with a gurney and a body bag. Bohannon thought to himself, not for the first time, that he ought to stop labeling these adults boys and girls. It was a mark of growing old, and he was only fifty-six. He said to T. Hodges, "How long are you stuck here? When can I take you to breakfast?"

"The Lieutenant will be back with Vern to look for the gun, now that it's daylight, but he'll want me to wait for

Celia. He'll want me to break it to her. Woman to woman. It's how he thinks."

"Right," Bohannon looked at his watch. "When did you notify her?"

"Four, a few minutes after." T. Hodges gave a little shiver. "Come on. The Lieutenant had me make coffee, earlier. Woman's work, you know. Maybe there's still some left. Kitchen's this way." The coffeepot was empty: Lieutenant Gerard and Clay Gilmore had sat here a good while, talking. Bohannon threw away the grounds, and made fresh coffee. T. Hodges sat at the table and read *Fletcher & Zenobia.* The only sound in the room was the grumbling of the coffee maker. Bohannon carried filled mugs to the table, and sat down across from her. She closed the book.

"What's it about?" he asked.

"A cat and a Victorian doll who have a party with cake and balloons and funny hats high up in a big old tree." She frowned, turning the book over. "I don't know what kind of child it was written for."

"Doesn't sound like a clue," Bohannon said.

And Belle Hesseltine came in and set down her kit.

"Coffee?" Bohannon stood up.

"I'd say the bullet's lodged in a bone." The old woman took a seat. "Rib or vertebra. It stopped his heart while he was still standing." She watched Bohannon set the mug in front of her. "We'll get it out at the lab. Then we'll know more." With a bony, age-spotted hand, she waved away the waxed cardboard carton of cream Bohannon offered. She saw a question in his eyes before he asked it. "No. Not a rifle. It wasn't some dim-witted deer-hunter's miss."

"Rifles are commoner than pistols in these parts," he said.

She nodded, tried the coffee, burned her mouth, but held the steaming mug instead of setting it down. She wanted the coffee. "You'll find the handgun in the woods, I expect. About the distance Clay Gilmore could throw it. He reported the shooting right away. Body temperature shows that. He didn't take time out to drive down and throw it in the ocean."

Jittery metallic rattling came past the kitchen window. They saw the heads of the ambulance pair go by. It was the wheels of the gurney with Chico Gilmore's body on it that rattled. That was below eye level. It continued on until it was out of hearing.

Belle Hesseltine tried her coffee again. "Don't mourn, you two," she said. "He hadn't much longer to live."

"Maybe that makes it even sadder," T. Hodges said.

"It was clean and quick," the old woman said. "AIDS is not. His suffering is over. Years of it, by the look of him." She drank a little more coffee. "He wasn't losing his life. Not what anybody'd want to call a life. All he had left was agony."

T. Hodges stared. "You think it was a mercy killing? You think his father did it to put him out of his misery? An act of kindness?"

The doctor didn't answer that. Her faded blue eyes were regarding Bohannon with a wry twinkle. "Go ahead, have your smoke. You've touched that pocket five times in the past two minutes. I'm leaving." She set the coffee mug down and stood up. "I have to find the bullet that's hiding in that boy." Her mouth twitched grimly, she picked up her kit, pulled open the door and stepped outside.

And not far off in the silence of the pines, a woman screamed.

"Oh, God." T. Hodges threw Bohannon a panicked look.

He laid a hand on her arm. "Take it easy." He got to his feet and told the blank-faced doctor, "That will be the victim's mother. She was out of town."

165

The lean old woman studied T. Hodges. "You stay here and collect yourself. I'll take care of it." And she started off at a stiff, long-legged stride. The screaming kept up, hysterical, broken by hoarse sobbing.

A young man's voice, panicky, ready to crack, yelled: "Hodges, where are you?" And Lundquist came running, dodging past Belle Hesseltine. He stopped in the kitchen doorway, red-faced, breathing hard. "Hodges, will you get out here, please? It's Mrs. Gilmore. She zipped open the body bag before I could stop her." He waved an arm toward the shrill crying. "She's going crazy."

"Right away," T. Hodges said, and went to him, and they trotted together out of Bohannon's window view, along the side of the house toward the front. Belle Hesseltine followed. Frowning to himself, Bohannon lit a cigarette, gulped some coffee, and trudged after them. He watched them run slipping down the ferny slope between pines to the crooked hilly road, and across the road, to where the green-clad youngsters were trying to slide the gurney into the rear of the County ambulance. A middle-aged woman, shouting, "No, no, no," clutched at them. "You can't take him. Don't you understand? He's my son, my son. This is where he belongs. He's just come home."

Now T. Hodges and Lundquist caught hold of the woman. She stared at them, wild-eyed for a moment, then went limp, whimpering, seeming to give up. The ambulance pair slammed shut the rear doors, ran and climbed into the cab. The doors banged, the engine roared. Celia Gilmore surprised the deputies, broke away from them, ran to the front of the ambulance and threw herself on the hood. "No, no. You can't have him, you can't have him. He's mine. He's all I have. I've waited so long."

The deputies caught her again and dragged her to the

brushy far side of the road and the ambulance roared off. The woman was struggling, keening, mad with grief. She stretched her arms out after the departing ambulance. Bohannon had glimpsed her often in the town, a good-looking woman, well-groomed, well-dressed, younger than her years, bright, brisk, businesslike. Not this morning. This terrible morning she was wild-haired Naiobi, weeping for her child, older than a thousand centuries, as old as motherhood itself.

"Come on," Belle Hesseltine said grimly. "She's a danger to herself. Or making a damned good show of it. In either case, I'll give her a shot to knock her out." She started down the slope. Worried that she might fall, he tried to take her arm, but she wouldn't let him. The Gilmore woman began screaming and struggling again. With a short, dry laugh, Belle Hesseltine said, "Do you know what they told me when I moved here to retire?"

"Sure," Bohannon said. " 'Nothing ever happens in Settlers Cove'."

Otis Jackson had come to work for Bohannon when George Stubbs was still alive and in need of care. Jackson, a hefty, good-humored young black man, was working as a rent-a-nurse, swatting the books, and saving his money for medical school. When Stubbs died, Bohannon, desperate for help that wouldn't walk out on him after a few days, weeks, months, coaxed Otis into staying on as his stableman. The pay was minimal, all Bohannon could afford, but room and board were free and the job would leave him time to study, so Jackson had agreed. But he'd never been near a horse in his life before, and was still a little spooky around them, and Bohannon was spooky at leaving him in charge of things for long. Horses could panic over nothing, and if a horse panicked, Otis might panic.

So, once Celia Gilmore was sedated, and an ambulance had come to get her to the hospital in Los Osos, T. Hodges riding there with her, to wait there to question her when she woke up, Bohannon headed for his pickup truck. But as he opened the door, a shout stopped him. "Where you going?" He looked. Phil Gerard had just rolled up in the patrol car with Vern.

"Back to minding my own business." Bohannon ambled over to him.

"That would be a novelty," Gerard said. He opened the trunk of the patrol car. Rakes lay there. They looked fresh from the hardware store. He handed one to Vern and one to Bohannon. "But for a change, this morning I'm going to be grateful for your help." He got a rake for himself, slammed the trunk closed, and started toward the Gilmore house. "That gun is out there in back someplace. We have to find it."

Bohannon and Vern trailed after him. Bohannon said, "According to Hodges, Clay Gilmore didn't own a gun."

"Technically the truth," Gerard said, climbing through the ferns, looking at the ground as he walked, maybe thinking the gun could be out here in front. The fog had pretty well dispersed now but dampness dripped from the trees. "It wasn't his. It was his wife's. She bought it a year ago after she unlocked the front door of a property to show it to some prospective buyers and surprised housebreakers at work."

"Hah," Bohannon said. "And you think it was here in a dresser drawer?"

"People at Principal Realty say at first she kept it in her desk there, took it with her in the car when she showed houses, but nobody's seen it or heard about it for months, now."

They trailed along the side of the house. "She got a com-

puter there?" Bohannon asked.

"Yes, and a Deputy Bruce Busby from San Luis is checking it out, looking for e-mail to or from Charles Chico Gilmore in San Francisco. To see if mom knew junior was planning to come home. Because mom could have told pop, right?" He grinned at Bohannon over his shoulder. "I'm on top of this, Hack. Been a long time since we were partners. Try not to worry about me, okay?"

Bohannon stopped at the open gate. "That swimming pool's got a lot of stuff in it. Must be two feet deep. Be the handiest hiding place for the gun."

"Check that will you, Vern?" Gerard said, and took Bohannon with him into the trees. He said, "This isn't going to be a big challenge. What is it—an acre?"

"Half an acre," Bohannon said, and stepped in something sticky. "Wait. Look at this." Gunk was on his boot, and flies were buzzing around the gunk.

"Somebody threw up here," Gerard said.

"Killing takes some of us that way," Bohannon said, and scraped his boot on a tree trunk to try to clean it. "It wasn't the coach. He'd have thrown up in his own bathroom."

"Not if he came out here to get rid of the gun," Gerard said.

"He didn't." Bohannon ran his gaze along the ground. For a couple of yards footprints showed. Spaced far apart. Somebody running. He pointed at them and Gerard saw them and understood what they meant.

"It wasn't Clay Gilmore. He must wear size thirteens." The lieutenant scratched his cheek. He'd had no time to shave this morning. "Well, we'd still better try to find the gun. If the killer was so disgusted with himself he threw up, he also probably threw the gun away."

They spent forty minutes raking among the ferns and

brush beneath the pines. Methodically. Marking off the areas covered one by one until they reached the side road and back road that bordered the property. Bohannon sat on a stump, lit a cigarette and, when Gerard walked across to him from where he'd finished off raking, nodded toward a dark shiny spot on the ragged paving.

"Some car with an oil leak parked here lately," he said.

"What sharp eyes you have, Grandma," Gerard said.

"He kept the gun," Bohannon said. "Drove off with it. In an old car."

"But who, for God's sake? It makes no—" Gerard's beeper sounded. "Gotta call in," he said.

Bohannon stood up, stepped on his cigarette, and went with him. As they passed the plank gate, Vern joined them. "No gun down there. Banana slugs, though. You ever see one? They're beautiful. Bright yellow. Great big. Eat decaying vegetation." He laid the rakes back and closed the trunk of the patrol car, while Gerard used the two-way radio. It crackled and buzzed and Lundquist's voice came out. "Doc Hesseltine recovered the bullet, Lieutenant. It's a thirty-two. Same as the gun Mrs. Gilmore bought."

"Ten four," Gerard said, hung the radio up, and looked at Bohannon. "I know how your mind works. Like a chainsaw. Hack, it wasn't Mrs. Gilmore."

"Because she doesn't drive a leaky old car?" Bohannon said.

"She was in Santa Barbara." Gerard peered at him, disbelieving. "You like her for it? Aw, Hack. She was heartbroken. You saw her, you heard her."

Bohannon shrugged. "After she zipped open the body bag."

"She expected it to be Clay. She didn't know the son had come home."

170

"Then why open the bag?" Bohannon said. "Phil, she knew he was coming. It wasn't grief that made her scream. It was rage."

"Oh, boy!" Gerard snorted, and drove away with Vern.

He kept Otis Jackson watching him, leaning on the rail fence of the oval where kids, mostly horse-crazy girls, were taught to ride, while he conducted the lessons. George Stubbs used to do this. And Manuel Rivera. Now Stubbs was dead and Rivera had long since become a priest. And Bohannon himself was losing patience with the chore. The delight and fear and joy and despair and all the other emotions so near the surface in children that accompanied the lessons gave him a happy sense of aliveness that any honest man past fifty knew full well he was slowly losing. But it was wearying too. He'd be glad when Otis got over the idea that he couldn't do it, and took over for him. Otis had bought himself a white cowboy hat. That was a good sign, Bohannon hoped.

And he had mastered saddling and unsaddling the horses, and most of the arcana of keeping their equipment and quarters clean and well-ordered, and the horses themselves curried, fed, watered, and contented. He had even got less visibly uneasy in the saddle, and would soon be out on the canyon trails leading the Saddle Seniors group on their Saturday morning outings. Most riders who rented his mounts went off on their own. Now, leading Stanton Criss around on her palomino, teaching her what to do with the reins when she wanted the pretty little filly to step over a length of telephone pole laid in the way, Bohannon suddenly had a recollection of coach Clay Gilmore coming here to ride, bringing his young son, eight, ten years old. A long time ago. The boy had been afraid of the horses, paralyzed by fear. His father had laughed at him, called him a little girl, bullied him. It was an ugly memory.

"He's still that way," T. Hodges said. She had come up to the ranch house at sundown, after her shift ended, for supper, as she often did. Tonight, though, she hadn't done the cooking. Otis had. Ham, beans and rice, collard greens, corn bread. They were all three gathered at the big round deal table in the plank-walled kitchen, while the slanting daylight turned to gold and crimson outside the windows. "Celia says he hated the boy until he learned to swim. It was the only sport he took to. And he was brilliant. His father forgave him all his earlier failings, what he regarded as failings. And Chico was so amazed to be doing something at last that his father took pride in that he doubled and redoubled his efforts to be good at it, to be the best."

"And here was a son his father could be proud of?" Otis said.

"Exactly. Until it all went sour. Very suddenly."

"Did his mother give you the particulars of that?" Bohannon asked.

She cheered with her mouth full. "Otis, I never liked corn-bread till now. What did you do?"

He grinned and chuckled. "Just what my mama showed me."

"Isn't it great, Hack?" she said.

"If you eat it all up, how will I ever learn?" Bohannon's face sobered. "Did she give you the details on what happened between the boy and his father?"

"Only that somehow Clay found out Chico was gay. She claims not even to know how. The subject wasn't fit for women's ears. But it completely outraged him, and before he had time to come to his senses and realize that, gay or not, the boy still had the potential to fulfill his father's dream by starring on the U.S. Olympic team, he had thrown him out."

"And now, after nine years, he was coming home? Did he write to her and tell her how sick he was and how broke he was and that there was no place for him to go and begging to be allowed to come home?"

T. Hodges grimly shook her head. "She says he wouldn't have done that. Chico wouldn't dream of coming anywhere near his father. Never. His father hated him, wished he'd never been born."

"And she thinks his father killed him?" Bohannon asked.

T. Hodges looked away at the windows and the view of the steep, grassy canyon walls with their rocky outcrops, grown shadowy now in the dying light. When she looked at Bohannon again, her eyes were wide and hurting, and her voice was low, and trembled a little. "Yes. She thinks he did that. She thinks he killed his own son, the minute the boy walked into the house."

Otis Jackson murmured shock and disbelief.

Bohannon asked, "With her gun?"

T. Hodges nodded. "She told me she brought it home from the office weeks ago, and it was in a dresser drawer. And, yes, Clay did know where it was."

"If she thinks that about him, why did she stay married to him?

T. Hodges said: "She meant to leave him. That was why she went out and got her license and started selling real estate, to be self-supporting. Chico had filled Clay's life because he was going to be a celebrated athlete, a champion. Hers because she loved the boy. Probably too much. In the end, I guess, she found she needed Clay to fill the emptiness." She shrugged, with a wan half-smile. "Who knows? Why does the moon rise?"

Otis reached out and switched on the light in the middle of the table. A converted kerosene lamp with a domed red glass shade, it cast a gentle glow. They ate for a time in somber silence. Then Bohannon rose to collect the plates and take them to the sink. "What about phone calls? Chico never called home?"

"Never," T. Hodges said. "And home never called him. Not while he had a phone. Evidently he couldn't afford one, the last few months."

"I'm not surprised. Lost his apartment too, did he?"

"San Francisco PD says he doesn't live there anymore. He checked out of the hospital two, three weeks ago. Where he went from there, nobody knows. When they get too sick to look after themselves, the officer told me, sometimes friends take them in. But it's our case, Hack. They were polite, but they're not going to do our legwork for us."

Otis hove up off his chair. "Who's for pecan pie?" he said.

Rodd Canyon was unreachable by television in the old days, and even after cable came in, Bohannon didn't bother with it. His days started early, and that meant he went to bed early. Prime time was sleeping time he couldn't spare. So he learned Clay Gilmore had been indicted for the murder of Charles Chico Gilmore only when Sorenson, the tall, towheaded fire warden, jounced into the yard in his red pickup around noon. The morning had been busy, with more than the usual number of customers wanting to ride the canyons this beautiful fall day. Bohannon was glad to take a break over coffee in the kitchen with Sorenson.

"Did they find the gun?" Bohannon said.

"Not that I heard, no."

"Then how can they indict him? There's no evidence."

Sorenson got up lankily and peered into the refrigerator. "Wife's testimony."

"What?" Bohannon stared.

Sorenson set the remainder of Otis's pecan pie on the table and went for utensils and plates and brought them back. "She says he hated the boy because he was gay, threw him out of the house, said if he ever came back, he'd kill him."

"A man will say that." Bohannon said. "Doesn't mean he'll do it."

Sorenson sat down, cut wedges of pie, eased them onto two plates, slid one across to Bohannon. "Depends on what man you're talking about."

"How's that?" Bohannon reached for a fork.

"The CA's office dug something else up. Seems back in 1972, the coach hounded an English teacher called Morton Lowry. Thought up a rotten nickname for him. Jeered it at Lowry at a basketball game in front of the whole school. The kids took to using it to his face in class." Sorenson filled his mouth with pie, wagged his head, and hummed at how good it tasted. He washed the bite down with coffee, and said, "Lowry finally went to the school administration and complained. They reprimanded the coach. But he didn't let it drop. Dug up a ten-year-old police record, multiple arrests in L.A., that proved Lowry was what Gilmore claimed, and Lowry got fired. Story was all over the news. With his picture. Finished him. Man would never get another job teaching school."

"That a fact?" Bohannon forked pie into his mouth.

"Clay Gilmore's got an obsessive hatred for gays. That's how the County Attorney puts it. School administration denies it, of course. But two of the other coaches bear it out, not giving their names of course. And the kids in the locker rooms. Kids these days. Gay bashing, they call it. And it is definitely uncool."

Bohannon drank some coffee. "The indictment won't stick. Somebody else murdered Chico Gilmore."

"Another crazy? Two of them in one case?"

"I don't think there's even one." Bohannon lit a cigarette.

"The kid was dying of AIDS, Hack. Who in their right mind would murder somebody like that? Anyway, his mother said nobody knew he was in town."

"And his mother is the soul of truth, right?"

"The County Attorney thinks so," Sorenson said, and carried the plates to the sink. They clattered. "Good pie, thanks."

"Otis made it," Bohannon said. "Thank him on your way out."

Next morning, at twelve past nine, Bohannon came out the back door of the Madrone bank into the little parking lot and the long shadow of a gnarled old California oak that made parking awkward there. He headed for the green pickup with the horse head in a circle George Stubbs had painted on the door. And a siren hooted. Only for a second. He turned his head. T. Hodges in her helmet sat in a brown patrol car on the street. Bohannon cheered up—seeing her always had that effect on him. He edged between the big terra cotta pots of tough, spiky native plants that margined the parking lot, and leaned in at the window on the passenger side of the car. "Everything all right?"

"All wrong," T. Hodges said. "After her deposition to the County Attorney, Celia Gilmore went home. I know. I delivered her there."

"Don't tell me," Bohannon said, "let me guess. She's disappeared."

"In her gold Mercedes. I should have parked where I could watch without her seeing me, right? And stayed till Vern or Lundquist relieved me."

Bohannon nodded. "You know that. I know that. Gerard didn't order it because he trusts her."

"She didn't go back to her sister's in Santa Barbara. Nor into her office. Nobody saw her here in town, none of the stores. Not the service station. Not the bank, post office, laundromat. She buys her groceries at Lucky's in San Luis. No sign of her down that way. Yet she didn't pack for a trip, Hack. Closets full, dresser drawers."

Bohannon straightened up, pushed back his Stetson, stood frowning for a minute at the flag fluttering atop its pole in front of the post office, blue sky and tawny mountains beyond—then bent again. "She make any phone calls?"

"We've checked. She didn't touch the phone. That's strange in a way. You'd have thought she'd be making funeral arrangements, for one thing. And talking to relatives. Her mother lives with Celia's brother and his family in Wisconsin. Not one call."

Bohannon opened the car door and sat inside, leaving the door open. "She had to do something, see somebody, and right away. No time for anything else."

"See somebody?" T. Hodges watched him light a cigarette. "Oh, Hack. What are you thinking?"

"That somebody threw up in the woods behind the house right after Chico was killed, and that somebody had parked a car that left a fresh oil leak on the road back there, and that this somebody was known to Celia Gilmore."

She cried impatiently, "Hack, that's all speculation."

"Then where's the gun?" Bohannon blew smoke into the clear morning air. "Somebody has it. I vote for the man who ran away through the woods. And he had it because Celia

Gilmore had given it to him."

"To kill the son she adored? Please. Can we get back to reality?"

"Sure. You said an expert checked out her computer at work. He didn't find any e-mail messages to or from Chico?"

"Not a thing," T. Hodges said.

"One of you should go to San Francisco," Bohannon said. "This is not an open and shut case. Phil Gerard always settles for the obvious. I'm sure Chico's father didn't kill him, and you're sure his mother didn't. So who did? Chico Gilmore lived up there a long time, one-third of his very brief life."

"It's his death we're working on," T. Hodges said. "That didn't happen in San Francisco."

Bohannon gave her a quick kiss, and got out of the car. "Let me know when you find the missing mother."

"Hack." She leaned across and peered up at him anxiously. "She wouldn't have killed herself, would she?"

"You saw her last," he said. "How did she seem?"

"Steely. She is one strong lady. When I let her off at her house, and offered to send a woman officer from San Luis to stay the night with her, she said there was no need, that she'd be all right. She'd rather be alone."

"Uh-huh." He stepped on his cigarette. "Too bad she didn't say where."

He crossed the highway into Settlers Cove and drove past the Gilmore house. Damn it, somebody ought to be posted here, keeping an eye out for the woman in case she returned. Her gold Mercedes was no place in sight. He drove up to the back road. No car. He braked and sat looking into the trees for a moment, then switched off the engine, got out, and tramped down to the house. He walked all around it, looking through the windows that weren't too high to look through.

No sign of Celia Gilmore. Well, hell, it wasn't his business. Horses were his business.

And Otis wanted to bring the stable's accounts up to date today. Which meant Bohannon would have to look after the learners, the owners of horses who boarded, and the folks who came to ride. That was okay. He could handle all that. He couldn't handle paperwork worth a damn. And he counted himself lucky that Otis reveled in it. He blinked, frowning at the house again, sighed, trudged back through the woods, got into the pickup, and drove home to Rodd Canyon.

But it nagged at him the rest of the morning, the need to find out what the woman was up to, where she had gone, and why. It wasn't a trip she'd gone on, it was an errand—by his reckoning an urgent errand. Maybe innocent, but then why hadn't she told anybody? Anyway, around a murder, innocence wasn't the factor you took for granted. Guilt was the factor. He kept busy until 11:30 or so, then stepped into the kitchen. Otis, wearing big horn-rim glasses, sat at the table, every inch of it covered—typewriter, calculator, ledger, ballpoints, staple gun, address card files, stacks of bills payable, and outgoing statements.

"There's no room to eat anyway," Bohannon said. "And I've got something to tend to in town. Take over out here, will you please?"

"Right away." Otis began tidying up. "But we have to talk about some of these bills."

"I'll be back." Bohannon lifted a hand and was out the door.

The pickup was parked beside the stake truck and Otis's modest compact, under tall, rustling, ragged-barked eucalyptus trees between the green-trimmed white ranch house and the stables. As he climbed into it, he thought he was acting like a fool. Still, his unease went deep, and hunches had served him in the past. It didn't do to ignore them. They could come back to haunt you. The truck rolled out through the parted white rail gates under the arch with the cutout letters BOHANNON on top of it, onto the narrow, pot-holed canyon road. He reminded himself sternly that his hunches often as not came to nothing. Still, he kept on driving. Maybe Celia Gilmore would show up.

He parked the pickup down the street, where she wouldn't take alarm from it, and he did not sit on the front steps waiting for her. He went inside. Breaking and entering, Gerard would call it. But then, Gerard didn't need to know about this. Bohannon looked around. He went from neat kitchen to neat dining room to neat living room, just resting his eyes on the good furniture and carpets, the polished tables, sideboards, with their well-chosen knick-knacks, the bookshelves, the pictures. Not surprisingly, the Gilmores had kept to separate bedrooms. Even separate bathrooms. He looked into a third bedroom, plainly Chico's before he'd turned into a pariah. His bed was still there, but storage cartons were piled on it. Discarded furniture cluttered the space. Spiders had made themselves at home. Mark Spitz in tiny swim trunks smiled from a poster on the wall. One of its corners had come loose and folded over. The mirror above the dresser was fogged by dust. Bohannon stepped out and closed the door.

He had saved Clay Gilmore's den for last. There were dozens of polished brass trophies on a mantel piece and in glass-fronted cabinets, commemorating football, baseball, basketball, soccer, track and swimming victories. Plaques hung next to the chimney. Clay Gilmore had been Dad of the Year in 1992, honored often by the Chamber of Commerce, Athletic Directors of California, the Presbyterian church, a long list. Framed, glassed photos covered the walls, of teams back to twenty-five years ago, coach Gilmore standing massive and proudly smiling among them. Pennants and banners hung here and there, some bright, some faded by time. A remote control lay on a tufted leather couch next to a jazzy plastic bag of sunflower seeds. Bohannon switched on the television set. A sports channel. Clips of baseball home runs and dust-up slides into second base. Noisy. He switched it off.

And heard a car stop down on the front road.

Heart bumping, he crossed the living room to look out the windows. To see the car well was hard because of the trees and brush. But it looked like a van, and not your ordinary paint job. More like an old-time circus wagon. Now somebody was starting up the hill toward the house. He stepped back from the window and went to the front door and unchained and unbolted it and waited for steps on the front deck. But first a voice called:

"Fletcher? Are you here? It's Zenobia."

Bohannon felt dizzy for a second, and then remembered the children's book he'd found in Chico Gilmore's pack and given T. Hodges to read. *Fletcher & Zenobia.* He'd looked idly at the pictures. They had made him smile. But he hadn't read the story for himself. Footsteps sounded on the stairs up to the deck and he opened the door.

A plump young woman stood there. Her face was painted like a China doll's. Her outfit you'd expect to find in a very old attic—short purple satin dress with a pink sash, long white stockings, Mary-Jane shoes, a puffy yellow bonnet decorated with daisies. And a war surplus safari jacket with a lot of pockets, which made some kind of sense. But fantasy reasserted itself in what she held in her hands, a cake, a big one, with raspberry-colored frosting. It bristled with green and

181

blue candles, and it had to be heavy. She stopped and stared at him.

"Where's Chico?" she said.

"He's not home," Bohannon said. If he had to tell her where Chico was, she might drop the cake. He stepped out. "Here. Let me take that for you."

"It's not heavy." She handed it over. It wasn't real. It was *papier-mâché* and thick paint and something that made it glisten. She eyed him, a little frightened. "Mr. Gilmore? She said you wouldn't be here."

"He's not. My name's Bohannon. I'm—house-sitting." He set the cake among potted geraniums on the deck rail. "Who are you?"

"Lettice Van Van," she said. "I'm Chico's friend from San Francisco. He was staying with me after he got out of the hospital. Before he decided to come home." She looked at the cake, blushed, snatched off the bonnet and held it behind her. "We had a silly game we played. To cheer him up. He has AIDS, you see. He was Fletcher the cat, and I was Zenobia the Victorian doll, and we lived in a tree and we couldn't get down so we had a party with cake and ice-cream and punch and waltzes on the phonograph." Her face changed. "I copied the cake from the illustration in the book. It's not a real cake. I never baked a real cake, but I'm a dab hand at *papier-mâché*. I'm a theatre designer you see, sets, costumes. I copied Zenobia's costume for myself, and Fletcher's little embroidered jacket. I can sew, of course. I just can't bake. Anyway, Chico couldn't keep real cake down. But we did have our pretend parties. All by ourselves. Like loopy six-year-olds. Sometimes we'd laugh so hard we'd fall down. It was lovely."

"Why did he leave?" Bohannon said.

"He wanted his mother. He was regressing mentally, you know. That happens. Turning into a little boy. He wrote to her and said he needed her and wanted to come home but he was afraid of his father. And she telephoned, saying she was coming to him. But he said no, it was home he wanted, here, in these woods. He was born here, and he wanted to die here. He loved this place." She turned to look. "And I can see why. An enchanted forest by the sea. No wonder he was pining for it. And his mother. He always did miss her." She turned back to Bohannon with a frown. "Isn't she here, either? What's happened? Did she take Chico to the hospital? Where? Tell me how to get there."

"He's not in the hospital," Bohannon said.

"He was very sick. The plan was that he'd fly down next week, on the twenty-fifth. But he had a terrible night on Sunday." A wooden bench was built along the railing of the deck. As if suddenly weary, she sat down on it. "And Monday morning he said to me, 'Lettice, I have to go home now. If I wait, I'll be too weak.' I reminded him she'd said she wasn't ready."

" 'If it spoils her surprise party or something, I can't help it,' he said. He was desperate. But it took all day to get him ready. He had to keep resting. It was long after dark when I drove him to the airport and put him on an SWA flight to Fresno." She peered into Bohannon's face. "He did make it, didn't he?"

Bohannon nodded. "He made it." This was getting damned uncomfortable. "But I need to know something. How was he in touch with his mother?"

"You aren't a house-sitter. You're a policeman. I can tell by how you ask questions." She made her voice deep. "I need to know something."

Bohannon tried for a smile, "Don't worry. I'm not going to arrest you for impersonating a Victorian doll." He drew a quick breath. "Something's happened, that's all. The plan

Chico and his mother had—it didn't work out. That's why I'm here. To find out what went wrong."

Lettice Van Van was poking into the pockets of the safari jacket. She came up with a little black ring binder and held it out to him. "The number where he called her is in there. I kept it for him because he was starting to forget things. Like some old man with Alzheimers."

Bohannon frowned at the book and leafed over the pages. Lettice Van Van wrote in red ink. In calligraphic style. It was like a tiny medieval prayer book. "What name?" he said.

"Morton Lowry," she said.

Bohannon almost dropped the book.

She said, "Some friend of his mother's. She'd ring him up from there, or he would call and if she wasn't there, he'd leave messages for her. They talked every day. But it had to be where his father couldn't overhear. His father's a terrible man. An ex-football player. You can imagine. He hates Chico."

Bohannon found the name and the number. The area code was in the next county. He sat on the bench and copied the number into his dog-eared notebook and handed the missal back to Lettice Van Van. "Thank you," he said. "You've been a big help."

She put the book back into her pocket without taking her eyes off him, searching his face, begging without words. It was too much. He couldn't keep this up. He moved to get to his feet, and she caught his arm and clung to it. She drew a shaky breath; tears came into her eyes. Her words were a quavery little squeak. "He's dead, isn't he?"

Bohannon nodded. "I'm sorry."

"They all die." She dug tissues from another of the pockets of the safari jacket, dried her eyes and blew her nose. "That's the trouble with looking after them. They become precious to you. And then they just die." She was weeping for sure, now, and her words were hard to understand. "Over and over and over again. So many." She got more Kleenex and tried to mop away the tears, but they just kept coming. "You'd think a person would get used to it. Maybe some do, but not me. Poor Fletcher."

She laid her head on Bohannon's chest. He put his arms around her and held her and stroked her while she sobbed. He didn't tell her poor Fletcher had been shot. It wouldn't help.

Shakespeare by the Sea. The sign was gold gothic letters on a black background and hung off the porch of a typical old saltbox house in Monterey. He found parking a little way along, and ambled back to the place and climbed the front steps. In the glass of the front door a sign hung off a string. *Closed.* He put his face to the glass. Bookshelves all around the walls. Tables with books on them. A desk with a telephone, cash register, computer at the center of the room. He knocked on the door, waited, knocked again. Nobody came. He read his watch. 3:35. Middle of the week. Why closed?

There was a combination greenhouse/flower-shop next door. He stepped into fragrance and color, dampness and dim green daylight, and asked a woman in a rubber apron. The slim hose in her hand had a misting nozzle with a trigger. She was misting a long table of plants in little green plastic pots. "I don't know, and I wish people would stop asking. How do I know where Morton Lowry is?"

"What people?" Bohannon said.

"First that fat girl with the funny costume. Then that woman with the gold Mercedes. If she didn't know who would? She's been in and out of there"—she jerked a head of short-cropped salt-and-pepper hair in the direction of *Shakespeare by the Sea*—"almost every day for weeks. Never bought a book—not that I saw." She sniffed. "Life's full of surprises. Who'd have thought Morton Lowry cared about women?"

Bohannon took out his wallet, let it fall open so it showed her his private investigator's license, closed it quickly, and pocketed it again. "I need to locate him. It's police business."

She stopped misting and blinked hard at him. "You certainly don't look like a police officer."

"Special assignment," he said.

"Try the back door," she said. "Wallace Finn might talk to you."

"Who's he?" Bohannon said.

She jerked her head back. "Why he's the owner. Lowry's just the hired help." She snorted and began misting again. "When he's sober."

Bohannon knocked on the backdoor of *Shakespeare by the Sea,* an aluminum screen door a little loose in its frame. The solid door inside it stood open. He called, "Mr. Finn? Bohannon, here. San Luis County Sheriff's Department."

"Oh, Lord," an old man's rough voice said. "Is it about Morton?"

"Need to know where he is," Bohannon said. "Can I come in?"

"I don't know where he is. Drunk someplace. Go away."

"Why don't you open your shop? Lots of people in town today."

"They just want to take photos of each other at Cannery Row." Finn appeared dimly. In a wheelchair, a coffee mug in his hand. "I can't run the shop on my own anymore. Doesn't matter. The public's lost interest in books. You watch TV enough, you haven't the brains left for reading."

"Where did he usually go to get drunk?" Bohannon said.

"Not far. That broken-down old car of his won't travel far." Finn grunted. "I don't honestly think it's just a drunk, this time. It's been too long. You'd better check the jails."

"They allow you a phone call," Bohannon said. "He didn't call?"

"He just disappeared," Finn said. "Why don't you try doing that?"

"First tell me where he lives," Bohannon said.

And Finn told him.

It was an old flat-roofed frame hotel, two sagging stories, once yellow, now in need of paint. Not on a street where tourists would see it. The buildings on those streets were tarted up. *John Steinbeck slept here!* But he didn't think about this. He was too startled. Because not only were Monterey County Sheriff's patrol cars parked in front of that bleak hotel—so was a patrol car from San Luis Obispo County. And Lieutenant Phil Gerard stood beside it, looking up at the sunstruck front of the building. Bohannon parked the pickup and jogged across the street.

Gerard stared at him. "I don't believe this."

"What's going on?" Bohannon asked.

"Drowned man was found a couple hours ago, washed up on the beach here. One Morton Lowry. Bookstore clerk and town drunk."

"And years ago a teacher at Madrone high school," Bohannon said, "until Clay Gilmore lost him his job. Moral turpitude."

Gerard's eyebrows rose. "Who told you that?"

"If you didn't know it," Bohannon said, "what are you doing here?"

"They found a gun in his pocket," Gerard said, "and they phoned me, because the serial number makes it Celia Gilmore's gun."

"Right. You missed the letter, but there was one. Chico was dying and wanted to come home. She knew Clay would never permit it. He'd despise the boy even more, now that he had AIDS. And Celia remembered Lowry. Clay had ruined his life. Lowry must hate him. She needed his help, and she got it. Such as it was." Bohannon tilted his head toward the deputies coming out of the hotel. "When they find Lowry's car, tell them to look for an oil leak."

"Jesus." Gerard wagged his head in disgust, looked down at his boots, looked up again, grimly. "All right. You obviously know all about it. Tell me."

Bohannon summed up Lettice Van Van's story. Then he said, "And if you drive over to the local Ramada Inn, right now, you'll find a gold Mercedes in the lot. I spotted it on my way here."

"She's here?" Gerard gaped. "What in God's name for?"

Bohannon shrugged. "She doesn't know Lowry drowned himself. She's waiting for him to sober up and stagger into the bookstore. I expect she'd like her money back. After all, he killed the wrong Gilmore."

Gerard squinted. "She paid him to do it?"

"He wasn't an avenger. He was a drunk. Of course, she had to pay him."

"So it comes down to the kid arriving home a week early. And Lowry sneaks in by that back door in the dark to kill Clay Gilmore. And the kid thinks he's a prowler, and yells and jumps up. And Lowry panics and shoots him."

"You have a better suggestion?" Bohannon said.

"Hell, no." Gerard got into the patrol car and slammed

188

the door. "But if my mind worked like yours," he said, "I'd never sleep."

"It's questions that keep me awake," Bohannon said. "Not answers."

Widdershins

It was January. Hack Bohannon hadn't seen Derek Fremont since last summer. The runty boy had suddenly grown, and it broke his heart. He had planned to be a jockey. It had seemed reasonable. His father stood only five foot two. His mother and sister were tiny. In the sweet hay smell of Bohannon's stable now, the boy stood beside the General, his big chestnut gelding, and with tears in his eyes asked Bohannon, "How did it happen?"

Bohannon said, "Where was it you went to? Wisconsin? Guess you should have stayed home."

"Yeah." Derek's grin was rueful. "Something in the water, right?" He threw a blanket across the General's back and crouched to pick up the bulky old Western saddle. "What'll I do with my life, now?"

"There's a hundred things a man can do around horses." Bohannon watched the boy heave the saddle into place. "You'll find one. How about quarter-horse racing?"

"Fine with me," Derek said, "but my Dad wouldn't like it. Thoroughbreds. Those jockeys make a good living. That's the only reason he let me plan on it."

"You said he wanted you to ask me something," Bohannon said. "What was that?"

The boy reached under the General to catch the end of the saddle girth. "While we were away"—he grunted, cinching the

191

girth tight—"somebody broke into the house. Made a mess."

Bohannon said, "Why not phone the Sheriff?"

"Dad doesn't want uniforms and patrol cars around. He doesn't want anything to get out about it. Sure as hell not on the nightly news, all right?"

Derek lifted the dangling reins over the General's ears. The horse nodded, snorted, gave his mane a shake. The boy put a foot in a stirrup, and swung aboard. Bohannon opened the stall door and Derek moved the handsome animal out onto the sheltered walkway that fronted the stable building.

"Doesn't want uniforms why?" Bohannon asked.

"It's weird, okay?" The boy rode out onto hardpan margined by flowerbeds and shadowed by tall eucalyptus trees. The sun was hot, but a sage-scented breeze blew up the canyon. It rustled the leaves of the trees. A leaf drifted down and the General shied at it. "Easy," Derek said to him, and told Bohannon: "You'll understand when you see it."

"When I see what?"

"It could start gossip. And this is the wrong time. See, he's selling the house. We have to settle back there in Wisconsin. At Gran's." He patted the General's neck. "She's, like, failing, you know? Alzheimer's. My mom wants us to be with her. The doctors say it could help her keep a hold on life." He shrugged. "I don't mind leaving. Not since Brad Yates died." The boy's face clouded. "He was my best friend, okay? Killed himself. At Christmas." He took a deep breath and gave a wan smile. "I like Gran. And it's a big old house. There's plenty of room for us all."

"What about the General?" Bohannon wondered.

"What do you think?" Derek was amazed. "I'd leave him, sell him?"

"I guess not," Bohannon said. "Snowy winters. He'll grow a shaggy coat."

"I'll take care of him." Derek nudged the General's sides with his heels and the two of them moved off toward the wide, white gates and the canyon road. "You going to look at the vandalism, now?"

"You've got me curious," Bohannon said.

Weird it was. He stood in the broad, handsome living room of the Fremont house among the pines of Settlers Cove, and frowned. The rugs had been rolled back, and into the hardwood floor a large circle had been gouged, three circles, one within the other. Gouged and then painted in black. A criss-cross five-pointed star was cut inside the circles. And runes in the segments of the star. Small burn marks scattered the floor around the circle.

A wall of sliding glass panels was closed off by drapes. One section of the drapes was scorched by fire at the bottom. Examining it, Bohannon smelled incense. Incense had saturated the fabric. Not the pleasantest incense he'd ever smelled. Acrid. He pushed back his Stetson and studied the ceiling. Smoke had darkened the plaster between the beams. He crouched and touched white drops on the floor. Candle wax. Grit crunched underfoot. He dampened a fingertip, picked up a few grains, touched them to his tongue. Salt. He got to his feet.

"Anything stolen?" he asked Grant Fremont.

"I don't think so. But they ruined this. Just look." It was a round, drop-leaf table, and there were scratches on it, scorch marks, more candle wax, salt, spattered ink. "They probably got in through a window in the half-bath at the back. It's usually partway open. We must have forgotten to latch it."

"You entertain a lot?" Bohannon said.

"Oh, it's open house." Fremont smiled a little wanly at his daughter Amy, who stood in a far doorway, watching. "When you've got teenage kids, they're in and out all the time. Swarms of 'em." The small man gave Bohannon a rueful smile. "From the perennial emptiness of the refrigerator, and the size of the grocery bill, I'd say, yes, we 'entertain' quite a lot."

Bohannon looked at Amy. "Can you guess who this might have been?"

She shook her long blond hair. Her face had no expression.

"You tell your friends you were going to Wisconsin?"

"My friends," she said indignantly. "You think my friends would do this?"

"Maybe they told their friends," Bohannon suggested, "who aren't as nice as your friends."

"They don't know any witches," she said, and went away into other parts of the sprawling house.

"Witches?" Her father's eyebrows went up.

"Looks that way." Bohannon regarded the scarred floor again. "A circle to fend off demons and cast spells in." He grunted a laugh. "I worked on a witchcraft case years ago. Never expected it to happen again." He looked wryly at Fremont. "You hang around long enough, things start repeating themselves."

Fremont stared. "They've been holding witches'— what?—covens in here?"

"A coven is a group of witches," Bohannon said, "sabbats are what they hold." He drew back the damaged drapes. Beyond a broad deck nothing was visible but tall slender pines and undergrowth. "It's a big property, isn't it? You bought the next-door lots for privacy."

"And to keep horses," Fremont said with an ironic laugh. "But, as you well know, the town changed the ordinance."

"Still, it's very private, and that's what the craft requires. Secrecy."

"Aren't witches supposed to be crazy old women, hags, crones?" Fremont said. "What would teenage girls have to do with it?"

"It was a fad with them in Salem three hundred years ago," Bohannon said. "It's a fad again today. Wicca, they call it."

Fremont touched the ugly circle with his shoe. "This is going to take a lot of repair work. I'd like to send the bill to their parents."

"No insurance?" Bohannon said.

Fremont's laugh was bleak. "The agent is Budge Walker. You know anybody who can spread gossip faster?" He regarded Bohannon worriedly. "You won't tell anybody, will you? If it leaks, everybody will be calling this 'the Witches' House.' I won't be able to give it away."

"Right." Bohannon settled his hat. "Let me see what I can find out."

"Thanks for coming." Fremont shook his hand.

"No problem. Better take Polaroids of the damage before you get it fixed." Bohannon blinked. "How will you keep the workmen from leaking the story?"

Fremont shrugged bleakly. "Bring them in from out of town, I guess."

Bohannon moved off. "Kids, these days," he said.

Fern Drummond opened the door. Short and pudgy, in her mid-thirties, she wore a blue smock with *Starstyles* stitched on the pocket in red. From his battered green pickup parked across the street, he had watched her arrive home. He hadn't wanted to upset her by interrupting her at work. He didn't want to upset her now. But he was after leads, and a missing persons report he'd chanced on this afternoon at the Sheriff's substation in Madrone gave him hope that she just might have one for him.

She lived on a street of overgrown oleanders and scrappy little old frame bungalows on cramped lots. Behind her, inside the place, a television flickered and there were beeping and buzzing noises that signaled someone was playing a game. Fern Drummond's hair was blonde and arranged in pile-ups and loops and falls that said they weren't so busy at *Starstyles* they couldn't fool with each other's hair at odd moments. She peered at him. "What is it?"

Bohannon touched his hat brim. "Your daughter Denise," he said.

She straightened, surprised and excited. "Have they found her?"

"She hasn't come home?"

Her shoulders slumped. "No, she ain't. And who made it your business, anyway?" She looked him up and down. Blue work shirt, faded Levis, scuffed cowboy boots. "You ain't no sheriff."

"I used to be." He dug his wallet from a hip pocket and let the wallet fall open to show his license. "Now I'm a private investigator." He tucked the wallet away. "Case I'm working on appears to involve some high school girls. And I just got to wondering if maybe Denise's disappearance could be connected in some way." He gave her a little smile. "Can I come in?"

"I just got home. On my feet all day. I'm tired. I have to cook supper for my ten-year-old. If you can't tell me where Denise is, what's the point?"

"I'd like a look at her room."

"Sheriff's already looked," Fern Drummond said. "Didn't find nothin'."

Bohannon smiled. "They didn't know what to look for. I do."

She tilted her head skeptically. "What would that be?"

"A pendant," Bohannon said. "That a girl would wear around her neck on a chain or a cord. Circular, probably. Maybe with a star in it. Silver? Gold?"

The woman grew pale under her makeup, and she blinked. "Now, how did you know that? Yes, it's here. I never knew she had it till after she run off." She hesitated, then said, "I'll get it. You wait here."

He nodded and she shut the door, cutting off the beeping and whizzing of the game. He leaned back against the gallery rail and dug a cigarette from his shirt pocket but there wasn't time to light it before the door opened and here she was again. He put the cigarette away. In her hands was a white cardboard box that looked like it came from a dress shop. She pulled off its cover.

"See here," she said, and picked the amulet out and held it swinging by its golden cord. It glinted in the sun. A pentacle. But something else in the box interested Bohannon more. A knife, not a kitchen knife, a knife you could use for carving big circles into hardwood floors. He took it out of the box.

"That could hurt somebody," Fern Drummond said. "I don't know what she was doin' with it. What if her little brother found it? Look at that writin' on the handle."

He was looking at it. Runes, again. Thinking where he'd have to go for a translation made him wince. He laid the knife back in the box. The box smelled of incense, the same as he'd smelled at the Fremont house. A little pot-metal goblet lay cradled in a cheap wok scorched on its insides. Cup and dish were painted with black runes as well. And under these lay a thin, hand-bound notebook, with the magic circle drawn on its cover. "Where did you find this?"

"High up on the closet shelf in her room, behind a lot of

stuff. She hid it. Why? What does it mean? What's it all about?"

"Oh, it's a new craze with high school girls." Bohannon tried to sound off-hand, though he didn't feel that way. "Playing at witchcraft."

"Witchcraft!" Fern Drummond laughed disbelief.

"She never said anything about it to you?"

"Not a word." She squinted against the late sunlight. "You serious? Witchcraft?" She said it to herself, looking past him at nothing, shaking her head. Then she focused on him sharply. "You think it's got something to do with her runnin' away?"

"She didn't go to her father's," Bohannon said. "Anywhere else she might have gone? You said she didn't have any money."

"Maybe she saved a little from her McDonald's job," the woman said, "but they don't pay hardly nothin', you know. Oughta be a law."

"There's a law," Bohannon said. "It's just not a very good law. What about her friends? Girls that age chatter a lot. None of them talked about witchcraft?"

The woman's face stiffened. "Denise didn't bring her friends here. She was ashamed of this place. A slum, she called it. It's not a slum. It's nice for the rent I can pay. But, you know, them other girls all live in fancy houses."

"You know any of their names?" Bohannon said.

"Madison, Cameron, it's them she yaks about all the time, their rooms with their own telephones, TVs, computers, the designer clothes they buy at the mall. There's girls her age in this neighborhood she could hang with, but it's gotta be them rich ones. She'd be a lot happier if—" Fern Drummond let that argument tail off. She peered up at him. Her eyes pleaded. "There's not even one report from anyplace on her?"

Bohannon asked, "Would she have gone to Hollywood? To get into television, movies, the music business?"

"She ain't pretty," Fern Drummond said. "Plays the guitar good. Don taught her—her old man. Sings real sweet. But show business? No. She didn't even take her guitar. She's too shy. Gets good grades, though. She got Don's brains. He's a rat, but he's smart. No way she got that from me."

"She ever say she wished she could travel? Far away places?"

"They get to their teens, they don't tell you their dreams no more." She touched his arm. "She's bookish, Mr. Bohannon. And that kind don't know much about life. People take advantage of her. I hope they find her before she gets in trouble. Before somebody hurts her."

"She'll probably come back on her own." Bohannon did his best to smile. "They usually do. Look, can I borrow these?"

But before she could answer, something crashed inside the apartment. A child howled, "Mom!" Fern Drummond said hastily, "Sure, you take 'em, honey, that's all right. You gotta excuse me now." And she charged indoors. "Dustin Lee, what've you done?"

When Bohannon reached the ranch up Rodd Canyon the sun had dropped behind the western ridge and was painting the sky red. He rolled the green pickup through the white gates, parked it beyond the stables beside the stake truck, the horse trailer, and Otis Jackson's old Honda Civic, climbed out and strolled back to where Otis was unsaddling Mousie and Seashell.

A big, strapping black youth, Otis had come here first to look after Bohannon's old partner, George Stubbs in his last days. After George died, Bohannon had talked Otis into abandoning nursing to help him run the stables. He couldn't pay high wages, but he could offer free room and board, and time to study: Otis was aiming at medical school. And serious about it.

Bohannon helped him wipe down the two mares, stable them and see to their water and food. They closed the stall doors on all the mounts, his own and those he boarded for others. Otis went to wash up. Bohannon got Denise Drummond's box off the seat of the truck, and set it on the big round pine table in the plank-walled kitchen. He was drying his hands at the sink when Otis came in and bent to take the makings of supper out of the refrigerator.

"Don't start yet," Bohannon got Old Crow and glasses from a cupboard, set them on the table, pulled out chairs. "Come sit and have a drink."

Otis sat down and eyed the box. "Lingerie for me? You shouldn't have."

Bohannon laughed. "I didn't. Open it." He clinked the neck of the bottle on the glasses, pouring, recapped the bottle, looked at Otis. He was scowling, his big hands in the box, rattling the cup, the wok, the knife.

"Where did you find this?"

Bohannon tasted the whiskey. "You know what it is?"

"It's incomplete. There should be a long braided silk cord with knots in it."

Bohannon lit a cigarette. "That part of your pre-med schooling?"

"Woman I dated at Cal State was into it," Otis said. "Scared all the time. Thought people were putting the evil eye on her. Foxy lady. Very intelligent. But she had this thing about witchcraft." He lifted the amulet out of the box. "Wore one of these day and night." Darkness had come indoors, and he switched on the lamp with its red glass shade in the middle of the table. Cradling the little circle of silver in his palm, he said, "Whose is this? Why isn't she wearing it? Because a witch would never leave home without it."

Bohannon looked at him sharply. "That right?"

Otis shrugged. "To ward off curses. What she said. I couldn't cope with the paranoia. I begged her to get professional help. She wouldn't. And in the end I just gave up." With a sigh, he dropped the pentacle back into the box, put the lid on the box, pushed it aside. "What's this all about?"

Bohannon told him. "If you can spare me tomorrow morning I'll go over to the high school and talk to a girl's gym coach I know there. Merle Parker. She used to come up here and ride."

"Why a coach?" Otis finished off his drink and stood up.

"Because if witches never take off their amulets," Bohannon said, "then they wear them in the shower, right?"

Otis switched on fluorescents over the stove and counters and began unwrapping the pork chops he'd taken from the refrigerator. "Not Denise Drummond," he said. "Wherever she is."

Merle Parker wasn't at the high school. But they told him where she was, and he found her on a white pier at Morro Bay, with a crew of girls in shorts and T-shirts. Shouting orders at them while they hopped in and out of the school sloop tied up there. He thought sloop was the right word. It had one mast, a large sail, and a small sail forward. He knew next to nothing about boats. The ropes the girls were tangling with, trying to raise the sails, were called sheets. He'd read that somewhere. He was always trying to learn. He'd had almost no schooling.

It wasn't yet 8:00. The breeze was fresh. Gulls circled against a blue sky. Sunlight glittered off the water. The great rock that loomed up in the middle of the bay cast a long shadow. It had always looked to him like the head of a gray whale surfacing for air. Only twenty times as big. He went down white wooden stairs to the pier. And she noticed him. He waved. She waved, and after a moment, came limping to him, a small straw-haired woman, cheerful, tough. The limp was from a skiing accident long ago.

"Hack Bohannon." She peered up at him, having to shield her eyes with a hand from the glare off the water. "What brings you here?"

"I'm working on a little puzzle for a friend," he said. "Maybe you can fill in some of the pieces." He pulled the amulet out of his shirt pocket and dangled it on its cord. "You ever seen one of these before?"

She took it and studied it. "Yes."

"Mind telling me where? Around whose neck?"

She nibbled her lower lip, frowning. "This one, I believe, is Denise Drummond's." She handed it back. "She's run away from home, I understand."

Two girls in shrill unison cried out, "Miz Parker!" She waved an arm and shouted, "I'll be there in a minute." She turned back to Hack, hand shielding her eyes again. "I should have brought RayBans. I'll be blind by noon."

" 'This one,' you said." He dropped the pentacle back into his pocket. "You seen others like it? Who wears them, Merle?"

She squinted at him. "What's this all about, Hack?"

He shrugged. "It's no big deal. Vandalism. Vacant house. Property damage, is all. Nobody's going to get in important trouble."

"I hope not." Now all of them were yelling for her from the sloop. She waved at them again. "I have to go. But yes. Two others. Cameron Chase. And Madison Schuster. The three of them are very close. Lots of whispers and dark, significant glances." She grinned. "Can you believe we were ever teen-agers?"

"I don't want to think about it," Bohannon laughed. "Okay. Thanks. I'd better let you go before they mutiny."

"Nice to see you," she said, and hurried off.

He started back up the white wooden steps. They trembled and he raised his head. Amy Fremont came running down the steps, breathless, flushed, long fair hair flying. Smiling, he took hold of both handrails, blocking her. "What are you doing?" she yelped. "Let me by. I'm late. You can't just—" And then she recognized him. "Mr. Bohannon. What's wrong?"

"Nothing," he said. "But I've got some questions for you."

She peered toward the sloop. "They'll leave without me."

"I don't think so," he said. "They have to figure out which end is the front, first. Denise Drummond, Cameron Chase, Madison Shuster. They ever been to your house?"

The wind was whipping her hair. She pushed it off her face. "Maybe. Once or twice." She shrugged, looking fretfully past him at the sloop. "But not by special invitation, all right? I mean, lots of kids come. You heard my Dad. I don't really know them." Then she caught her breath and her eyes opened wide. "You think they're the ones who—?"

"I think they're into witchcraft," he said. "What do you think?"

"Everybody says Ms. Oritz-Laredo got sent a doll with pins in it. So there's witches at school, but I never knew it was them."

"Nothing's proved yet," Bohannon said, "so don't tell anyone, all right? Who's Ms. Ortiz-Laredo?"

She couldn't believe his ignorance. "The principal, of course."

"Of course," Bohannon said. "Tell me about your brother's friend. Yates?"

"Boring old Brad," she said. "He killed himself. Please, I have to go."

"Why did he do that?"

"He never went to classes. They warned him, but he didn't listen. So at the end of the term, they expelled him. A Christmas present, right? All he cared about was computers. I don't know why Derek liked him so much. He even flew back here for the funeral." She fluttered her hands and jigged from foot to foot. "Can I go now, ple-e-ase?"

Bohannon stood aside. And she went.

Bert Shuster and Bohannon had met more than once down the years, when property owners had felt threatened by developers in and around Madrone and the town's activists had organized ad hoc committees to fight them off. So when Shuster, a big, bluff oil geologist found Bohannon at his door now, he smiled, invited him in, and sat him down in a living room big enough to hold Fern Drummond's whole house, and fetched him a mug of espresso. He took an easy chair and asked:

"Who's trying to wreck our paradise, now?"

"Nobody I know of." The mug had a New Guinea tribal design on it. "Good coffee," he said. "Thank you." He looked around. African masks, a totem pole in a corner, a kayak suspended overhead. "Tanya not home?"

"Meals on Wheels today," Shuster said. "Tuesdays, Thursdays, Saturdays. You need her for something?"

"Maybe not." Bohannon poked into his shirt pocket again for the amulet. "Maybe you'll recognize this." Morning light was in the room. The silver circle turned and twinkled when he held it up. "Madison own one of these?"

Shuster sat forward, brows knitted, and blinked at it. "Why, yes. I think she does. Likes it too." He gave a half laugh. "Even wears it in the pool." He tilted his head. "Where'd you come by it?"

"This one"—Bohannon dropped it back into his pocket— "belongs to Denise Drummond. I'm told she and Madison are friends."

Shuster grew guarded. "Well, I don't know about that. She's been here once or twice when I happened to be home. That's not a lot, you know. I travel all the time." Bohannon knew. He flew to Alaska, Siberia, the Gobi desert. Places most people never heard of Bert Shuster was at home in. "Funny girl, a little mopish, mousy. Not sunny and full of life like Maddy. And Cameron Chase. Now those two are like sisters, they're so tight. This Drummond girl was different." He sipped his coffee and had a sudden thought. "Didn't I hear she'd run away?"

"Right," Bohannon said.

"And you think Maddy can tell you where she went?"

"That would be wonderful," Bohannon said. "But I think the Sheriff's people asked all Denise's friends at school. That would be the routine. No, I wanted to learn if she wore one of these too."

"Why? What would that prove?"

"It's a pentacle," Bohannon explained. "Witches wear it to ward off evil."

"Witches!" Shuster stared.

"It looks as if some girls at the school have taken up witchcraft, formed a coven, and recently made some mischief."

Shuster pushed up out of the big chair. "Well, Maddy wears one of those things, and she can be a handful these days. But witchcraft, Hack?" He was skeptical and not pleased. "Mischief? What does that mean?"

"Damaged a vacant house in Settlers Cove, carved up the floor, got careless with fire." He set down the coffee and stood up. "It's an isolated place. They were holding sabbats there, Bert. Private. Secret."

"Oh, come on!" Shuster chuckled and shook his head. "You lost your common sense? You mean these little girls were casting evil spells? Dancing with the Devil?"

Bohannon nodded. "Midnight, naked, with incense, and candles, and incantations in dog Latin. It's the latest teenage craze."

"Her latest craze would seem to be a movie actor. Leonardo diCaprio?"

"She go out with any boys? Brad Yates, maybe?"

Shuster's face clouded. "The one that killed himself? No, she didn't know him. It's a big consolidated school, Bohannon. Anyway, he was older, two classes ahead. Yes, she was upset. Whole school was upset. Terrible thing."

"Any books in her room on witchcraft? You might want to check on that."

Shuster bridled. "You don't have kids, right?" Bohannon closed his eyes and opened them. "Well when you do, you start out teaching them the right values, and then you trust them. The same as you expect them to trust you." He worked at a smile. "No, Hack. I don't think my princess has taken to witchcraft. And I'm not going to search her room." He clapped a hand on Bohannon's shoulder and steered him toward the door. "She's got an obsession, all right. She's still too young to get a driver's license, but all I hear from her these days is when am I going to buy her a car." Out on the deck, they shook hands.

"Don't bother her with it, then," Bohannon said. "Forget I came, all right?" And he went down the steps.

"No problem." Shuster, plainly not wanting the encounter to end sourly, called, "How's the horse business these days?"

Bohannon stopped and turned. "I'm still there. You know where to find the place. Bring Madison. A couple hours ride up the canyons on a kindly horse, maybe she'll forget all about cars."

"I might just try that." Shuster smiled, lifted a hand, and went back into the house.

A rosy-faced, middle-aged housekeeper in an apron answered the door. She looked blank when Bohannon asked for Wayland Chase, but she went away and he soon appeared, around forty, thin, frail looking, slightly stooped, a book in one hand, finger in the place where he'd stopped reading. Glasses had slipped halfway down his nose. Over them, he regarded Bohannon without warmth.

"I've heard of you. You're adept at solving crimes." His thin mouth twitched. Maybe he meant it for a smile. "I've sometimes wondered if this little place even had crimes before you came "

"I go back a long way," Bohannon said, "but not that far."

"And is the local Anglican priest involved in the latest wrongdoing?"

A blue jay squawked. The cry echoed through the silent woods. Bohannon looked upward for a moment. Then he said, "Property damage? Vandalism? Doesn't sound Anglican to me."

Chase did not smile. "Then what brings you here?"

"Just a question. About your daughter." Bohannon held up the glittery little circle of silver. "Does she own one of these?"

Chase pushed up his glasses, craned slightly forward, then

jerked his head back. "That's a cabalistic symbol. A pentacle. Certainly not."

Bohannon nodded, put the pendant away. "Her mother here?" he asked.

"Long dead," Chase answered. "I've raised Cameron on my own since she was four years old. We are good friends. We understand one another. She is, in the deepest and least outwardly showy way, the truest Christian I ever knew."

"No changes in her lately? Anger? Depression? A boy named Brad Yates killed himself at Christmas. Did she react to that?"

The clergyman nodded. "Oh, yes. We all did. I delivered a sermon on teenage suicide. Tragic." He tilted his head. "Are you asking if Cameron knew the boy? No. She grieved, but the whole school grieved."

Bohannon said, "Grieved, and gossiped, I expect. Surmises. Wild guesses. They've been gossiping lately about this witchcraft business. But there's a kernel of truth in it. Somebody in our little town has been holding sabbats this winter. I've seen the evidence. They were careless not to have tidied up after themselves. Maybe they were careless elsewhere. With their secrecy. That's why I think they may be youngsters. That's why I'm asking around. Forgive me."

"You simply don't know Cameron." Chase's smile was thin and cold.

"Thanks for your time." At the foot of the steps, Bohannon turned. "One more thing: Cameron was friendly with a girl called Denise Drummond. She's gone missing. I'd like to find her. Cameron ever bring her home?"

"Fairly often." The clergyman frowned to himself. "Shy girl, homely, withdrawn. An odd choice for Cameron, I thought."

"Did Denise ever talk with you at all?" Bohannon asked.

"Say anything you remember that could help us find her?"

"No, apart from hello, we never spoke." He narrowed his eyes. "That amulet you showed me—is it hers?"

"You'd make quite a crime-solver yourself," Bohannon said.

A picture window at her back, with a breathtaking view of the ocean over treetops, Alicia Ortiz-Laredo sat at a big, busy-looking desk, facing the open door of her office. She was eating lunch with chopsticks out of paper cartons with red Chinese calligraphy on them. She was a slim, handsome young woman, dressed simply but, Bohannon guessed, expensively. Her look at him combined a smile and a frown. He took off his hat.

"Bohannon," he said. "You've ridden my horses a few times. Don't like to interrupt your lunch, but I need a minute of your time."

She stuck the chopsticks into one of the little cartons, touched her mouth with a paper napkin, laid the napkin down. "Come in," she said. "Sit down." He did these things, resting his hat on his knees. Her large dark eyes were puzzled. "A minute for what?"

"A couple questions. I was a deputy sheriff before I opened my stables. And I still do investigations now and then."

She nodded. "For the County Attorney."

"And private parties, if they ask me. It's that kind of case I'm working on now." Without naming names, he sketched in words the damage at the Fremont house. "Looks as if somebody's taking this witchcraft mania a little too far."

Her expression lost its hint of humor. She bent and opened a desk drawer. "This is what you've come to see." And she laid a ragged, newspaper-wrapped bundle on the desk. Her telephone yodeled. She picked up the receiver, murmured into it, hung up. "Open it," she said to Bohannon. Rubber bands bound the wrapping. He pulled these off and laid the bundle open. He looked at the ugly clay doll and then he looked at her. "You knew I'd heard about it?"

Her smile was wry. "It's impossible to keep a secret in this place. Someone was bound to tell it to someone else." She shook her head and took another bite of whatever was in the carton. She managed the chopsticks elegantly. Bohannon had tried that once, and given up. "In confidence, of course."

A needle was stuck through the doll's heart. Between crudely made breasts. "Somebody out there doesn't like you," Bohannon said. "Have you shown it to the Sheriff?"

"I don't think it's worth bothering him with," she said.

"Any idea who made it?" Bohannon said.

"I don't." She studied his face. "Why do I think you do?"

He pulled the pentacle from his pocket and pushed it across the desk to her. She blinked at it. He said, "Witches wear these. To ward off evil. Never take them off." He told her where this one came from. "And Merle Parker says two other girls in this school wear them."

He had her attention now. She didn't ask. She waited for him to speak.

"Madison Shuster," Bohannon said, "and Cameron Chase."

"Really?" Frowning, the principal pushed the amulet back to him across the desk. He put it away. She said, "Well, they're certainly a tight little threesome. Were. Denise has disappeared. Suppose that could mean a guilty conscience."

"Possibly, but what about the others?"

"A lively pair, Mr. Bohannon. Bright, restless, imaginative. If they came from different backgrounds, they'd be rebels, not A students and class officers."

Bohannon said, "I spoke to their fathers this morning. They tell me one is a princess and the other is a saint."

"Fathers." Alicia Ortiz-Laredo gave a dry laugh. "Why don't you ask the girls themselves if they held a sabbat at that mysterious house?"

"I don't have the authority. This isn't official business. The owner of the house is a friend. He asked me to try to find who vandalized his living room, ask them not to do it again, please, and to pay for repairing the damages. Nobody's going to jail over it. Could you question them?"

She blinked. "On what pretext?"

"That rumor has it they were the ones who sent you that puppet." She thought about that, keeping her gaze fixed on him. She didn't speak. He spoke. "It's hocus pocus, but the makers of dolls like that mean for them to do harm." He reached out, withdrew the needle, put the needle back. "This tells me they want you dead." He looked into her eyes. "Why would they hate you so?"

"If I take it seriously"—the principal was grave, chose her words carefully, spoke them slowly—"the whole school will know it in a day or two. It could turn what were only sparks of superstition into a wildfire." She shook her head. "If they'd done something like—what?—slashed my tires, I could react. But I must not, cannot be seen as giving witchcraft any credence. Do you see my point?"

"I see." Bohannon got to his feet. "Thank you." He made to turn away, changed his mind. "One more thing. Very important. Were any of these girls close to Brad Yates?"

She dismissed that. "Not possible. They're so much younger."

"Young girls can get crushes on older boys. And this older boy was expelled for not going to classes. Kids don't look at these things the way grownups do. It's never the kid's fault.

211

No punishment is ever deserved."

"I've noticed that," Alicia Ortiz-Laredo said drily.

"When Brad Yates committed suicide," Bohannon said, "some young girl who loved him could have blamed you for his death. You follow me?"

She turned pale, stiffened in her chair, opened her mouth to speak. And loud electric bells clamored through the halls. Whenever he heard such bells, Bohannon remembered why he'd quit school young. It seemed as if these would never stop. But they did, and in a voice trembling with outrage, Alicia Ortiz-Laredo said, "I don't know where you got that idea, but it's insane."

"So is witchcraft," Bohannon said. "I'm sorry if I upset you."

"You're tactless and cruel," she said.

"Clumsy," he said. "Forgive me." He gave her a half smile, put on his hat, and went away.

Bohannon had stayed away too long today, leaving Otis to manage the place on his own, and he was contrite. "You're asleep on your feet," he said. It was getting on for six. The daylight was dying. And two riders hadn't yet returned to the stables. "You've been working since four in the morning. Get yourself a glass of milk and go to bed. I'll wait for them. I'll close things down."

"You sure?" The black youngster peered down at him. His face was drawn, eyes bloodshot, lips dry and cracked. He gave his head a shake, and managed a tired smile. "It sounds like a beautiful plan."

"Go." Bohannon nodded toward the low, long line of the ranch house. "You sleep in your room tonight. I'll take the tack room."

"Bed's not ready," Otis Jackson protested.

"I've slept in unmade beds before," Bohannon said.

"All right." Otis limped off. "See you in the morning. Likely be two or three mornings from now, but I'll see you." His big form was silhouetted for a moment in the lighted kitchen doorway, then the door closed.

Bohannon heard the clop of hoofs and creak of saddle leather out on the canyon trail, and ambled toward the gate to meet the riders. When he'd wiped down Buck and Twilight and got them watered and filled their bins with oats, he closed the doors of their stalls, went into the white-washed tack-room, sat on the iron cot, pried off his boots, and before his head hit the pillow was dead asleep.

The most familiar sound can wake us if it's in the wrong place at the wrong time. And he woke and sat up in the dark and listened for it to repeat itself and it did. Horses were moving on the hardpan of the yard. He flung himself across the room, yanked open the door, and ran smack into a horse. He fell backward. The horse shied off. Bohannon scrambled to his feet. "Otis!" he yelled. The yard was milling with shadowy horses. Why was it so dark? What had happened to the ground lights?

But that wasn't the worst. The gate was open. And horses were moving out onto the road. Two, three, four. "Otis!" he yelled again. And ran for the gate. Wrong tactic. They took fright and bolted up the road, ears laid back. He closed and latched the gate. He'd round them up later. Given time to think it over, they might even come home on their own. For now, he had to wrangle the others back into their stalls. All the stalls stood open. But Buck was still inside his, a little old for midnight adventuring. Bohannon swung aboard his bare back, nudged him out into the yard. "Otis. Wake up!"

Otis didn't. Bohannon rode to the fuse box. Its door hung open. He bent and groped inside and worked the switch. The ground lights came on. Which panicked the horses all over again. "Come on, old guy," he said to Buck. And together they followed and cornered and caught the bridles of the seven bewildered, eye-rolling, head-tossing fugitives, and led them back where they belonged. The youngest were skittish, of course, darting off just when he thought he had them. One clattered along the ranch house porch, sending potted geraniums flying. Still, eventually he'd boxed all of them safely in their stalls. He found carrots for them and treated them all, not quite losing fingers in the process. Then he pulled on his boots and went to the kitchen. It was 1:00 a.m.

"What's happening?" Otis came tottering in, blinking, rubbing a hand down over his face. "I had a nightmare." He dropped onto a chair at the table. "And I do mean mare. Tried to climb in my window."

"That was no mare," Bohannon said, "that was a filly." He got coffee brewing, and in its grand aroma, sat down, lit a cigarette, and told Otis what had happened.

"Those witch girls?" Otis said.

"You can spell it however you want," Bohannon said.

"Oh, no." They were at the table eating eggs scrambled with chopped onions, grated cheese, salsa, when Bohannon heard a sound and looked up. "Not rain." He shoveled in the last of his food, washed it down with coffee, got off his chair and headed for the kitchen door. "Should have got those horses first."

"Aren't they waterproof?" Otis said.

"They are." Bohannon took down the old yellow slicker that hung by the door and shrugged into it. "But I'm not." He put on his Stetson and pulled the door open. Cold damp air met him. "I'll see you."

"You want me with you?"

"I'll be fine," Bohannon stepped onto the porch. "Go back to bed."

Otis called, "Wait. Flashlight."

"There's a big one in the stable." Bohannon closed the door and jogged down the long porch and into the rain and then was sheltered again by the walkway in front of the stalls. He saw movement outside the gate. And he went there. Sure enough, Bearcat was waiting in the road, looking hangdog, and the Steinberg horse was with him. "Ashamed of yourself, aren't you?" He opened the gate. "You should be." He led them to their stalls and dried them off. Then he saddled Buck, got the flashlight and a couple of lead straps, and rode up the canyon through drizzly darkness to find the last two.

Nobody was coming to ride in this weather. Otis was poring over medical textbooks in his room with rap music on the radio. Bohannon, wearing glasses, was slumped in a deep chair in the living room, reading an encyclopedia article on witchcraft. And a car came into the yard. He heard the tires splashing, and stepped onto the porch for a look. The car slewed to a halt, throwing arcs of rainwater. Derek Fremont got out and came running.

"The General," he panted, pale-faced, wide-eyed. "Is he okay?"

"If he wasn't," Bohannon said, "I'd have phoned you." He gripped the boy's shoulders. He was trembling. "Hey, relax. Everything's fine."

"The whole school's talking about it," Derek said, following Bohannon inside. "How your horses got away last night, ran wild all over the county."

"Most of them just took a little turn around the yard. The others didn't go far. And the General wasn't one of them."

He led the way to the kitchen. "You want some hot chocolate?"

"What? No. Well, yes, thanks." The boy dropped onto a chair at the table, and gazed up at Bohannon. "You sure he's all right?"

"I'm sure." Bohannon got milk from the refrigerator, mugs off the shelf, cocoa from a cupboard. "I'm also sure who let him out."

"The witches." Derek nodded. "Amy said you told her they're Madison Shuster and Cameron Chase and Denise what's-her-name. The ones that messed up our house. And now they did this to you. Why?"

"It was a warning." Bohannon set milk heating in a pan on the stove, and spooned cocoa powder into the mugs. "They know I'm tracking them down, and if I don't stop, they'll do something worse to me next time."

"But what are they so serious about? It doesn't make sense. I mean, chewing up our living room floor, that really doesn't qualify as a major crime. Even if they got caught. And sending that stupid voodoo doll to Ms. Ortiz-Laredo. I mean, it's all a fantasy, isn't it. Games?"

"Your friend killing himself is not fantasy, not games." Bohannon poured the steaming milk into the mugs and stirred the brown mixture smooth and brought the mugs to the table. He sat down, lit a cigarette, and said, "I think the time has come for you to tell me about Brad Yates's suicide."

"All I know is"—Derek watched his fingers turn the spoon in the cocoa—"no way was it about school. He's a genius. He didn't have to attend classes to get A's. It's a stupid rule. He knew he wasn't going to stay expelled."

"Then, what?" Bohannon said. "Derek, was there a girlfriend?"

The boy looked away, shrugged. "He dated around. Like all of us."

"Not that," Bohannon said. "A serious relationship?"

The boy winced, shifted on the chair, tried the chocolate. He started to speak, closed his mouth. Finally he looked at Bohannon and said miserably, "Yeah, there was something going on. I mean sex. And it was with a younger girl. He felt terrible about it. He was very depressed."

Bohannon said softly, "And do you know that young girl's name?"

Derek looked across to the kitchen windows, the gray rain falling steadily outside. He shook his head. "He wouldn't tell me."

"But you found out," Bohannon said. "You saw them together, right?"

"She's just a kid," Derek pleaded, tears in his eyes.

"Tell me her name," Bohannon said. "A boy is dead because of her, and a girl has disappeared. Derek, something very ugly is going on. Was it Denise? Is that why she ran away?"

"No." Derek got up sharply, scraping the legs of the chair on the wide plank floor. Hands shoved into his pockets, he went to the kitchen door, opened it, and stared out. Cold air blew in. For a long minute, the only sound was the rattle of rain on the shingles overhead, the heavy plop of drops off the porch eaves. At last he said, almost too softly for Bohannon to hear, "It was Cameron." He turned and held his hands out. "Brad and I were in and out of each other's place all the time. So, yeah, I walked in on them. I didn't think he saw me. But the next day, he explained. She wouldn't leave him alone. That was why he started cutting school. To keep away from her. But it didn't work. When he told her it had to stop, what they were doing was wrong, it could ruin their lives, she said if

217

he ditched her, she'd tell, claim he'd made her do it."

Bohannon smiled as best he could. "Your cocoa's getting cold." The boy shut the door, came back and sat down. Bohannon said, "Don't feel bad about telling. She needs help. She's running out of control, Derek. She has no mother. Her father thinks she's an angel. Someone has to stop her. Your dad really ought to let me turn the case over to the Sheriff, now."

"He won't be able to sell the house. We need the money if we're going to move to Wisconsin. He'll have to start over, there." Derek's eyes pleaded. "You can do stuff the Sheriff would never even think of—that's what my dad says."

Bohannon sighed, stubbed out his cigarette, and stood up. "Let's go see the General," he said.

Guadalupe sat beside the old highway, a row of 1880s houses, tall and spindly, turreted, bay-windowed, and porched, painted bright colors. Most of them were places to eat, now. Mexican food. Good, too, as he remembered. But he hadn't been to Guadalupe in a long while. A stretch of dunes backed the town. In fair weather, people with crash helmets and nothing better to do snarled over the dunes in little cars made for the purpose. He hated the noise. Luckily, since he had to come here, the weather had kept the dune-buggy crowd away. Nobody much was around in the steadily falling rain.

The house he had never wanted to return to he found without having to search. Turning up the collar of his old cowhide jacket, pulling his hat down, hunching his shoulders, he trudged a long, rickety duck-board walkway to a porch just as rickety. He poked a corroded bell push. The woman was old and slow when he'd been here twenty years back. He figured his wait would be long, and he stood shivering, shifting from foot to foot, and tried to be patient. Sure enough, at last the door opened. Not far. And a face of old wrinkled leather showed itself from the shadows beyond. In wry recollection of her powers, he hadn't phoned ahead.

She didn't disappoint him. "Hackett. I've been expecting you." She backed her massive form, pulled the door wider, and a large hand crusted with sparkly rings motioned him inside. He entered glumly. There was a strong smell of cats. One came and bumped his ankles. As his eyes grew used to the dim light he saw cats everywhere. Asleep. Cats knew what to do in rainy weather. The gigantic woman layered in scarves and shawls plowed along ahead of him to a corner of a tall Victorian parlor where a floor lamp with a Tiffany stained glass shade glowed on an immense, threadbare armchair. She sank into it with a groan. "Sit down. You want me to help you find a missing girl."

He dislodged a warm fur bundle of curled-up cats and quickly sat on a red plush sofa hard as rocks. "And you probably know her name," he said. "Right?"

"Drum," she said. "Something about a drum."

"Drummond," he said.

"Hah. I'm not as sharp as I once was." Her snaggle-toothed grimace was meant for a smile. "But one receives what one receives and when it is taken away, one accepts that in the same spirit."

How this huge Englishwoman had ended up in Guadalupe on the Central Coast of California some sixty or more years ago he couldn't understand, or why she had stayed. The house was fantastic. Probably it hadn't been surrounded by hills of sand when it was built. Now it stood up paintless with not a tree or green growing thing around it, shingles, stained glass, jigsaw work, a place from a bad dream, out here all by itself. He said, "I expect you're still sharp as ever. That's why

I came." He told the story from the beginning. "I was going to ask you for a translation of the runes, but something told me they wouldn't get me anywhere."

"With young novices," she said, "the inscriptions on the athame, the chalice and thurible would be conventional, copied from books. And so would the witch names these girls would choose. You're right, Hackett. The runes would tell you nothing." She gave a shout, "Rosa!" and told Bohannon, "We'll have some English tea. Against this English weather." She chuckled, and it was a chilling sound. "I summoned the rain in your honor." He half believed her. Rosa appeared, a middle-aged Latina, plump, comfortable, un-witchlike as possible, learned what was wanted, nodded, gave Bohannon a little smile, and went away.

The old woman looked at him again with her strange pale eyes. "Your black friend was right. There should have been a long red cord. It's called a girdle, but it's more than that. It is knotted at certain lengths. It's used like a compass, to measure and lay out the circles like the one you describe on that living room floor. It was she who did that. At someone else's bidding. When we wish to do a great evil, we get someone else to perform the ritual. That way if the curse is deflected, it does not come back upon us." The thought pleased her, and a smile deepened the creases of her face. "The cord was not with the Drummond girl's other tools, because she is—um, wearing it."

"Where?" Bohannon said. "Where is she?"

The old woman lit a cigarette. Smoke wreathed her tangled white hair and curled lazily up into the colored lampshade. It smelled of dried camel dung. Turkish tobacco. Hard to believe. She coughed, and said, "Not—far away."

"How do I find her?"

"You ask the girl whose father is a priest," she said.

A cat jumped onto his knees. Bohannon stroked it. It curled up on his lap and began to purr. "Cameron?" he said.

The great ugly head nodded. "She knows."

"Yes, but how do I get her to tell me?"

"Ah," the old woman said. "You must frighten her, of course."

Then Rosa brought in the tea, which was surprisingly good to taste, and bracingly strong and hot. They smoked, and drank the tea. And after the pot was empty, and Rosa had cleared the tray away, the old woman told him how to scare an answer out of Cameron Chase. The ritual was called fetching. When he rose to go, he felt sickened by its meaning. Bidding him goodbye from the doorway, a cat on her huge, stooped shoulders, she said, "Don't forget. Backward, counter-clockwise, against the sun. Widdershins—that is the ancient Scots word at the heart of witchcraft. The secret of its power. The power of the perverse."

"Yup." On the shaky old porch, he settled his hat on his head, and said, "It's complicated. Don't see how I can manage it alone."

"Help will come," she said. "From a quite unexpected source."

"Truth is," he blurted, "maybe I don't want to know where she is."

She gave him that awful smile again. "Oh, yes you do. It is your principal failing, Hackett. The nagging need to know. It will always overmaster your better instincts. It is what makes you human."

And she closed the door.

The rain was still rattling on the shingles overhead. Otis Jackson had served big bowls of homemade chili for lunch, with slabs of his fabled cornbread. And Bohannon was washing up the lunch dishes, when he heard another car come into the yard. He dried his hands, crossed the kitchen, opened the door and looked out. The car was a new Jaguar, dark red. He didn't know the car. Then the door opened and the driver got out. He was wearing rain gear, but Bohannon knew him. He pulled something out of the trunk, slammed the trunk shut, and came at a jog toward the house. Bohannon went out to meet him. Bert Shuster said, "Hack," and hopped up onto the covered walkway. He took off his canvas hat and shook it out. "I owe you an apology. More than one."

"Come inside," Bohannon said. "Hang up your coat." He reached out for the case in the geologist's hand. "I'll take that."

"Yes, right." Shuster hung up his hat and coat. "Maddy's mother was looking through her closet for stuff to donate to the start-the-year-with-a-clean-house rummage sale at the fire station, and found that." Bohannon had set it on the table. Shuster sat down at the table. "Cold. Got any coffee?"

"Absolutely." Bohannon moved to the stove. "What's in it?"

There was a click of spring latches. "Come look."

Bohannon did that. It was the same as Denise Drummond's collection, but not in a discarded dress box from a cheap shop. This was housed in a velvet-lined case that held not only the basin and cup, the knife and book, but a wand and a braided red cord as well, each wrapped in black silk. The case was also fitted with little segmented drawers of herbs and incenses.

Bohannon asked, "You know what this is?"

"Tanya found books in that closet, the books you said would be there. I looked through them. These are witch's tools. And from the well-worn condition of those books,

Maddy's learned how to use them. I was a jackass before."

"Forget it." Bohannon brought mugs of coffee and sat down. "The girl know her mother's found this stuff?"

"Her mother went and yanked her out of school. Maddy thought she'd learned about her coming up here last night and turning loose your horses." Shuster's laugh was brief. "The witchcraft matter was almost an anti-climax."

Bohannon stared. "She came up here by herself?"

Shuster shook his head. "With Cameron. It was Cameron's idea. And Cameron who had the car. The house-keeper's car. Mrs. Reilly. She's deaf. Cameron had the key copied at the mall. She only takes the car at night, and of course the woman never hears it. Cameron's panicked you'll expose the witchcraft. Wanted to make you look like a fool, so no one would believe you."

Bohannon grunted. "She's panicked, all right. But I'm afraid it's about matters far more serious." He drank some coffee and lit a cigarette. "Bert, I need your permission to question Madison."

Shuster turned his head, looked at him sideways. "What about?"

"Denise Drummond's disappearance. Brad Yates's suicide."

"Oh, Christ." Shuster sat back in his chair, hands gripping the edge of the table, forehead creased. "Don't tell me Madison's involved in those."

"Just Cameron—that's how it looks. I've only got part of the story. I'm hoping Madison can fill in the blanks for me." He raised his eyebrows. "Okay?"

"You know what you're doing." Shuster's smile was rueful. "I'm not going to forget that soon."

Bohannon held up a hand. "There's more. If she seconds my suspicions, then I'm going to need her help. Her active help. Late into the night." He got to his feet. "All right if we start now?"

Shuster took another gulp of coffee and stood up. "Let's go," he said.

The rain had blown off inland, over the mountains, and the sky was filled with stars. No moon. When Bohannon had told her that this afternoon, it had made Madison Shuster extra sure Cameron would be here. "The dark of the moon—that's the absolute max for witches."

Now, six hours later, in a clump of old oaks at the steep top of Bohannon's spread, Lieutenant Phil Gerard, head of the local sheriff's sub-station, yawned. "What am I doing here?" he asked. "It's cold. It's pitch dark. Everything's wet. Why do I let you get me into these crazy things?" And he turned night binoculars on the line shack below, a hundred yards off, by the side of a rutted service road.

Bohannon used the line shack to store fence repair tools, a roll of barbwire, spare posts, and bales of hay for the winters when the grass was gone from the long, sloping meadows, but the weather could still be fine, and he wanted to loose horses up here. Tonight it was serving another purpose.

"No sign of her, yet." Gerard squinted at his watch. Again.

"She'll come," Bohannon said.

The shack was as plain a structure as could be. But now, with candlelight from inside glowing through the cracks in its weathered siding, it managed an air of mystery that ought to satisfy Cameron. Her friend Madison had told her, at the Smoothie Shop after school, that she'd located the perfect place to summon the demon, and put an end to Bohannon's prying. "It's deserted. Nobody will see us. My dad's out of town. I'll drive myself up. Here's a map. Meet me at midnight."

Hours ago, on the splintery plank floor of the shack, using her knotted witch's girdle, Madison had laid out the pentacle, copying it exactly, runes and all, from one of her books. Vern, the tow-head deputy had carved it, and Otis had filled in the routed circle, star, and runes with black paint. A little table stood by, with the chalice of water, incense glowing in the thurible, and flickering candles at the corners. Everything was ready early. Madison was dressed in her black tabard, with the red girdle tying the waist. She pleaded one last time with her father. "I should really be naked. She might suspect something if I'm not."

"No way," Bert Shuster said. "Just tell her it's too cold."

"Listen!" Madison ran to the door and peered out. "Is that her?"

Nobody else heard anything. Not even crickets. It was too cold for crickets. But by ten past eleven, Madison, rattling with nerves, certain that Cameron's curiosity would bring her ahead of time, begged them all out of the place. As she closed the rickety door after them, her last quavering words were, "Oh, God, I hope I can remember the ritual."

"I hate leaving her here," Bert Shuster said.

"We won't let anything happen to her," Bohannon said.

Shuster's red car remained. Otis had taken the man with him in the green pickup truck back to the stables. Vern had driven the patrol car down to the start of the service road, and parked it, lights out, in a clump of brush where Cameron's headlights wouldn't find it. Bohannon and Gerard had hiked up here to the oaks. Breaths of wind shook cold leftover raindrops down on them.

And Gerard's walkie-talkie hissed. "She's coming," Vern said softly.

Gerard pressed a button and spoke into the gadget. "Okay, Madison."

225

"Ten-four." Her voice was a frightened squeak.

Far down the night slope, the headlight beams of a car, jittering and erratic from the potholes of the twisty road, came into view. How feeble they seemed in the dark canyon, under the vast black curve of the heavens. The car crawled slowly toward them, till its lights brushed the red Jaguar and the line shack. The car halted. The hand brake rasped. The engine died. The lights went out. A car door slammed, and a girl's voice, thin and far, called "Madison?"

"Let's go." Gerard and Bohannon stepped out of the trees and started down the hill. The ground was wet and their boots made little sound. Cameron never once looked their way. The door of the line shack opened. She stood silhouetted in the rectangle of candlelight.

"Madison, what are you doing? You said you'd wait for me. It isn't even midnight." She plunged inside. "Stop. Wait. I'm not ready."

Nearer now, Bohannon could hear Madison's voice. Chanting.

Cameron shouted, "Talk to me, damn you. Why won't you talk to me? Madison! Walking backwards? That's not what we planned. That's fetching. Oh, no. Oh, my God. You're fetching the dead. Stop it, Maddy. Don't do it."

The chanting broke off. Madison spoke. Jeered, really. Fear was nearly choking her, but she kept her promise to Bohannon. "Don't you want to see Brad? Why not? Because you made him kill himself?"

"I didn't. That's a lie." There was a scuffle. Screams. A crash. The table must have tipped over. Metal went clattering and gonging across the floor. The candles fell. Still burning on the floor, their light grew eerie. "I loved Brad. That Mexican sow killed him. You know that. Madison!" A shriek. A thump. Bohannon and Gerard ran for the shack.

"What about Denise?" Madison came backing out of the shack now, screaming at the girl inside, "She wouldn't help you do the death spell on Ortiz-Laredo, and you told her you'd kill her for that. I heard you. You said she ran away, but she didn't run away, Cammy. You killed her, didn't you?"

"Strangled her with her own girdle, and buried her, and that's what I'm going to do to you." Cameron came hurtling out the door, straight into Bohannon's arms. She flailed at him, kicked him, a raging fury. Fighting to keep his balance, he put a foot wrong and fell. On his back. With the hell-cat girl on top of him. She clawed at his eyes. He squeezed them shut, turned his head away, and hung onto her. Gerard dropped to his knees, handcuffed her, hoisted her off him. She still struggled, kicked, and cursed as only a preacher's daughter could.

Fighting to control her, Gerard asked the walkie-talkie, "Vern, where the hell are you?" Bohannon picked up his hat and climbed to his feet, wiping with the back of a hand at the scratches on his face. Madison, fingers tangled in her hair, sat on the ground in her torn robe, rocking and sobbing.

And inside the line shack, the last witch candle flickered out.